BEFORE ALL WHO HAVE EVER SEEN THIS DISAPPEAR

Michael Gills can flat out write fine sentences. His writing is part Old Testament prophet, part Cormac McCarthy. It's not as violent as either, but it's not without its moments of violence, betrayal, and the attendant tragedies those things bring. All of Gills' novels are rooted in the Stepwell family's history, which is dark and shiny in turns. This, his fifth novel, *Before All Who Have Seen This Disappear*, is, to some extent a baseball novel, but not as much about baseball as the cover might lead us to believe. Like all good baseball novels, it's about life, love, loss, and most of the time rallying, finding enough strength to persevere. This season, 1949, after the war against Hitler has been won, is cut short by the buck saw that takes Weldon Stepwell's leg, and soon his marriage. It does not end with a shot into the gap with the winning run in scoring position. No, Weldon, like the mighty Casey, strikes out. He's "sorry to beat the band. Sorry like no one's business. The sorriest man on a planet full to the sorry brim with sorry people." And yet, his grandson Joey forgives him, as we are wont to do, and loves him to the end of his days. This novel will leave you a bit bruised and battered, but it also will help you find your way through the dark times, past and yet to come.

—Rick Campbell, author of *Sometimes the Light*
and *Gunshot, Peacock, Dog*

Michael Gills' brand-spanking-new novel begins with an avalanche and never slackens pace thereafter. These pages jangle with incident, present a pageant of unforgettable personages, and speak a language of ruefully humorous lament and celebration. Every phrase exhibits the generous outlook of its author. Every sentence reveals and affirms a surprising truth we already know. The ornery humor is truthfully mordant, energized by sprightly melancholy.

—Fred Chappell, author of *I Am One of You Forever*
and *Midquest*

BEFORE ALL WHO HAVE EVER SEEN THIS DISAPPEAR

A novel

Michael Gills

Lake Dallas, Texas

Requests for permission to reprint or reuse material
from this work should be sent to:

Permissions
Madville Publishing
PO Box 358
Lake Dallas, TX 75065

Cover Design: Jacqueline Davis

Author Photo: Jill Gills, a selfie with her husband on a bridge just up from Notre
Dame (the black spire in the background) in Paris, Sunday July 2, 2017, on a
Berlin, Prague, Vienna, Paris trip celebrating their 30th wedding anniversary.

ISBN: 978-1-956440-31-7 paperback
978-1-956440-32-4 ebook

Library of Congress Control Number: 2022944368

For Lyra and Jill, always

PART 1

1.

Avalanche. Two days ago, in the high country. Seventeen dense inches fallen on the rotted base. Lara told us about it, me and Renee, while I was baking Sunday biscuits. Super Bowl Sunday, for what it's worth, and the rescue crew had been up there on skis all yesterday afternoon. Two parties, one of five guys, mostly in their twenties, and another of three girls, twenty-six year olds, they were nurses up at Intermountain where I had the prostate surgery. Maybe one of them had ministered to me, brought a glass of water or adjusted my catheter. Story was the girls had gone in quiet, made the turns to mid-mountain, then the guys came in above and started the slide, tried to outrun it and couldn't. All eight buried. Four were able to dig out, guys. And if you've never heard one of those beepers go off, then good for you. They dug out the buried ones, all dead. Made the call. The helicopters came in and hoisted the living out. They were in shock, the avalanche victims. And the slope was too steep to risk a rescue that late. So the bodies, the three nurses and one guy, lay out there on their backs, face to the sky, overnight. In full gear. Their backpacks still on, the little shovels sticking out. They hadn't been ID'd yet. Their parents didn't know. Laying out there on that new field of snow. It had cleared. The stars were out, the moon. And they lay there like that overnight in the snow. After a year of lock down and mask wearing, handwashing to the happy birthday song, the sheer hell of hearing the ventilators going in ICU. They'd been vaccinated. The cavalry had come. And snow to Utah, finally, fallen on a rotted core. They'd skinned their ways to the top bowl and were having a go at it in the morning sun. And a football field of snow rolled over them and that was that. February 2021, Saturday of Super Bowl weekend. Only a few years older than Lara.

"Did you hear about the avalanche?" she said.

She was supposed to be skiing. She'd changed her mind. Side country and backcountry, it was all red alert. Not to mention the crowds at the resorts. One died last week near Park City, a skier, you had to be crazy. But the lure was there, pretty much lockdown since March, ten full months, young people were stir-crazy, they wanted out. The backcountry was not so crowded, it wasn't supposed to be.

"Four died. I think the rest got out. Beat up pretty bad."

I'd sworn off the news, men wearing cow horns storming the Capital in DC, defecating on the Senate floor, hang Mike Pence, where's Pelosi, this on a day when we hit half a million dead from the virus, which it turned out was eight percent of our own genome, retrovirus. Renee'd had the vaccine by then, her second dose. She'd printed out a notice saying anyone who'd had cancer in the last year could make an appointment for the next round on March 1. My day was coming. Down in Florida, her dad still didn't have it yet, the vaccine. Lara, who knew when she could get it, about to graduate college, virtually. Twenty-three in January, living in the Honors Dorm up on Officer's Circle by Stillwell Field, where my office was, and we played baseball sometimes when the snow melted, and we had the view of the mountains.

"Oh," I said. There was a dozen, the biscuits. A bright sunshiny day, the light pouring into the kitchen. We'd snow hike later, me and Renee, above the upper Avenues where glacier lily bloomed on mornings like this. You could see Nevada, nearly, on a clear day from up there. "Did you hear helicopters? From the hospital?"

"No."

"Neither did we."

Renee'd finished her fruit bowl, the honey bells her father'd had mailed from sunny Florida in a case, each one of them wrapped in green paper. My ears were sagging. I noticed it the day before, along with the cracked windshield on the truck. We'd be a generation of people whose ears sagged. Wear a mask for a while. I guess you have.

We'd decided to buy her a car for graduation, Lara. She deserved it. Taking math three times. Forget a vacation or alternative Spring break. Any break. They'd all been cut. No parties, unless you were frat or sorority and wanted to risk the Black Death. You couldn't even get married or buried in person, I don't think.

"One of them lived in my dorm," Lara said. "Before she graduated."

"That's awful."

She'd come home for biscuits. What I'd learned from my grandmother, Mom Dee, back in the Old World when she lived in Park Plaza, and we'd go hear jazz at the mall and swim in her pool and never dream in a million years what had come. Or had I learned it from Mama, hadn't hers looked like toads?

"She was a nurse."

And there was this dream going around. Of being stalked. Having to hide. From men with guns. For me it was of me and Mama, and I'd somehow remembered how it felt when Jimmy died. I forgot about it for a while and then it'd come back, that sucker punch and grief. No getting away from it. Wake up and right there it was. I was trying to tell her how it felt, Mama, that he'd have a family by now, how it wasn't right. How utterly and unspeakably oppressive that felt. But of course, Mama already knew. She knew and knew and knew. What was I thinking in my dreams, telling Mama that?

Of course it wasn't right. Out there lurking, just beyond our line of sight. Hear the rumblings. About to roll down on us all, or not. Wear your mask, social distance, take your temperature, cover your mouth when you cough, wash your hands—happy birthday to you, happy birthday to you—sing it till it becomes a charm, the singing. Pray to God and Jesus and Holy Ghost.

Get vaccinated. Twice.

But you don't know, do you? How or when or why or if. Your daughter, your wife. All of us suckers for the ambush.

Blindsided.

Alone.

2.

August 21, 1949

He knew the way up Chickalah Mountain, could drive it in his sleep, which he might just have to do before this was all over. Ease on over Petit Jean River, a silver gleam in the dark, 27 North to Starfire and the old Hallowell hunt road where he'd killed his first whitetail on a morning when it rained and the rain turned to snow. Red eyes shine at every curve, coon, possum, skunk, too hot to roll the windows up, he'd lost the staticky baseball game just off the highway. The road's still muddy, climbing, yesterday's ambulance tracks clear, coming and going. What must that have been like for the girl and Dee? Jane Ann had been the first to see the scene inside, and all she could say was dear God. A rafter of turkeys steps out from the deep dark wood, jakes and hens, the old bearded gobbler staring golden-eyed from behind a tree trunk. Him and Stepwell had hunted this very wood, going *shreet, shreet, shreet* on homemade calls—Mr. Gobbler hear that from a mile away. Lord God if he could turn away this cup, how it had come to him to do this. Horace Hicks, who'd been up here when it happened, he'd flat out refused. "I aint'a gonna go. I can tell you exactly where it is. But aint'a gonna go."

Back at St. Mary's in Russellville, on blankets scattered all across the front lawn, they'd all given blood, all the Little Johns, even the ones who weren't a match. The church had brought food for anyone who could stomach it, fried chicken, mashed potatoes and gravy, pie—he'd had none of it, and that'd come back to bite him in the butt. What he'd give for one of those thighs now. Have to be a rooster to get a better piece of chicken, what old Ruffin said. His headlights graze the crowns of pine trees way up the road, hunt club property designated by the Guv as Ozark National Forest land. Still a few lived up this way, the old-timers with their trees hung with snakes to bring rain, don't kill a toad or you'll get bloody milk, or days like yesterday when the rain fell down in full sunshine, the devil beating his wife, they call it. No good comes out of a day like that, when the devil beats his wife.

In the passenger floorboard, Jacky's mail bag, still half-full of yesterday's undelivered mail, bills, paychecks and court summons, the odd letter home from kids who'd moved off to live in cities, St. Louis, Kansas City, Springfield. He'd finish it up today, even though it was a Sunday. Was it even today yet? Sixteen miles in from the highway, Hallowell wasn't much to look at, no lights nor running water, outdoor john, a pen for the dogs and poles lashed together for skinning. Lew Bland, their second baseman, had plumbed the place for gas, poured a pad for the butane tank they'd all donated for, so the club cooked with gas, give them that. But this was fire country. One hell of a hearth laid down in stone on the north side, where the wind blew snow through the cracks in winter on mornings before light, and it was keeper's job to stoke a fire, lay in splits from the pile out back, the one each member was sworn to replenish—that was the deal.

The wood had a smell to it, all those locusts out there making their locust racket, so it got under your teeth. The scene he'd left behind at St. Mary's radiates through his blood, will come to define who he is as a human being. As a ball player. A friend. A husband. Father. It'll be like that for every one of them who was there tonight, or was it last night? Where they'd prayed and wept, some of them, and waited for word from the surgeon's mouth. Floradee and the girl, misted in the fine spray from all those loosenings and tightenings of the tourniquet, they moved from inside to out, what they'd seen blasted on their faces, in their eyes, so when you met their gaze it came as a jolt into you too, the vision they'd have to carry from here on out, sweet Jesus.

The mailbox he'd built himself shines yonder. The shiny red flag visible from a quarter mile, marking the turn off to the hickory fence with its rusted creaking gate he'll have to open and the short drive into the stand of timber where he's been sent.

A barn owl flaps up in his headlights. He makes the turn in, little Vs in the soft mud where deer have crossed from thicket to crabapple some far off ancestor'd planted, so they'd eat the sour fruit till their bellies bloated, and the meat would be sweet come first frost.

The gate's wide open. Sure it is.

He wonders if a place could recollect what had happened there, if it was any trace of the previous passage? The sound of it. Terror. I aint'a going back, Horace had said. Center fielder, pitcher in a pinch, he wasn't a man you'd think on as faint of heart. Not Horace.

He drove on through, on top of the other tracks, deep, heavy. Twelve gauge behind the truck seat, loaded with number one buck. Dee'd been afraid of dogs, she couldn't live with that, not matter how it ended up. Rural mail carrier, only job he'd ever had, he'd had his run-ins with dogs, though what Dee had in mind had gone through him like a knife blade.

"Okay. You aint'a going back. Tell me where to look," he'd said.

Horace had drawn a little map with ball point pen on a piece of unopened letter from Jacky's bag, a federal crime, to mess with mail. There it sits right now, in the passenger seat, beside the flashlight and garden gloves somebody'd gone down and unlocked the hardware store for. Thirty burlap feed sacks in the lean-to back home, and not one of them here when he needs it.

Must be 4:30, quarter till 5.

He kills it aside the hunt club, just a darker piece of dark. Above, the summer triangle had sailed west, the first of the Hunter showing, his belt, the tip of the club he was about to whomp the bull with. The locust had shut down, just sudden as that. No morning birds yet. It's quiet. Terribly so. He let down the tailgate, decided to stand. Shook out one of the three cigarettes Horace'd rolled him, said, "You'll need these."

He wasn't a smoker, Jacky. Didn't carry a lighter. He used the one on the dashboard, the red eye glowing. And he stood out there for a while, smoked the Prince Albert tobacco under the good sky. Postponing it? Maybe. He was thirty-one to Stepwell's thirty-two. Could've been him transfused up to St. Mary's, little Jack with those blasted out eyes of Josephine Stepwell, Jane Ann beating off the dogs from nightmare. Stepwell up here smoking a cigarette this second, he'd of seen the wild turkeys, the V'd hoof prints, thought of Opening Day last year when Dennis Hargrove took down a spike before first light, how they'd barbecued it all day long in a hole dug in the ground so by supper meat fell off the bone, and there was good whiskey, he liked that, Stepwell.

Best friend he'd ever had. Handsome. Boy liked to fight some. They'd all went out to this night spot once in R'Ville. Stepwell was back there in the alley going at it with someone. They'd all scattered by then. Police came. They all got away— he was the only one caught. Stepwell. And Floradee refused to go bail. Coach Stringham had got Stepwell out. Made him run the perimeter of Little John Field till there was a regular path out there shining. Called it Stepwell Alley. He liked a fight, Weldon did. Good thing.

He ground the butt out on the tailgate. The light just won't come, maybe because he's wishing so for daylight to shine down on this sorry path he's about to follow. Past the pump house and summer garden with its burned-up beans, the dirt road down to the first tree stand where they'd been clearing. Over by the bucksaw, one tree felled, wedged up against another, he must have tried to push it, Stepwell. That was where. Horace'd drawn a little black x, circled it. "I aint'a going back," he said a third time, visibly shivered in the ungodly heat.

He started it, column shifted to first, let off the clutch and went. He'd grown up out in these sticks. Built his own house in the wood, even though Jane Ann preferred town, where the Stepwells ran the flower shop. Eternally Yours, it was called. There was the Methodist church where he'd been baptized, pools of stained light shining on the floor only last Sunday, the Call to Worship bell peeling. Danville, Arkansas, tail end summertime, nothing's supposed to happen then save the Dixie League ball games at Little John Field, where they'd borrowed $4000 from Danville Bank & Trust for light poles and lights, promised to repay the debt in two years with half the gate receipts, and they did. Swept the by god league, Stepwell catching, him on first, Bland and George and Moore, Hicks, the rest.

Two games next week. Who on earth would catch? Would they cancel? Did any of that even matter ever again?

His headlights sprayed the bucksaw, a hundred yards off, a good shot with a .30-ought six. Too far for the shotgun and number one buck. He eased on up. So far, no dogs. The ambulance track is deep here, tread prints splayed in the soft mud. They could have got stuck. Doc Jenkins and the women, Stepwell when they got him in. What then? One tree had fallen into the cradle of another, the wheeled saw there, silver-bladed, teeth big as two fingers made into a V. A bucksaw is like this giant tiller, push it right up to the tree and let her go. He'd cut one down and it fell into another. Jacky let his headlights rest on the scene in front of him, clicked them up on bright with his left foot and put her in neutral, sat there idling. Thirty yards off now, close, what he wanted was to lay her into reverse, bass-ackward his way out of here, up through the gate and out onto the road, just keep on driving till he was home, get in bed and forget this day ever was, so help him God, that's what he wanted to do but couldn't. There were no dogs, none he could see. Right there that second, up on Chickalah Ridge in the Ozark National Forest, Hallowell land, not far from deer camp—this thing should not be.

He took the second cigarette out of the ripped open envelope where Horace'd traced his map, lit it with the dashboard lighter, pulled out the ashtray that'd never been used. His hand was shaky, Horace's. There's the saw. He'd drawn it, exaggerated the teeth in an out of whack circle, the road up to it where he sat that second. The smoke smelled like something he couldn't remember, how here began a story he'd tell for the rest of his life, how he'd driven here in the dark, right up to the bucksaw, cranked a shell from the magazine into the chamber of the twelve, gazed long into the silly map, opened the door, stepped out on mother earth, truck running, headlights on bright. He'd have to use the mail sack, it hit him, to carry it. Stupid, stupid, stupid. Not to have thought about that. He could use coffee. Dumped out a good fifteen pounds of undelivered mail. Why on earth hadn't they thought of this yesterday? Again, it flashed through his head, how he pictured it happening. A wonder they got him down alive at all, a miracle, folk out on the lawn had said. Somebody should have thought to bring it. Shouldn't have been him have to come out and do this.

With the truck lights behind him, his shadow was twenty feet tall. He walked into it, the shadow, afraid. Gun in hand, mail sack strung from his shoulder, mailman from hell.

Close now, in the harsh light, he remembered what the smoke smelled like. When he was a kid, he'd wandered upon a place in the wood very much like this place. Fresh dirt, still wet from the digging, marked the doorway into this straight down tunnel he'd crawled into, no light save the daylight behind him. Who knows why boys do what they do? He'd crawled on in, gone on crawling, and in a while the tunnel'd opened into a room with barely enough light to make out the walls, cold to the touch, alive. And he'd just leaned his back up against a wall when he heard their voices, the boys who'd dug the secret fort he'd trespassed into. Their knees thump-thumped through the tunnel. It was a small world. Everyone knew everyone. Of course, he recognized them by what they said, a whole lot of damns and shits, a fuck from the older. They came on in, the brothers. Jacky'd crouched into a corner, still, breath held. Heart hell bent for leather in his chest. One was Jeryl, the other Beryl. The Dempseys, everyone mixed them up. Eyes adjusted, their dark forms were close enough to spit on. Beryl or Jeryl lit a match, yellow flame guttering, then the cigarette. They stared straight at him, smoked. They went to the same church, ate the Lord's Supper off the same plate. That's what the cigarette in the truck had put him in mind of, being stuck underground that day with the Dempseys.

There's blood, then there's a whole lot of blood. Dark, it stained the sawdust. Hunks of flesh, skin and gore mark the trail where they must have dragged him when it first happened. The smell. Vomit burned up his throat, and he bent to let it go. That's when he saw. The boot and pants. The leg. He'd forgot to wear the garden gloves. They were Stepwell's pants, spattered, cut clean through. The laces were still tied. On the boot. Got him just below the right knee. This time nothing came out. When he vomited. It was heavy, the length of it with the boot. Filled the whole goddamn mail sack. He tried not to look. Seemed like it could be used for something. Light came

11

then from back behind the low growl of the pickup. He had two choices. Bury it in the cemetery or burn it. He walked, almost ran back to the truck. Forgot the shotgun his dear departed daddy'd surprised him with the far-off Christmas when he was twelve. Would've left the thing, if not for that, the strap of mail sack finding the groove in his shoulder blade. One more time.

Then he aint'a going back.

The Yell County Incinerator's out Highway 10 East toward Ola, so he had to drive through town bright and shine Monday morning, where news waited on the lips of those who'd ordered eggs over-easy and hashbrowns, grits buttered please, black coffee and toast at Coger's, where he'd have to eat if he was ever going to do this deed. He parked out front, locked it in the front floorboard, Stepwell's leg, leaking through the sack onto the heap of undelivered mail. He'd never locked his doors before, double-checked them just to be sure. Inside, all eyes were on him, getting warm already, a Monday morning. Went quiet when he walked in, like a light switch had turned off the sound. Every soul in the room knew his lot, the task he'd taken on himself. And more than a few of them in there'd just driven from the front lawn of St. Mary's where they'd stayed up all night in prayer vigil, though they wouldn't have called it that then. Jimmy Patterson and Bill Lordes had a table to themselves by the plate glass window. Jacky said, "Mind, fellows?" and they both shook their heads, that blasted out look in their eyes.

"He lived," Lordes said. "He made it."

"That's good."

"Yea."

"Dee? The girl?"

"They all torn up. Tired. We all are. You?"

Ruby Goodno stood off to the side with a pad. She looked

scared to ask what he was having. He told her the special, whatever it was. Hot coffee, black. That'd do. And thank you.

Lordes and Paterson were done, the check beside a plate, clean save a scrap of bacon fat.

Out the window it was tail-end August 1949, a team practice day at Little John Field. They'd cancel, of course, though Stepwell wouldn't like it—if he ever found out. He was alive, turned out, but not conscious. That would come later, that awakening.

"I'm fine," Jacky said. "Found it."

"And?" Lordes said.

"Taking it to the incinerator."

Both men nodded. It was the right thing to do. They took refills on coffee. His food came. He salted the eggs. Peppered them. Spread jelly on the toast. Grape. Horace Hicks walked in staring at his shoes. They made a place. No one talked. Not in the whole place. Jacky tried to eat, realized he'd forgot to wash his hands. This time he fought it, the wretch.

Won, for the time being.

At the incinerator door, pulpwood smoke, trash from neighboring towns, run-over dogs and what went unused from the birds at the chicken operation, Jacky'd hauled open his mail sack, said, "Can I throw this in there?"

The operator'd given him a funny look. Jacky sat the bag down, opened the flap, took it out. "This," he said. "Can I throw this leg in there?"

The two things didn't go together, the cut-off leg with the boot still laced on a foot. The mail bag. He gave a second funny look, the operator.

"Well, can I?"

The fire shone on their faces, hot, smelling of everything fallen.

"Well, I guess so," he said.

It hit him to say a prayer or something, before he threw it in. But he didn't. He heaved the thing into the living flames, and his U.S. Post Office mail bag after it, turned just as it caught. He'd have to get another.

3.

They'd kept giving him blood, morphine for the pain. But he wasn't out of the woods, Dr. Coffin said. What kind of name was that for a doctor—Coffin? He'd of thought that funny, Weldon. The punch line to a joke or answer to a riddle. How many coffins does it take for an amputee? Two. One to do the sawing and the other for the patient. She didn't know what day it was, Floradee. Isn't that something, how the swirl of purpose sweeps you up tumbles you around and drops you in the hospital room with your sleeping husband. Not sleeping, really. The morphine drip in his vein, what must he be dreaming of, her brown-eyed man? That house of horrors operating room. Good God. The lot of them slumbering on the lawn? They'd all given blood, taken turns, the men, the women, traded their life's blood for Weldon's. How many thank you letters did it take to summon a man from death's door? For that's surely to God where he'd been, where they'd all walked. He'd live, Doc Coffin said. They'd stanched the bleeding. His heart was good. His lungs. None of the organs had failed. His head was a whole different thing. When he woke up. What he'd know. How he'd take to it. No way to tell. No way on earth. He had a temper. Everyone knew. He'd get mad. Eventually he would. He'd study up on it, Doc. More was unknown than known. Be there for him. When he woke up. That's all she could do.

Earl and Josie, someone had taken them home. They'd eaten. Everyone had come together for them. The world was good. Wasn't it?

Floradee'd been lacing baby's breath into a bridal bouquet, the scent of it mixing with the odd heaviness of that afternoon's air. Yellow roses and thunder, the smell of it. Josie pouting out on the front step, listening for the storm to come and likely wishing herself a million miles from Yell County when the Methodist church bell rang out and a flashing ambulance slammed up to the front door.

"Get in, Josephine," Doc Jenkins, a cousin on one side, screamed. "Dee," he hollered over the siren. He reached a big, palsied hand out the door and pulled her in, and the ambulance took off with such a jolt that all three fell on the metal gurney that had a chill to it even though it was summer, the sort of cold that stays.

The road up Chickalah Mountain was like running your tongue over missing teeth, the truck slip-sliding through fresh mud.

There'd been an accident. With a bucksaw, Doc said.

Weldon was up there. And another man. The call'd come from the hunt club. Hallowell. Did they have a phone now? Weldon had cut a leg off. He was hemorrhaging.

The girl shouldn't see this.

When the doors opened, a calm came over Floradee, the way it did when she arranged a piece bound to be important in her client's life, color and space, dominant and minor motifs. He was white, the second leg cut half-through as well. She ripped a strip of hem off her dress, twisted a tourniquet beneath the knee, what was once a knee. Fine blood misted their faces with each loosening.

On the way down, when Doc said "tighten," she tightened. Josie'd said goddamnit to hell, her daddy's phrase, goddamnit to hell. Where was it, the cut-off leg? The sun was out, rain still falling all lit up like silver bullets. The devil beating his wife, hill folk called it.

A hundred or more stood waiting on the hospital lawn

when the ambulance wailed up. Everyone agreed that the hospital lawn was entirely covered that August evening with men and women and families who'd driven over from Danville. The Little Johns were there, Coach Stringham, who'd lost a son to sniper fire in France. Jacky Thorpe's wife, Jane Ann, a nurse, the first to see the scene inside the ambulance.

"Dear God," she'd screamed when Weldon's gurney was wheeled out. The hospital's double doors opened and right there in front of them, Jane Ann Thorpe stripped naked, wrapped herself in a sheet, and disappeared into the operating room for emergency surgery.

Danville folk stood on the rain-sweet grass. Flowers bloomed. The war was over. This should be a happy time. They'd got him to the hospital. There was hope. Anything could happen, anything at all.

They'd moved from blanket to blanket out there, her and Josephine. Accepting sympathies from kith and kin. She'd lived long enough, Floradee, to know something of sudden change, that sucker punch life's liable to throw at you, laying over there with one eye open.

He'd live. The rest only God knew.

Stay in the room. Somebody said, stay in the room. It's hot. Can't open a window, germs, the threat of gangrene, another amputation, the knee joint gone already. The third day? Fourth? They've made up a cot for her. So she can be in the room. Stay in the room.

He cried out.

A while ago, he did. It was the same cry as the one in the ambulance, when he was going into shock and the devil was beating his wife. Goddamnit to hell, Josie'd said for him, because he couldn't. All he could do was make that cry like he did a while ago.

I love you, I love you, she'd said into his face. Unshaven these however many days, a shadow. A handsome face, brooding, he could smile, God could he. She'd fallen for him because of his letter jacket if anyone could believe it. His name, Weldon Stepwell, writ in white cursive inside the right pocket. Three bars on the D for how many times he'd lettered in basketball, a star, they'd invented a cheer for him, the cheerleaders. He'd noticed her in the stands one night. Who was she? What grade was she in? The seventh or eighth, daddy jobless for the whole year, nearly, she'd dropped out. She wasn't in a grade, didn't matter. He let her wear his letter jacket that night, his musky smell rough against her neck, her shoulders, heart. The same smell in the room right now, only different.

He could hear her. Saying I love you.

From the cot, his breathing's steady. Drip, drip, drip from the IV. They'd quit transfusing. His body was making its own blood now. Good.

Mama and Daddy'd driven over from Subiaco. One of the monks from the monastery'd brought them in a cloister car, Daddy looking older than she'd ever seen him, his heart beating sideways in his chest. Mama cold as ever, as if it had been her fault him up there cutting firewood. What kind of thing was that for a man to be doing on a Sunday?

"It was Saturday, Mama. *Saturday*." Silence. That look in her eye. Poor daddy. Poor all of them. She'd fallen for Weldon's letter jacket, and for that she'd never be forgiven in this world, nor the next nor the next.

When the door opened, Sofi, the night nurse said, "Knock, knock, it's just me again." She took his pulse, listened to his heart, held the stethoscope to his chest's rise and fall. Checked for bleeding, should the gauze be changed? The bandage seeped through, morphine drip, glucose. "What day is it?" Dee asked. She lay folded in half a sheet, cotton, all she could stand.

"Why it's Wednesday, Mrs. Stepwell, August 24th. The full dog moon's putting on a show out there right now."

"Four days we've been here?"

There was no sign of moonlight, neither day nor night. Here sleep was dotted around the edges, perforated, something to be torn down the middle, one part kept, the other thrown away.

"Five," Sofi said. "If'n you count the day you come."

The sound was the first thing she didn't want her daughter to remember but knew she would. It got at them through the ambulance walls as they turned hard, thrown up against the window with that noise coming through it, over the siren, pouring into their hearts as the driver hit the brakes, skidded sideways.

Truth is strange, how it can be walked up on like a sleeping dog that's deaf in one ear. August. Lunchtime. She should have brought food. He must be hungry. Flowers, her hands smelled of baby's breath and cut roses. Dr. Jenkins gripped a hypodermic in each hand. That sound. She tore her dress, made a tourniquet, and they all became part of the sound, it was who they were now. The morphine from Doc Jenkins' twin hypodermic found what the saw had made of him. They somehow got him loaded, the metal gurney blood-slicked cold.

"Daddy? I'm here now. Mama's here. Goddamnit to hell," Josie kept saying, her face down next to his, pleading, breathing the fine mist each time the tourniquet loosened.

Strange words from a girl to her father.

Fifty miles from Chickalah Mountain to Russellville and St. Mary's. She asked him not to die, said I love you with all my heart, that she was his for all time. When he stopped breathing, Josephine beat his chest with hard fists, screamed *No, No, No.*

Weldon's breath caught—a tear in his throat.

Up in the cab, the driver's face distorted. Somewhere beyond him the cupola atop Arkansas Tech's dining hall, then

19

downtown Russellville and the big lawn with people on it, standing, holding their breaths. Coach was there. His wife. Perry Wiseman, of course Perry was there. At the heart of the frenzy was a quiet place where he stood. The story of the story of the story.

Through the double doors of their lives.

The war was over. They'd survived Hitler and the A-Bomb, the genocide of the Jews. Weldon's name had been mentioned for a run at the county seat. Aunt Ella'd traced the Stepwells back through the Adamses, all the way to John and John Quincy. The blood of presidents ran through his veins, Weldon's. They were business owners, the town florists. Fall was coming. The heat would let off. School for the kids. The hunt season, venison barbecued the way he liked it. The holidays. Their tenth anniversary. Daffodil was the flower for the tenth, first color of springtime, jonquil some called it. They could be forced in a hot house from separated bulbs. Weldon'd surprised her with third year sunflowers—about a thousand years ago when the season was young, and anything could happen, anything at all.

On the morning of the fifth day, his color returned. Dee opened the curtains halfway, cracked the window so a gust of sweet morning air rushed in. Bird song, the notes repeating every so often, a clean melody to fill the empty space. She asked the morning nurse to send for flowers, and when they arrived, she'd arranged them in the window so the light shone on the petals, Brown-eyed Susans, her favorite. Outside, it was Wednesday, the pivot day for the week. She lay her hand on Weldon's forehead, and it was cool. The fever'd broken. The stench they'd breathed for forty-eight hours eased off a little, there was light and the flowers, more in the waiting room, she was told, a whole slew. They brought her oatmeal, coffee on a tray, a bowl of fresh blackberries with a touch of cream. Buttered toast.

She said grace.

Of course she'd promised God the Father everything under the sun if he'd pull Weldon through; she'd quit smoking, be less like her mother to the kids, join the new Outreach Program over to Logan County, be a better wife. She'd break the silence that had come on them these last two years, the long, brooding emptiness that had blanketed their lives since the day she refers to simply as the day. When Weldon was out making deliveries, and she'd forgot something at home, what was it? Walked the blocks to their house, a wood frame with yellow roses blooming on the trellis they'd put up on the south side. It was rainy springtime, these huge white clouds with purple bruises, tornado season in the River Valley—but not that day, another. The brisk walk had her thirsty, and she'd run a glass of water from the sink faucet. And that's when she'd heard it, a woman's voice, a girl's.

From her bedroom. Theirs.

She'd flipped the light switch on and saw. Walked calmly into the kitchen and took the eight-inch butcher knife from its wooden block, turned back into the room and threw it. Hard. And the gash in the cherry wood headboard was there this second, shining its reminder. The Day.

He'd always been afraid of the knife, Weldon. It had been a cigarette she'd gone home for. Smoke was forbidden inside Eternally Yours. Like everything else, Floradee'd learned the hard way—tobacco mosaic virus in a room of forced tulips, blight ripping through the carnations.

Her husband. Like she'd thrown that saw at him sure as the world.

The food brought her back, what it took to stand up and take leave, walk down the ICU hall its scarred walls where other gurneys bearing the afflicted had bumper-carred. Splashed water from the sink faucet on her face. She brushed her teeth, her hair out, put on some blush, lipstick. Looked like she was the one who'd been in a four-day coma, five if you counted the day they landed on this odd planet, with its funny light and air, the curious focus on the fleshly body at the cost of what it served. What did the body serve? You could slap it down and cut it in half, offer it to another, or not. There was no escaping it, the body.

They bled and wanted and weren't ever satisfied, were they? She was twenty-nine, thirty come January, mother of two, wife, Methodist, smoker, graduate of Memphis School of Floral Design, who'd thrown an eight-inch butcher knife at her husband's head. So, what did that make her? Someone willing to take a life in anger? A could be murderer? A person who could be overcome? And *now*?

If Weldon made it out of the woods?

What on earth?

She went to the bathroom, tried to press the wrinkles from her blouse, off-white, Jane Ann had brought it from the house with the other stuff. Where Josephine and Earl are. What would she have told her little brother, Josie? How would she carry that ambulance ride with her hemorrhaging father, how would it weigh on her heart, nine-year-old girl, what would it do to her? All that time, this rocketing toward them. And what would become of them? If he made it, Weldon would need therapy and God knows what else. Earl was seven, about to start school, show and tell, see Dick run.

Dear God was right.

The kids could go live with Hallie, go to school at the monastery in Subiaco. The thought of that cold, dark place with all the ghosts and guilt she'd run away from with Weldon, wearing his letter jacket, his name in white cursive just inside the right pocket. The man she'd loved. Who could hit a baseball to China. Who'd swept her off her feet. Who she'd die for. Whose features mixed with her own in the faces, the limbs, the blood of their children.

Dee needed her family back. The best part of her. No matter what else, that one thing. She needed her family. They'd save each other.

On the way back, she hit the fountain, its water cold and good, a delight to the flesh and blood. It was a new day. They'd make it. They would. She made her way toward her sleeping husband—they'd vowed to cherish one another in sickness and health. Till death do them part. The heft of those words. Their meaning. The moment the door opened inward on her newly amputeed husband, when her heart beat hard with the flood of newfound hope for her babies and her man, how they had it fully in them to save one another, another thing. When they met eyes, he'd come to. And she knew. Knew and knew and knew. She should have stayed in the room.

She should have.

4.

The runner, big son of a bitch, he was coming home, spikes first. Light from the big poles, the ones they'd borrowed for and promised to repay in two years with half the gate, and by god had, it shone from the silver spikes, the mitt stiff on his left hand, he blocked the way, Weldon, go ahead, try me. In the fecund night, the stars crisscross crazy, moon shadow, her voice spliced with the others from the stand, the last inning, the last out, the last run to block. Coming in hot, feet first, cleats high, the gleam in them, like a buzz saw, a spinning blade. Between him and home, the lime white line. He took the full blow, the weight of the man, with his body, right leg first, left, chest, felt spikes rip flesh, blood, could smell it, old and new. Weldon screamed. And then he screamed again, tangled between third and home, with the man, they must have been a mess. Their uniforms were hot. Jack'd taken his jersey off. His white undershirt had dirt on it. The moon was out, big as a buffalo. He'd stolen. Hatless. The crowd had gone quiet. Held its breath. Coach made the signs. Somebody screamed no. Spiked him good, burned like fire, like whiskey, tomorrow.

She'd laid his head in her lap, smell of her dress, skin. Her voice, the one he'd recognized first time he heard it. I know you, he said. He'd be okay. They'd get him to the dugout. Cold water there. Ice.

Josephine's face, down from the bleachers. Goddamnit to hell, she was saying. Goddamnit to hell.

A sound, part train, part bone. A third thing. The knife blade singing just over his scalp—I thought we were over that. Should throw the fucker out of the game, come sliding home like that—all spikes.

Funny thing, how you had to take blood to see how much'd been lost. Jane Ann filled one vial, then another. His color was coming back. Breathing, good. Blood pressure up. Stable heart rate, 72. Temp, 99. Up a tad. Infection trying to sneak in the door? What they needed was some fresh air in here, Dee on the cot, breathing in and out. They'd stopped transfusing, but kept the spikes in both arteries, just in case. No sign of him coming out, but the color was good, just the slightest bit.

Bandages needed changing. Again. They'd had to take off an extra two inches, suture the flap over where the knee joint had been. Not pretty. She could pass it on to the next shift, new bandages. Back home, Jacky sorting mail on the kitchen table. Had had to deliver that one batch on Sunday, despite. Some of it had been a mess. Whole thing a mess, really. All of this.

Just a crying shame.

A touch of wheeze in his lung. She held an eyelid open, clear. The utter shock of it had been enough to kill a horse, the trauma. Dee and the kid, Jesus. It was all a bunch of baloney, the business about not caring, not getting invested, staying removed. Before her lay husband, father, friend, a living being who'd walked right up to death's door and knocked. Who'd walked in and got back out. Looked like. Not out of the woods yet.

The color was a good sign, always the good to counter the bad. Almost always. Her own self? 1949. A Wednesday. Her moon over for the month. Jacky Junior. The drought had broken. There'd been word of a team benefit for the Stepwells, a game, donated proceeds, blood drive, fish fry, all of that. But they had to get him out of the woods first.

"Weldon. You hear me?"

Was fake light better than no light at all? It darkened the crevices of every run into wall, the baseboards, just lay on the floor like a pool of skim ice, what's wrong with her today? It had been a long week, and now this. Everybody was on edge, and Jacky wasn't the same since hauling that thing to the incinerator, the stains of it.

"If you hear me, you're gonna be alright. We've got you in a good place. Dee's here. Jeanine Wiseman's with the kids. We're holding you up in prayer."

The water in the wash basin was warm, not hot. She made a lather from the soap bar, spread it on his face, where the color was coming back, under his nose, down his cheek to the neck. He needed changing. The bed.

It was Jacky's razor, his idea. There in the lukewarm water. She held it the way she shaved her legs, between thumb and forefinger, started high on the right cheekbone, worked down.

"There," Jane Ann said. "There."

She put herself in Dee's shoes. What might this look like from over there on that cot, a nurse in a silly white hat shaving her husband before daylight on a Wednesday in August. Poor thing.

She worked the bristly stubble above his lips. They'd shaved what was left of the leg, the other, too. It works better when she pulls up, not perfect, better. She'd watched her father shave a hundred times, her husband. Slap their faces with hot water then cold. Towel off. How that somehow gave them energy, set the day going in a good way.

She had to switch to her left hand for the other side. Just the slightest cut below the ear. "I'm doing the best I can, Butch. Hear?"

What Jacky called him. The men.

"Butch," she said. Leaned down close to the clean-shaven face. "That's better, now, isn't it?"

One eye twitched, and then the other.

Close now. Today might be the day.

WELCOME HOME DADDY, the sign Josie'd outlined in block letters, free hand on butcher paper from the grocery store—they sent her enough to cover the whole front door when she asked. WE LOVE YOU would come next, and then they'd all sign, the dog too, she'd make their handprints and footprints—he loved dogs, Daddy did, Suzi best, the beagle. Each letter had to be its own color. She was sure of that. For her half birthday, he'd brought home a tackle box with her name writ on it in his hand. He'd smiled that crooked smile with the light in his eyes, said maybe he'd take her fishing after they'd finished the flowers for the Lordes girl's wedding. Open it on up, he said, and she did. But instead of hooks and sinkers, inside was the brand new that year Crayola No. 48 drawing crayons she'd seen at the pharmacy, coveted, and never told anyone in the world about, not even little Earl, to whom she told everything up until five days ago, or was it six?

There was red and dark red and Indian red, all of which she chose to skip the morning of that day when Daddy'd wake up and come home and they'd be a family again just like Christmas. The four oranges didn't seem right for the W—first letter of Daddy's name, so she went with gold ochre, a fitting color, seemed to her, for August, and the beginning of welcome, she went with gold ochre, and it was right.

The yellows were too close, so she skipped to dark green, which was perfect for the E, and matched outside, and if it could talk would say I am she of living things, or the force that through the green fuse drives the flower, or something like that she'd read last year in Miss Baskin's class. Blue had too many choices, cerulean, Prussian, azure, she went with cobalt, color of the hard cloudless sky all summer before the rain. For

HOME, she ran through mahogany and burnt sienna, interlacing them with the yellows she'd skipped earlier, and by the time she got to Daddy, she'd run right up against flesh.

He used to get them after wind sprints, charley horses, forty yards at a pop, come up slow, hit half-speed, three quarters, wind it on down and walk back. After a dozen you'd sweat out all your salt, and they'd get you at the dinner table or in the middle of the night, the fist-sized knot in the calf, sweet Jesus, how it hurt. Stand up and walk it out, somebody get me a banana, warm salt water, anything, goddamn. And he'd be on his feet in the dark, walking wall to wall, sometimes out in the dark, down the street, bats chasing mosquitoes above his head, come back and she'd be awake, Dee, would massage what was left of the hard knot out of the muscle until it let loose or another one came, or didn't. Thank you, he'd say to her, thank you. That kind of hurt, there's no words for. Like walking out past the railroad tracks, on a rabbit path then off, pant legs loose over your boots. One step, then the ground collapses, wasp burrow, a whole swarm up his pant leg. Yellow jackets, the worst kind. So he was running while they stung shit out of him, ripping his belt loose, his pants, and they kept on, the pain in his veins, worse and worse, little injections of kick ass till he got naked and hit Four-Mile Creek, crying sweet Jesus, come out of nowhere, straight up his leg with fire in its teeth. What words for such a message? What was it trying to say to him, that voice?

From a deep dark place, swimming to the light, and the closer he got, the more it hurt, so that sometimes he'd stop, look back, and be lonely for what he'd left behind back in that world, the Old one, back there, where the ball game was in the bottom of the third, and it was one of those peaceful nights when you know you're in the right place, doing the right thing. Nobody's coming at you from behind. Big son of a bitch has turned down his spikes, shaken hands, you've made peace and the game is just a game, something to have fun doing, wasn't that what it was about, that life back in the Old World. And the charley horse and yellow jacket and fist-sized knot that seized up your heart and brain, it had turned loose of you for a while, lay back in that place you swam up from, up and up, toward the fierce light in the hard sky all summer before the rain.

No turning back, no turning back.

Today might be the day.

She opened the blind, light coming. Clouds still thanks be, half-moon with a star, or was it a planet, Venus maybe, the goddess of love she'd learned about somewhere way back, off to the right, three fingers held at arm's length. Her favorite time of day, Jane Ann's, that sliver of in-between when it was quiet in the hospital, like the empty church she'd snuck into one day on a dare, she doesn't remember whose, doesn't matter. In there, the faintest glow through stained glass, where she could make out a white lamb and green grass, the tree of Jesse, the silver casing between panes. The front door had been open and he'd walked right in, the middle aisle falling away to the pulpit where it got darker, until the choir loft where she sang beside the man who'd be her husband one day on Sundays, their voices twined. And behind them, the baptismal font with its wedge of silvery glass so the congregation could see the water when the preacher laid his hand atop her head and lowered her down for long enough to need breath, to breathe, really, really *need*.

There'd been the silver plate with little bits of broken bread left over from last Sunday, a tray with little holes for the shot glasses filled with Welch's unsweetened grape juice, awful stuff mixed together. Dents in the hardwood from PaPa's casket stand. Her daddy after he'd walked her down the aisle to give her away, all of that way out in front of her that day she'd snuck into church before daylight on a dare from someone she didn't even remember.

The place had had a smell about it, a feel, all those marryings and buryings. Now why would she think of that? When she was a girl with twin braids and someone had come in, she'd heard the door open and hid behind a pew, in the still dark till light came in, when she'd crawled the aisle's length and got out through the double door so no one ever knew but her, and she didn't tell. Not a soul.

She pulled the curtain to. Her shift'd be over soon and she could go home and sleep, sleep, sleep. A Wednesday, little Jacky'd run off through the woods to school and she'd have the place to herself, maybe go out to the garden and pick a mess of okra that hasn't been picked in three days, good God what she might find out there. Squirrels after her geraniums. Deer chewing the collards. Ripe muscadine, some of it gone to ferment grown half up a hickory, so birds, sparrows, a crow once, sip the sweet wine from golden husks till they're drunk as Cooter Brown. Fall down a-thunk in green grass and lay there for a while, till they come to, fly right up there and do it all over again. Beats all.

"Good morning, Butch," she said, took the clipboard in one hand, the wash basin with Jack's razor blade-side down in the other. She was forgetting something, *what?*

The color for flesh was nothing like it, not at all. She stared at the box long and hard, Josephine, the little circle with Forty-Eight Reubens Colors in it, painting of the man Daddy'd called a prissy little fart with a paintbrush in his right hand. An artist, painter, had the colors spoken to him the way they did to her?

The four reds? Dark green? Gold ochre? Cobalt blue speaking the tongue of hard sky? Magenta? Salmon swimming in a river called Fourche la Favre? Mahogany and burnt sienna interspliced with yellows, had they talked to him, the prissy little fart artist, had they spoken of home? Of flesh? What on earth caused him to get that one so wrong? Was the voice of flesh a liar? Had it misled him with stories from the hunt fires up to Hallowell on Chickalah Mountain? Where the road had been like running your tongue over missing teeth and Mama'd twisted the tourniquet when Doc said, loosened when he said to loosen. When naming the color flesh, had this artist with his Forty-Eight Reubens Colors not been to the woods where Daddy's leg lay? Had he not seen saw teeth? The boot with its laces still tied. The bow. Had the color told him a dirty joke? Run away from home? Did it need spank-a-butt? Was it hungry or laughing or full of piss and vinegar? Did it goddamn the world to hell? Had it arrived in a surprise tackle box? Where there were supposed to be hooks? Was it some kind of joke, flesh?

Was it a prissy little fart, just like Daddy said?

The finished sign would cover half the front door, just under the little window where she'd stand on the stool and watch him coming, yell SURPRISE, DADDY, WELCOME HOME when he walked in, and Earl would be there, Mama, the four of them like they were supposed to be.

And flesh could go jump in the lake. Couldn't it?

He woke up thirsty.

And afraid.

And not exactly sure of what. His foot itched. The sheet was wrapped around him. It was wet. Spot on the ceiling, a fly? On a bed in a room wrapped in a white sheet, cotton-mouthed, his foot itched, afraid of something, he'd tried to get away from.

Big son-bitch, spikes blazing. He'd been shaved by a woman. Had heard her voice. Not Dee. She'd said his name, called him from the deep. Light, a window to his right, Dee'd been there, he doesn't know how he knows. He knows.

The kind of thirst you write home about—you just wouldn't believe it, Mama, like his mouth would break. *Mama?*

He had to shit. His stomach was messed up. His teeth tasted salty, like he'd eaten a mouthful straight from the shaker. There'd been a preacher praying, touching his head, callus on the middle finger. Not a day he'd want to remember any day soon, sound of the bone saw, preacher's callused middle finger crying out for Jesus to have Mercy.

Mercy.

The sort of itch that made you crazy, if not for the thirst, which was sharp enough to take the itch off for the few seconds to need to scratch again, his little toe, a tug of war for those first few moments of consciousness that he did not think of then as moments of consciousness, the first time he rose from the dead, the other thought just brushing his periphery. Scraping it. Hauling off and waylaying him so bile came with the retch.

And for a second, he felt himself as he was. Flashed through it, the odd dance in the deep dark wood, how it hurt, the bleeding, silly-ass Horace whipping off his belt, gone to use the phone, the embarrassment of Josephine seeing him that way, the fire come on her, Goddamnit to hell. Yes. Goddamnit to hell.

That first injection, first taste of morphine.

A cliff he'd climbed off Denby Cove on Ouachita, the deep hole, quartz crystals shine up through clear water he'd dived into, held the one breath down to sixty feet, gripped the one with the knife edge in his right hand, braced both feet against the bed and pushed, lungs hot now, afire. One stroke, another, kicking, the thought he'd never make it on that one breath, the translucent crystal cold in his palm, from the blue-deep morphine to the light, the sky-world with its dark fly on the ceiling.

A swarm of yellow jackets, the worst kind goddamnit to hell, all up his pant leg and he'd jumped into the dance but the water kept on burning, his mouth dried to breaking, skin split, you'd think he'd take a drink of water, turn loose of that breath and let be.

And at that very moment, the door opened inward, and there stood she to whom he'd pledged his troth, which they'd both laughed at behind Preacher's back, because it sounded like trough, what a pig ate out of, *oh darling, I pledge to you my trough*. Baby, in sickness and in health, woo pig sooie, till death do us part.

The stone-cold hand. Breath.

Weldon Stepwell stared down the length of his bed. One door opened and another closed. Yellowjackets up his pant leg.

Green-eyed, Floradee.

Color of life, living.

Yellowjackets all up his pant leg. That itch.

"Water," he said.

5.

They didn't expect him to make it through the night, but he did. He liked a good fight, Stepwell did. They'd all gone to this night spot in Russellville after a double header, thirsty to beat the band. Still in their uniforms. It was the day they'd taken the picture of the eleven of them with Coach Stringham, and Jacky'd taken his jersey off. Hell, it was hot, he had an undershirt on, white as anybody else's. Hat with a D for Danville centered. Exactly half of them had looked straight at the photographer, and the other to third base—in the picture, the one taken on the day of the fight. Stepwell glared at third, had something on his mind, who knows what, he played them tight sometimes, catcher, back there getting knocked around for two games, first one under sun, second under lights. He'd pitched the bottom half, Jacky, Stepwell back there flashing signs: one for fastball, two for the curve, three for knuckle and four for change up, five for a dust off, and a closed fist, bean the son of a bitch. Fist-one finger, in the head; fist-two, in the ass; fist- three, in the foot. They'd won that second half of the double without beanballs, though he had something on his heart, Stepwell did, you could tell he wanted to fist-one it.

Lewis Blanding'd joined them that night, driven the car, in fact. All he had was a thumb on his right hand, but could he ever throw the ball, drift over from short and make the scoop, turn the two-one double, one-hand it sometimes, make the toss.

Lew could do with a thumb what anybody else could do with their whole hand. Hold a pencil, comb his hair, pump gas, pull the trigger on a ten-point opening morning. Only that one night after the double-header, somebody'd said something, made a joke on Lew's lack of a hand, something about the Little Johns being so hard up they had to field a one-armed man.

Stepwell wasn't having any of it. He'd turned to the guy, that look in his eye. "What's that?" he said. "Say again."

"Must be hard times," the man who didn't know he was about to be shit-kicked said. "Have to field one-armed boys."

He was a big redhead, into his bourbon and branch, squeeze of lemon.

Stepwell gave Jacky the look, made the sign with his left hand, because he'd put the right one behind his back, where he kept it while he cold-cocked the redhead, and then the red-head's friend, and the redhead's friend's friend. Three of them down just like that, broken nose, teeth, you could hear it, that awful sound, his right hand still tucked behind his back, that look in his eye. Something was on his heart, had been all day, don't know what. But when he tore into a fourth R'Ville boy and the fight moved outside, they'd all scattered, and the police came. They all got away—he was the only one caught.

Threw him in the pokey.

Dee refused to get him out. Flat out no, she'd said to him over the phone, and that was that. Coach'd made the drive, brought him home, still in uniform.

He had the fight in him, that was for sure. They hadn't expected him to make it through the night, but he did. With his right hand behind his back, he'd hemorrhaged blood fast as they could give it, one leg gone, the other half in two. Lived to see another day, which just might be today, Jane Ann said. His color'd come back that morning, today might be the day.

He'd cooked her a breakfast supper, done the dishes, sorted the mail, hefted it in a burlap sack to the truck where the smell of Stepwell's leg lingered. How the incinerator man'd looked at him funny when he'd asked could he throw it in there. "Well, I guess so," eyes full on it like it might jump up and bite him.

Dee'd been afraid the dogs would get at it, up there camped out in that room, waiting. He aint'a going to be happy, Stepwell. No arm behind his back on this one. Fist-one, fist-two, fist- three.

Even with the windows down, it wouldn't go away. He'd have to spray out the floorboard later, scrub it with ammonia, Pine Sol, maybe.

Practice this afternoon, first one since. They'd have to try out a replacement catcher, track down Stepwell's mitt.

Learn the signs.

There's the sweet morning smell, too. Cruise on to where his route starts, Jacky Thorpe, rural mail carrier, what it said on his paycheck, the one he'd been cashing for ten years over to the Bank & Trust, where they'd taken out the loan for the poles and lights, big ninety-footers to shine over the ballfield for night games, swore in ink they'd pay the two thousand back in two years with half the gate receipts, and they were halfway there, weren't they? Perry Wiseman's daddy, Codger okayed the deal, and they'd built bleachers with lumber donated from the Petit Jean mill, oil dealer bought them their uniforms.

The Dixie League Circuit, they played teams from Bald Knob and Crossett, Hamburg and Ft. Smith and Jonesboro. Boys drove a bus over from the Oklahoma side, an all-Indian team called the Chickasaw Warriors, farm boys from Tulsa and a real good group of ballplayers from Texarkana, the Texas side. The war was over, all of that beeswax. They'd won. Why not play ball?

Why not?

Stepwell's bat made a sound when he hit it, you could tell it was him with your eyes shut. A right-hander, he hugged the plate, dared every pitch to hit him, number thirty-three Louisville Slugger just over his shoulder, light in his hand, good eye, hum babe, hum babe, all coiled up there like a truck spring, the ball flashing white under the torchlights, and then that sound. Of a sudden. And everybody'd go quiet for a second to see where it was going, usually a long goddamn way on a string line. Once he hit a power line, made sparks, set the fence on fire. Another, a line drive clean over left center, smacked against a hickory and bounced clear back to second, just like that. Ump said, "Play ball," and he circled the bases to our opponent's catcalls, and next time we played that team they'd cut that tree down, they sure had.

Newspapers, Little Johns with that permanent sidebar about where the name came from, all rolled up with little rubber bands around them, go right in the box with the mail. Billingsly then Tucker then Patterson, there were Blands and Stringhams and Kemps, Elliotts and Taylors and Paynes and Baggotts, Sextons and Lordes and Hicks, Mathisons and Baskins and Moores and Masons, you know exactly what's in the envelope. Tom Baty's son Tom Baty writing from the Marine Base in San Diego, his once-a-week letter with FREE Marine Corps Base written where the stamp went, give mama a hug, tell Cisco I say hi.

Yell County census forms and phone bills, electric, the Sears & Roebuck catalogues that were heavier each year, the return envelopes with bank checks for guitars and fishing reels and sewing stuff, shirts and socks, they did some business out here in Yell County, Sears & Roebuck.

Reverend Day had condoms mailed to his P.O. and his old lady found them, opened up the box and cooked one into the Sunday meatloaf, made sure he got the right piece. Word was he didn't say a thing, just pushed it off to the side with his fork and cleaned his plate.

Sometimes he came across their own mail, his and Jane Ann's. A letter from school, was he still up for calling the Little

John High School games this season, his press pass, the words to the song like he needed them. Pea seeds, too late for the planting. A card from his mama who'd likely follow daddy to the Gloryland Way this year or next. See you on Sunday. Proud of you for what you did. Will he make it, the Stepwell boy?

He pictured himself in that bed, all cut up and sawed on and half bled to death. Waking up like that. Not being able to walk, to get up and go piss, even, man alive, Jesus, it was too much to think. A man like that on crutches, in a wheelchair. Thirty, wasn't he? No fishing nor hunting nor R'Ville kick ass. Jane Ann said they could fit him with a wooden one, paint it the same color as his skin, match the foot size. But he had to make it out of the woods first and be willing. There was the head part, getting his mind right.

Last time he saw him, Stepwell'd hauled off and threw out a runner stealing third, just beamed it down to Elmer Moore and you could hear it hit the glove, wa-pop. Out of there.

He'd smiled that crooked smile. Stepwell smile.

It's again the law for anyone to tamper with the mail. To open it, add to it or take away, sort of like that last part of the Bible where it says that if any man shall take away from the words of the book, God will kick his ass out of the Lamb's Book of Life and the Holy City and he'll get visited by plagues of frogs, get warts on his tongue, and be visited by all manner of affliction. Don't mess with the mail.

The idea comes to him just about the time he tops the hill where Jimmy Simm's white horse stands shining in the sun with that look like he's figured it all out, that's when the idea hits him, the moment he sees White Horse. The hospital, all that blood, the transfusions and surgery and probably more surgeries and more transfusions, all the drugs and penicillin and morphine and days upon days in St. Mary's—there'd be hell to pay by the time they got Stepwell out of the woods and home.

And for that matter, it's not like you just drive down to the hardware and order up a wooden leg, match the skin color and foot size, throw in instructions on how to walk on the thing, a warranty, tips for maintenance and repair. He'd have to fly off somewhere, Stepwell would, to have such a thing fitted. That family, Dee and those two kids, they were in for it. There was the floral shop, but that wasn't but a drop in the bucket they'd be looking at. Thousands. A whole lot of thousands.

White Horse lifted his snout and neighed. Right there on that hill yonder, not ten in the morning, all lit up in the bitter weed, his silver voice ringing.

Jacky neighed back, so the horse nodded its head, snorted, pawed the ground. The two have met each other at this exact spot for about three thousand days, and it's always the same thing, the neighing, head nodding, snorts. Only this time, something different happened.

Behind him, the green field shimmered, the diamond shaped roof, the tin bar right where home should be, the outbuildings situated exactly where bases should be. It was more than a game for grown men. Women played it. Colored. Cuban and Puerto Rican and all those South American folk. You couldn't shake a stick without a team rolled up with their own colors and uniforms and lights to pay for with half the gate. One-armed men and midgets, Indians and ex-cons, rich folk and poor.

His idea blazed before him and he knew it was the right thing, and that he himself, Jacky Thorpe, part Indian himself, a relative of Jim who had all his medals stripped for petty bullshit, he had the means to make it happen, Jacky did.

He ticked off the particulars with each box, the silly red flags waving when it was a pickup, some of them knocked clean off their rockers so he had to get out the truck and stick mail into their dark mouths, down in the green grass and briars and thickets in places. Run over snakes. Dogs. Beer bottles.

By the time Jacky finished, it was a done deal. But they'd

have to get him out of the woods first. Stepwell needed to wake his ass up. They'd give him time. Not push. He'd almost died, Stepwell. With wife and daughter watching, he'd almost breathed his last. Who knew what that did to you, wake up after all that? He pictured it, headlights on the bucksaw, teeth like a man's fingers splayed. Hunks of flesh and skin. The boot laced over a foot. The rest. They'd seen it, the wife and girl.

He shook the vision from his head, turned toward home where Jane Ann, his good wife, must be waking after her grave-yard shift. It was a golden afternoon, a Wednesday in August with fall's break from the heat around the bend, dove hunt-ing in September, squirrel and rabbit after first frost. Deer in November. Then the holidays, and there'd been talk of heading down to Stuttgart where Jimmy Patterson knew a man owned a field of flooded timber on the flyway, so many mallards the sky turned black, hog-gobbling all that rice and milo. Take little Jack down there and stay out at the Quack Shack, set a run of yo-yos on Bayou Meto, bait'em with shiners, go to town on smallmouth and crappie and home potatoes, raw turnip, eat it like an apple. Get up before light, slide into waders and fire the flat bottom down the ditch to the clearing, blow the feed call, sky call, set out the decoys, hear the *tu tu tu* wingbeat and fire some number four up into the just light, ducks rain down, manna from heaven, little knock of Crown from the side pocket. He'd take his boy to Stuttgart come January, they'd all be over this by then, surely they would.

And in spring, about the time the redbud bloomed, dog-wood with Christ crucified on every white petal, daffodil and tulip, when Yell County woke from winter and was washed clean with April rain and the tornado sirens howled to beat the band, when they'd linseed oiled their gloves and rosined the bats, run the lime straight down left field and right, laid in syrup and food coloring for the snow cone machine and fifty pound sacks of popcorn, when they were all a year older and wiser, Jacky'd have about a thousand flyers printed up announcing the benefit at Little John Field, a fish fry all you can eat ball game to benefit Mr. Butch Weldon Stepwell and his family, to cover doctor bills and the fitting of a prosthesis by somebody who knew what they were doing, so he'd learn to walk and maybe even play again. So help him God. He'd print a thousand of them, stuff them in boxes from here to Morrilton, two dollars a pop, they'd put on a show. By summer, they'd have him on his feet again.

He drove home in a rush of goodwill, past Petit Jean creek and the sawmill to his turn off into the wood to the clearing where stood the A-frame he'd built with his own hands. After five now, Janey in the garden wearing the white shirt that had been his Sunday shirt once, and now she wore it for the sun, fair skinned Janey.

She was knee-deep in purple hulls, they'd grown sixteen feet high, up one side of an eight-foot trellis and down the other. Beat all. Purplish-white blooms, pretty, the leaf make your skin itch. There she was, Jane Ann, a number 12 galvanized bucket hooked through her left arm, little Jack nowhere to be seen. Dog-dog in her spot out under the sweetgum. The rain had done the place good, greened the grass. The chickens were out, hiding in the shade under the shed with his tiller and posthole digger, old waders look like a half a man, shovel and rake, hoe, antlers all strung up on a single rafter, rattle together like a buck in rut.

He smelled them, the purple hulls. Tomatoes just touched on the low limbs by summer blight, okra about half crazy with blooming, pick it every day or else, no need to water today.

The wave of goodwill he'd come in on broke at the garden gate and was completely slack by the time she met his eye. Tonight was her off night. The shirt was too big, rolled to the elbows.

"I'm home," he said.

She said, "You are."

A creek named Pea Vine marked the property line to the West, where the wood got heavy with hickory, and they'd spotted an Ivory-billed in May. They'd only seen it once, dog'd barked. Maybe it was still out there, Lord God Bird, watching them from a distance, big as a banjo.

"It's so hot after a rain. You forget about that." She handed him the bucket, turned loose a fistful of peas on top of the others. "He's conscious."

"Stepwell?"

"Who else."

A few years back they would have hugged right about then, and a few before they would have kissed. Ivory Bill out there watching from a tree: woman, man, bucket, dog, house.

"Is he okay?"

One chicken strayed from the shed, chased a horsefly. School started next week, little Jacky'd be in third grade, same as the Stepwell girl. He wanted to ride his pony to school. People didn't do that anymore, they'd told him.

"Coffin called," she said, waiting for him to shut the gate behind them. "Okay was not the word he used."

The dog raised its head, wagged its tail, then went back to sleep. It *was* hot. Get in your bones kind of hot. Rabbit-squealing hot. Inside smelled like ham. Biscuits. Best get those peas on a burner. Slice tomatoes. Fry up some okra. Not yet, outside was better. Shade. They sat on the porch, hulling. Stripping the pods and running thumbs along the groove, light green peas, purple dabs in the middle. Boil them up with a hunk of ham, sprinkle salt and pepper, best thing you ever tasted. He never got tired of them, purple hulls.

"What was it? The word he used."

From the tongue and groove porch they saw the silver wire

of creek run into the woods, the twin Catawba to the east, armed with ten-inch spikes that fell in fall. If one stuck in the ground, that was good luck Jacky'd been told, so it was always the first place he looked if he wanted to be lucky, if he needed a sign or good mojo. It was too early, but there'd been the rain. He'd walk out there, directly, see. What they all needed was a bucketful of good luck.

"'He's come to.' That's all he'd say."

It was his favorite time, pretty much. Her off night, summer still, hulling peas on the front porch he'd tongue and grooved himself, dreaming of what it would be like to have a family sit here with him, hull peas, crank ice-cream, stack a cord of firewood against the far-off cold that would surely come.

"Well good."

Stepwell had game. They'd see him through.

6.

Water. When their eyes met, the very first thing, water.

Can I have a drink of water. She'd pressed the wrinkles from her white skirt, brushed her hair. His color'd come back. He was conscious. After the long slog. Was that a word, slog? She'd pushed the door inward. Their eyes met. Looked each other a question. It was one of those moments, the kind your whole life can pass through, slippery slide, outside of clock time, like the Bible, like the monks, like I love you, like a burial, a birth, like seeing somebody laugh out loud or cry, a birthday, a song, the sound a train made the second it passed you and went from coming to going, the hot breath on your face, out in a field where you could walk forever and never be anywhere, his eyes that second, earth-colored, he'd passed them to Josephine, so her daughter looked at her through her husband's eyes, the way he'd turn his head to the side, smile crooked, shotgun wedding, her mother'd never let it go. Like bug poison sprayed in the kitchen, like being up all night, what had she dreamed? What? The way Mama'd knife-blade corn from the cob, coax the juice out, turn it to sauce, knee-deep in Isbel Creek saying *I do, I do*, touching a tree root with her toes, wasn't that what it was like to marry a man, standing in the murk and flow, saying she would, a thing you couldn't see but felt down there amongst the root of all things.

Looked each other a question.

44

Like the day you die, how it came up on you every year, September 27 or March 26 or May 9 or June 14, when the sun'd come up, and you'd get out of bed and maybe walk outside just when the light came, and it was pink sky in the morning, sailor's warning, only you didn't know, did you, the day you'd give birth, dear God, and she'd breathe and cry and look like your daddy. A daughter, a son, and their cries would turn to laughter, and it wouldn't be just about you anymore forever, no matter the headboard nor the butcher knife, the sound of rain on tin in the afternoon, low thunder far off canceling the game. Like poetry, like prayer, a song sung by a stutterer for whom melody keyed the inner lock, like blood, flowers, water, he'd asked for water, the very first medicine.

There were eight of them, Fankhauser children, Floradee second to the youngest, Hoyt Howard, who'd been named for Jesse James, who went by the alias Mr. Hoyt Howard, and had been a family friend who'd drift down from Missouri time to time before Bob and Chucky Ford shot him in the back. They'd fought for the stars and bars, they'd done it for Dixie. Son of a preacher man, Mr. Howard, little brother's namesake, over to Scranton, not far from Subiaco where she'd made it to eighth grade before Weldon Stepwell, a basketball game, wasn't he something, wasn't he?

There's a light that comes when the moon's out full in spring, full Flower, or was that May? Moon that she was named for. Comes floating through the cedar slats of a barn where last summer's hay is nearly gone, all stripy on your skin, your chest, across your face, his. The moonlight.

Eyes of hoses shone from buckled straw. Wasn't that the line, how he'd put it? When it was spring and the moon was full flower, or was it pink? How a moment, a heartbeat, can stretch out so you can crawl in and out of it for the rest of your life, and then for the other lifetimes, the ones you'd conjoined to make.

Do you want me to live?

Do you want me to?

I should have stayed in the room.

You didn't.

Remember the cedar barn?

Eyes of hoses. Or was it horses?

Hoses.

Hoses.

In a movie, this would be the moment when everything hung in the balance, the amputee awaking to see he's no longer whole, an athlete, a ball player for the Danville Little Johns, Catch, sugar pie, honey bunch, *Ding Dong Daddy from Dumas*, he'd always said that *Ding Dong Daddy from Dumas*. Would he be violent? Cry? Curse God? Shout her down? Ask for the kids? Say never let them see me this way? Ask how it happened? For the preacher. Twelve gauge? Whiskey? Why did you throw that at my head? You could've killed me. See what you've done. Would he blame her? Who was keeping the shop? What day was it? Where's my leg? What happened to me? Goddamnit to hell. Tell Mama I love her. What are you looking at? My foot itches. There. Yellowjackets stung me. Son of a bitch slid into me. How long have I been here? What's that smell. I love you. *Deedee?*

Can I have a drink of water?

Thirsty. The morphine was like that, make you crazy for thirst.

Other things.

Yes.

He'd asked for water, first thing. Yellow medicine killed you that way, but of course none of them knew that then, on that Wednesday in August when Weldon opened his eyes and rejoined—for good or naught—the world of the living.

She stood to her full height, Floradee, put on a face she'd

practiced for just this moment, neither happy nor sad nor anything at all—neutral, there, willing.

"Of course you can."

She half-filled a glass from the hallway fountain, walked back through the door and held it to his lips. The way a man whose head is on fire wants a bucket of water, how bad he wanted it. Years later, when she told the story to the grandson who'd record her talking through the whole thing, finally, the accident on Chickalah Mountain, the scene on the lawn of St. Mary's that far off and swiftly receding afternoon and night, who'd one day track down the very last Little John and hear from his mouth the riddle of what had happened to the leg, when everyone who'd ever heard the story was gone or about to disappear, she'd remember how he woke up thirsty, the way a man whose head's on fire wants a bucket of water.

Then the nurses were on them, Doc Coffin, everyone. They put tranquilizer into his vein, looked into his eyes, unwrapped the stump and began the impossible task of cauterizing nerve ends.

She was whisked out, Floradee. That was best now. She'd done her part. Stayed in the room. She had.

Daddy was coming home today, it hung over the house like a fog waiting for the sun to burn off, neutral gray, white almost, not quite. First day of school, Miss Blue for homeroom mornings, Miss Redd for afternoons—blue then red. What Daddy'd call bass-ackwards, because in the Crayola No 48 with the prissy fart holding the paintbrush it's the other way around, red before blue. Would her days be upside down? It was a sign, surely, her teachers being named that. Blue then Redd. Mix them together you get purple, a color missing from her box, the shade of royalty, of muscadine and certain clouds, those peas Daddy likes to mash up with mayonnaise and make a sandwich, of bruise, blood when it dried, the color inside your head when you held your breath for a really long time trying to make something happen, only it wouldn't. He'd be home when they got home, Josephine and Earl. She'd go by Josie this year. Daddy called her Joker sometimes. Happy hour happy—Joker, go get me my catcher's mitt, I'll teach you the curve. Mama wouldn't let her go by that, Joker. Her color is medium yellow and olive green, peaceful colors, the Ouachita hillside turning to fall. It was best this way, for him to come home, get his footing.

That wasn't the right way to say it.

They'd have to watch out, be careful, not stare, keep it on the upbeat, be positive. Mama'd been through it with them, her and Earl. Poor Earl, he'd quit talking. Cat got his tongue. Gone stone-eyed. It wouldn't be easy being a family again. The house was officially dog free, let Suzie in and it was spanka-butt city. They were to wash their hands every time they went, twice after number two. Use soap. Hot water.

Germs were everywhere, even in your breath, on your words. She'd wash her hands until they bled, if it'd help daddy.

They'd been through it all after church yesterday, Mama with that look. Earl hadn't said three words since, what was he thinking? No dogs. Wash your hands. Don't get dirty. No dirt eating. Don't bake your brother dirt brownies. Bedtime early. Help with the dishes. There'd be medicine, don't touch it. A whole lot of things they didn't know yet but would learn. Like going to school. Her pencils sharpened. First day.

Promise?

Promise.

Cross your hearts?

They crossed their hearts.

And hope to die?

Hope to die.

Good. She hugged them then, Mama. Her color was

rose-pink, like Codger Wiseman's Cadillac. Shined up, what Miss Dardanelle waved from in Little John parade.

Dressed like fall, Mama drove them to school. She'd only ever walked, mostly. Daddy was the driver, pick up the flowers, haul them to the shop, lay them in the cold room she'd sneak into sometimes of a hot day, until the smell about made her crazy. Through the fog to school they went, her and brother, first day, Mama driving, just like she'd drive him home where the WELCOME HOME DADDY sign covered most of the front door, and Earl had built a handrail out of two-by-fours. Hand sawed them himself. He'd see it from the drive, know they made it and that they loved him and were happy to have him home and be a family again, and it would lift his heart and everything would be A-okay.

She'd hold her breath till her head turned purple, if she had to.

A pair of geese, or were they ducks? Jane Ann wondered, flew over that morning, him awake, surely ready as a man can be to get clean of this place, going on three weeks now, vitals good, breath, no sign of gangrene, backing off the morphine now, though the nerves were still jangled down there, charley horses in the phantom calf, so the only way was to massage the stump, pass on directions for that to Floradee, what a mess. If such a godawful thing ever happened to Jacky, he'd best go on and bleed to death, she did enough nursing work, not about to take that home. No way. If she lived to be a thousand, she'd never get it out of her head, that first look inside the ambulance, the surgery after, how the night stretched out into sounds and smells and the touch of it between her fingertips, on her tongue so she could taste it, even, what had happened up on Chickalah Mountain. Best would be to take him to Little Rock, let the Vet's Hospital take care of him for a while, let him work

49

his way back into things under supervision. Keep a watch on him until the flesh had healed, especially the flap, which had been tricky, taking off the extra two inches, stitching the fold. Maybe they could work sending him to have a prosthesis fitted. Teach him to use it. He'd walk again. Drive a car. People did it all the time. Jump the gun and who knew what could happen. Inside those stone eyes, he was one pissed off *hombre*, Weldon Stepwell. Best take him to Little Rock.

Dee'd have none of it. They'd been through enough.

He'd go home. He sure would. They'd take care of him. And that was that. It was nobody else's business. The decision was hers.

Fine.

The new crutches leaned again the headboard. Stepwell'd mastered them in nothing flat, whamming up one side of the third-floor hall and down the other. Stand breathing hard by the far window that looked out on the lawn where they'd all waited all night, that brooding stare like he wanted to kill someone.

They'd bathed him, let him shave. Dress in his own clothes, the one leg pinned up, the other'd been a mess too, the stitches clean out now, scabbed. A watch, wedding ring, his wallet, all there on the nightstand, ready for him to take possession of himself again.

And he did want to, didn't he? He was to blame, no one but. The pain, infernal itching, loop-de-loop the morphine went when it hit vein and artery, whoa. The way the crutch dug into the underarm, there was no one to blame but himself. Goddamnit to hell. And what was he going to do now? Just what? Go home and lay in bed? Write some letters? Get them to haul his ass out to practice and watch goofball Perry Wiseman try to be a catcher? Give him pointers? Be the mascot? The one-legged Little John, say? Maybe he'd sit in the bleachers with an ought-six and fend off the crows, pop a few over the Visitor's Side bleachers, *bap, bap, bap*. The outhouse. Shit fit.

The nurse was their first baseman's wife, Jane Ann Thorpe. She didn't like him, never had, not since that time they'd got in the scuffle over to R'Ville. When that big mouth'd gone off and laughed in Lew's face, made fun of his hand, must be hard up fielding one-armed men.

Right.

Not for the first time, he took his own measure. Thirty-one last June. Married. Two kids. Runs the floral shop, Eternally Yours, Dee did, mostly, he made deliveries. Private in the war. Marines. San Diego. He played ball, was batting .400. Right-handed. He could pull it or lay off, either way. Behind the plate, he'd only been stolen on twice since May, Black man from England, Stegall was his name. Outrun a wildcat—he'd take one Stegall for every Perry Wiseman, stand out in left thinking about how his daddy was the town banker and their shit didn't stink, the Wisemans. Sneak a look at Dee. It was the medicine made him think this way. They were teammates. Were.

His sweat smelt of shame. Aftershave, shame. It oozed out of his pores, was under his nails, in his hair, under his tongue, that taste. And the truth was, his foot itched. The kind of itch like he'd got on his scalp one winter, psoriasis, little white scales wake you up in the night, so he'd had to coat it with salve, sleep with a plastic bag over his head.

But of course, he had no foot. How can his foot itch if he has no foot? Or even better, how's he supposed to scratch something that's not even there?

What he needed was another shot. That helped, knocked it down a notch. Didn't it.

The nurse could read his mind, over there doing the paper-work, writing it all down for Dee, the medicine schedule, bandages, penicillin. To think it was made from mold, what grew on the toilet, on drainpipe, on the rag he'd left hanging on a nail outside the shed one whole winter. They were going to save his ass with mold. And morphine. What he needed was a little jolt just then, take the edge off, right his wrongs.

"Should I dress now?"

Jane Ann Thorpe had the clipboard on her lap, sitting in the visiting seat where Dee had so often, that sad look on her face that made him feel like busting a glass pane, swallowing it, as if he needed to hurt any worse.

"I can finish this out there," she said, nodded, earnest, in full support. Let him do for himself.

He said, "Thank you," meant it.

The transfusion spikes had left red holes inside his elbows, big as a first grader's pencil.

Their first day of school, today, September 12, little Early in first, Josie in third. The teachers, Principal Higgs, Coach, everybody'd know and know about the Stepwell kids, what'd happened to their daddy. Pitiful things, on the free lunch program. Was there a free lunch program? He missed them. Deep down, he missed his kiddos.

They'd brought him a blue shirt, light blue, short sleeve, button up. Dee's work. She'd pressed it, little creases down each sleeve. Cotton trousers, the leg pinned up on the right side. His brown belt because who knows on earth what ever happened to the black one. A pair of socks folded into one another. Shoes, his favorites, Hushpuppies.

The shirt felt good against his skin, clean, the smell of his wife, of home and food and biscuits and his daughter and son and the way the light came in the two front windows in the afternoon. The catalpa tree out there growing. His trousers were another thing. He'd stood on his left foot, holding onto the headboard, then tried to reach the pants and couldn't. So, he sat back down, tried it that way. In his whole life, Stepwell'd never put on a pair of pants sitting down. He looked at it. He hadn't yet seen what was under the bandages, already leaking through, he could smell it, the flap of skin they'd folded over, sewn it shut. He touched it like it was someone else's. His leg. Not his leg.

He had to lay back on the bed to get them on, the pants. Laced the belt through the loops, pulled it two holes deeper, he'd lost weight. How much? 207 before. How much did it weigh, the leg?

When he tried the laces of his left shoe, his back cracked, in the old spot. He threw the right one under the bed, the Hushpuppy. He'd forgot to put on clean underwear, there they lay, a triple-fold, white.

He'd have to have the talk with Doc Coffin this morning before he left. Equinox coming on next week, time to plant collards, a fish head in every hole—have 'em on New Year's with a fat ham and peas—collards for money, peas for luck, he'd forgot about ham, what was it supposed to stand for?

He hadn't been outside in twenty-three days, one month had slid into another. He unlaced the shoe, slid off the sock, knocked the stump on a bedroll, fire screaming all up his back into his head. Jesus goddamn.

Morning out there, first day of school. He'd see his kids today, and they'd see him. Lay back and hauled the pants off the waist, one leg at a time. The clean underwear smelled like summer air of an afternoon when Humphrey the Camel was getting poured into a tumbler of ice. God what he'd give for a drink, three weeks without, hopefully she'd bought whiskey, probably not. Nor pipe tobacco, frosty cold beer nor wine. He didn't want to push it. He's a lucky man. Hasn't he heard about it? How the Lord had looked down on him, had mercy, mercy me, mercy. Answered prayer. He was a walking miracle. Would be. Praise be, glory hallelujah. Amen.

But no whiskey, no. Didn't sit right with the morphine. That's what Doc wanted to talk about, likely. He liked a nip, everyone knew it. So what? In the civilized world folk were allowed to have a sip time to time. Didn't he need that, didn't they all, didn't they? Goddamnit to hell.

The elastic on the leg hole got the fold of flesh sewn over where his knee used to be. That fire again, yellowjackets swarmed, stung all around his brain, inside his inner ears, under his scalp. Holy moly.

But he got them on, the underwear. Then the pants, belt buckle, his belly shrunken, white, the sock, shoe, tucked the shirt in, the one his daughter'd picked out for this day because it went with his eyes, the color blue from a crayon box he'd given her in a tackle box, thought they were going fishing. Well, wasn't that a thought. What cripples do. Surely to hell they could fish. His arms were fine, hoss a Devil's Toothpick out into the shallows.

The thirst again come on him of a sudden.

He could drink a bucketful of ice water, just like that. And then he'd have to piss, which meant he had to get out of bed and put the goddamn go to hell crutches into his underarms, fit the little rubber ends into the bruises there and hop his way over to the piss pot, where his bright yellow pee had stained the porcelain, and he could smell it from a mile away, his piss. And so could everybody else in Yell County, take a good country shit in it, try that with one leg, slide the cover on and somebody'd dump it once a day, three times that once. Lord, thank you, but I'd rather never have come here, to this place, hear that?

That?

Swam up from the deep eye to eye with his Floradee, who'd hurled that buzz saw at him sure as shit, just like that hissing butcher came spinning from her right hand, just to the side of his head. Would he have to sleep in that bed? The one he'd made for himself?

She was a good woman. Very good. God was good.

He crutched to the one mirror, felt the comb wetted in a glass of water go through his hair, over the scar where he'd split his head open on corrugated metal, the shed roof under which was to go the firewood that he was cutting off the tree that had wedged into another, so he'd had to reach out and push it with one hand, hold the bucksaw with the other, and it fell wrong, onto the right tiller handle and then he was wedged between the tree and it, and he hadn't expected that, to be dancing there on Chickalah under a tree with a buzz saw, one two three, one two three, dance all night, dance a little longer.

She just couldn't get enough of him, that old waltz.

Stepwell caught a glimpse of himself, almost prayed, didn't.

He was ready to go home. Past ready. The Doc'd show soon, they'd have their talk. Then Dee. They would have talked about it, how they'd let him get out of his own accord, the elevator to the lobby where all those framed pictures of mule-faced nuns stared from the walls. The parking lot, door to the Chrysler already open for him, radio off, St. Mary's in the rear-view getting smaller, and smaller, about to disappear.

And he'd made it, if not in one piece.

7.

She'd of course had to get someone to help, Dee. There was her brother, Hoyt Howard, who Weldon hated, he'd been a referee for high school basketball way back when and they had bad blood from that somehow. Jacky Thorpe had to deliver the mail. Coach Stringham offered, but they still couldn't really look each other in the eye after him having to bail Weldon out that time, make the drive to Russellville, get him out of jail, sort of that all over again. She'd said no thank you and Coach had nodded, sweet big-nosed raw-boned man. The Little Johns had all given blood, every last one of them. To the river now, oddly named Petit Jean. A sign on the way out of town retells the story of the Danville mascot, a clear morning, twenty-five miles to St. Mary's where Perry Wiseman, the team's left fielder, had agreed to meet her, help get him in the car, follow them home just in case. She'd dropped Josie and Earl off for their first day of school for Fall 1949, the decade about to end thank God.

The Petit Jean sign pointed the way out of town, to St. Mary's to pick him up and bring him home, oh God give them luck, let this come off, let them get him home in a good way and this nightmare end for a minute or two.

Petit Jean, the block letters said, Little John. And then Russellville, 25.

The story was that there was this nobleman from France who was engaged to be married, only they'd had a revolution there, the world was crazy. The guillotine mouth yawed open for anyone and everyone. The king and queen had lost their heads, Robespierre even. And he was an expert cartographer, this French nobleman who was engaged to marry a beautiful woman named Adrienne in Paris, where they'd invented the instrument of execution and were putting it to use. It was a dangerous time. Anything could happen. Anyway, this nobleman, call him Chavet, he was hired to sail across the Atlantic to map the New World with Lafayette, who was powerful and might one day rule New France. They'd had to put off their wedding, Chavet and Adrienne, so he could map the New World, a whole lot of which would one day be named Arkansas, after the Akansee tribe which plied its rivers, mound builders and fish eaters, who DeSoto had once convinced he was son of the living god. The very earth she was looking at that second, driving across the Petit Jean, north toward R'Ville, where her husband would be waiting. Monday morning, first day of school.

But the beautiful French woman, she was clever, cut her hair off and somehow slipped onto the ship dressed as a cabin boy, calling herself Jean, to whom the men added the adjective little, so that even her lover didn't recognize her during the long passage over the great blue ocean. How she must have wanted to tell him, the night in the hole with the sailors snoring, other things. The ocean was crossed in springtime. The sailors called her *Petit Jean*, the beautiful French girl, *Little John*.

Their vessel sailed up the Mississippi from New Orleans, to the mouth of the Arkansas, and then to a cold flowing river whose confluence was marked with emerald-green water, cold flowing and good to the taste. Indians walked down from a mountain to greet them, to bring fruit and squash and fish for trading. They invited the crew to spend summer on the mountain top where all manner of comforts would be furnished them. There were hot springs, healing waters, venison, and chokecherry and poke salet.

And so they did, live the summer on top of the mountain. Right over there.

Paris had been a dangerous place. But she couldn't live without him, could she? Her father had stayed true to Louis, the family was marked. The crazed mob's voice called for blood—they could not get enough. Everyone knew someone who'd lain their head into the curved cradle below the blade—nobles, a monarch, beautiful women, the queen in time. The world had gone mad, she could not stay, not in Paris, not in France. So she sneaked her way to the New World, New France, to the mountaintop where her and her unawares lover took their retreat for a summer overlooking the Arkansas before it was called Arkansas. A land so vast and green and living, far from the awful sound of severed necks.

A day came when the maps were made, the rivers charted, they must return to the mouth of the Mississippi, and east into the Sun, to their dead sovereign whose father had been named for the Sun.

On the night before departure, she got sick. Real bad sick. Fever, throwing up, delirium, coma finally. He discovered her then, Chavet, how she'd deceived them all and was now dying. And she opened her eyes to his, kissed his lips, and begged that, if she should die, he'd carry her to the mountaintop where for a summer she'd gazed unmolested at him, and, unknowing, he her.

Away from the muddy river they carried her, on a stretcher made of deer hide, the fur turned to her flesh. And she was buried up there, on the mountain now named Petit Jean, in Arkansas when it was New France, a vast green forest growing from the Old World to the New, her story the bridge.

Had that tree not grown roots already, the one Weldon laid hand and blade to. Had it not lived and breathed in the day of Petit Jean? Was it not already living when she gazed down that last summertime? She who'd been baptized in Notre Dame on a day in April when the grand old cathedral would one day burn, and the season of violence that followed would rival Robespierre's wildest dreams.

It was a sign, morning sunlight falling on the letters of the old legend. Surely it was. A climbing vine turning fall colors already. Like rain falling through sunshine. Behind her, the church bell rang, just as she crossed over, and it was a morning when there was nothing to do but turn loose and have faith, walk the path that's been laid for you, even if it led into a great burning.

Baptism by fire.

He'd said yes, what else could he say? But it wouldn't go well, how could it? For the hundredth time he put himself in Stepwell's shoes, in that hospital the three weeks now, waking up like that in a world of hurt, the medical bills, on the other side of the river, and now another man shows up escorting your pretty wife to take you home where you're supposed to do exactly what? Say? A man like that? Look at him sideways he'd slap you silly. Perry'd seen it happen, more than once. On the ballfield, he was afraid of nothing, nobody, not a thing. From left, he'd watched Stepwell at the plate with a sort of awe, how he'd throw down the runner, take them coming spikes first, stare down the opposing coach, the dugout, say something to take the batter off his swing. Dugouts never cleared when he was on the field, never happened. He had that presence, heat, monkey foot, mojo. That look in his eye when he saw you look at Dee—and who could help that? Stepwell'd kill you, best not even think about it, no sir. Gone off to college, college boy, you think you're smart, your daddy runs the bank, huh? You look at my wife again, I'll take your head off, that's what his look said, and that was enough for Perry, he didn't need reminding.

But God, Jesus, what did he step in to deserve her, Floradee, green eyes shining behind the plate glass of Eternally Yours, up to her elbows in flowers, none of which was remotely sweet as herself. She'd seen him, and she knew. She knew.

He shook the thought from his head.

Hoped for the best.

Meet her at the hospital, St. Mary's, in the lobby, 9:30, he was early, crossed the river bridge from Dardanelle over the Arkansas, good catfishing spot down below the dam, a couple black men down there now running lines before the heat comes on. Over to the Pope County side, Arkansas Polytechnic off in the distance, where he'd met Jeanine that fall when the Wonderboy Band played "Dixieland" at half-time and he'd seen her eyes glowing on the fifty, a silver flute horizontal against the green of her uniform, tassels, the horns like elephants on the moon.

St. Mary's, that green front lawn where they'd stretched blankets and waited it out, he'd hemorrhaged, breathed his last, no, still alive, wouldn't make it through the night, he'd made the turn, no, going again, he lived. Stepwell'd made it, no one knew how. God wanted it to be so. He'd gone in and given blood, they all had. Gill Stegall'd driven over from England, Black shortstop, only man steal on Stepwell, twice, England Lions, he'd walked in and given blood and no one had said a word. That serene look from his wife and little girl, the boy, out on a blanket of their own.

Dee and the girl'd been in the ambulance. Good God.

Early, Wiseman was good to his word. What would come of it, he could not guess. What they needed was a goddamn preacher, Reverend Day from First Methodist, couldn't do it, had to drive over to Memphis for a funeral, or was it a wedding? Didn't matter, they needed a preacher and a boatload of prayers to God and Jesus and Holy Ghost, the whole nine yards. To tell the truth, he was scared, Perry was. Jeanine had sniffed it on him earlier, did he want her to go with him? It was a Monday, slow day at the store.

No. Say a prayer.

Will he be on crutches? A wheelchair? Will you have to lift him? He's heavy as a horse, has to be.

Perry didn't know. Maybe they need two men. Three. Maybe the whole team should have come to see him home. Why hadn't they thought of that, the team, the Little John short bus, that was it. Stepwell could have his old seat to himself, the whole thing, maybe they'd play catch, swing a bat.

The nuns hanging in the hallway scowled at him as if to telepath the error of his thought, there'd be no baseball today.

The Ford needed oil. Dee was sure of it. Air in the tires, they all four looked low. And the spare, what if the spare was flat. The wipers needed fixing and the spark plugs changed, was there enough gas? Did she need to fill up in Russellville before heading home? There was this thing called dead battery syndrome, and when that happened, you were supposed to get the lug wrench out from the spare tire compartment, hook it to the latch up front on the grill and twist. Could she do that? If it came right down to it? Turn on the radio or not. Windows up or down? It was still hot, what if they overheated? The list of everything that could go wrong flooded over her. The smell of catastrophe.

She'd wanted to do this right. Had fussed over every detail of her dress, not too pretty, not too plain. Easy on the eyes and rouge, not a spritz of White Shoulders, it made him sneeze. The ring she'd once froze in an ice tray, he'd cracked it open to make his bourbon and branch, and there it was, the gold band his mother'd worn, not even a diamond set against it. The front end shimmied some, that was normal, wasn't it? She should have washed the Ford, cleaned the tire wells. Front seat or back. Her breath came in little gasps.

A clear bluebird day, not yet time, she parked far away as she could, took one of Weldon's cigarettes from her purse and lit it with the lighter on the console dashboard, aglow when she smelled the smoke. There she was in the rearview, all quiet the way it gets on a snow day when the tree limbs make white Vs and one thing's over and another begins.

Her throat burned, her lungs.

A man pushed a mower in squares around the big front lawn, so it reminded her of a checkerboard, how she'd play her daddy on the days he'd not even try to find work, Mama with her stern look and meanness. It mixed with the smoke, the smell of cut grass. Too early to sweat, hot already. Could he hear it from the room where he'd be sitting dressed already, waiting? What would he be thinking, was he as nervous as she was? Of the twenty-nine Septembers of her lifetime, and fifty some that were left to her, when three crisp minutes were severed from each day and you could sense the world diminish and not know why, surely this was the one that would decide all, that's how it seemed, breathing in the smoke and mown grass, a hint of gasoline from the mower as it made smaller and smaller squares, little boxes, perfect jails.

He'd be thirsty, she should have brought water. A bottle of it. Ice. Twenty-five miles home, and then? Doc Jenkins would come around. Reverend Day. Coach. Earl and Josie home from school this afternoon. She'd bought a fryer, mangled it in the sink, that had always been his job, slicing the backbone out, separating drumsticks, leg from thigh, sectioning the breasts into six pieces. He liked the little wings crispy. Save some of the oil with cracklings for gravy, peel the potatoes, wasn't that what they'd fought about last time, peeling potatoes? Her people used a paring knife, how Mama'd turn the potato with her left hand, the peel coming off in one long piece. Only Weldon'd said that's how bumpkins peeled potatoes and brought home a peeler which you sort of had to flick at the potato with, take the skin off in little wisps. She'd refused that first time, went back to doing it the way Mama had. Any time she wanted to get his goat, make his heart beat fast, all she had to do was peel with the knife, he was scared of the knife, to tell the truth, temper sudden as heat lightning.

She'd already baked biscuits, his other job. Hers came out looking like toads, but she'd tried, and they weren't so bad.

He'd smell it on her, the smoke. Already had. "So you keeping on smoking," he'd said to her day before yesterday.

"Yea," she'd said. "Guess I am."

They hadn't talked about it, not yet. It was like this fog hanging out there that wouldn't go away, and if you said anything about it then it'd only get thicker, till you couldn't see anything at all, and you'd start to bump into things and that was dangerous.

"Well, save some for me," he'd said.

"I will."

"And you know what else." He'd looked her in the eye.

She did.

But back home, where they'd be driving to today, to get him settled in and unload all the gauze and tape and pads, the salves and ointments for bedsores, liquid morphine with its paper instructions marked *must and must not*, she'd poured it all out, the bourbon and clear stuff, even the little pint of Ancient Age hidden under his tackle box in the shed. It didn't mix well; Doc Coffin had told her in no uncertain terms. Best not to open that can of worms.

Best not.

Inside, all she had to do was sign to have him released. Promise that he'd be in her custody, let them write down all the stuff from her driver's license. There were promissory notes to sign. She'd asked how much, but the woman behind the desk said she hadn't a clue. Accounts Payable would be in touch. They surely would. Mr. Stepwell had been through a lot. They'd come through the mail, the woman said, both hands flat on her desk. "Just don't worry about that today, sugar. He's waiting for you, Mrs."

Stepwell, the woman said, an odd name, she sees now, something not right about it.

"Thank you," Dee said.

And if she could have turned away from it right then, just hopped in the Ford and flown, gone back to Subiaco and hidden in the monastery with the dark-eyed monks, she would have. But she didn't, did she?

Perry was in the room, in a chair across the lobby, looking at her like he'd seen a ghost, a car wreck, a train come slamming into St. Mary's. They met eyes. She smiled. Signed her name, and there was nothing left on this earth to do but what they'd come for, 9:37 on the big round clock, add up to nineteen, unlucky number. The releasing nurse was assigned to them, her and Perry—and Weldon, yes—Jane Ann Thorpe, who'd stripped naked that eternity ago, that other world, when it could go either way. Could it still?

"Morning, Dee."

He reached to shake, his right hand, and she took it, just for a second, awkward, pulled back.

The white floor was darkened where people walked, little trails, cow paths.

"You ready?"

They were coming, going, pushing linen carts, wearing work uniforms, ties, some of them, flowers in their arms, God knows what had come of hers, baby's breath locked with yellow roses in the stifling room, iris, a case of carnations, what else? Somewhere here, the maternity ward where they'd taken Josie while Dee was sutured.

"No, you?"

"How is he?"

"We'll see. Ready to go home."

"I bet."

"Josephine and Earl?"

"It's been a haul."

He'd dressed, Perry. Worn a tie, silly man. 9:41, fourteen, good. Jane Ann stepped from the elevator, clipboard in hand, that look on her face they must train you to wear in nursing school, reassuring, not too. Her hair, her shoes, the I.D. hanging from a little silver chain around her neck. The elevator, thank God. She'd never even thought about it, stairs—the front porch, how he'd carried her up two steps at a time on the bright shining morning they'd moved in, Josie toddling behind, Earl on the way. Springtime, and now almost fall, winter coming. Everyone locked in the house, all of them.

"He's stable," Jane Ann said. She held one hand behind her back, so the elevator stayed open, clicking for some reason.

"Doc Coffin. Have they talked?"

"They have."

The door dinged wide open. Inside, the creak and jolt, the feel of rising, smell of people, food from other floors, 2, 3, 4, added up to 9, bad number. Weldon on 5, fourteen again, good.

"Perry."

"Jane Ann."

"He doesn't know. That you're here."

"Weldon?"

There was a pause, a moment when the floor inside was made to match outside, a brief lowering, the bell. And then the door opened, and they were on the fifth floor and the sense of dread washed over her for a second time that morning, then

65

passed. There was the water fountain with its cold sweet relief, and down there the door she'd walked through when he'd first come to, there was no more putting it off, was there? They walked a line, one behind the other. The rooms numbered, 506, 507, and then his. Where she'd seen him that first morning, when he'd asked for water and she'd filled a glass from the ice-cold fountain, held it to his lips, listened to the sound of him drinking. How he'd said *good*, and *good*, shut his eyes for a while, then opened them and saw.

How she'd said *I love you*, the only thing that came to her. And he'd just looked, that question in his eyes. Jane Ann shoved the heavy door with its dents from the throng who'd entered a world of hurt, where had passed those who'd come to bring comfort, to soothe, and there they were, the four of them.

A good number.

8.

Everything had gone according to plan. He was dressed and waiting, polite to Perry, contrite to death, almost, to Jane Ann, Dee, who he'd greeted as Deedee, the name he alone ever called her, and never in front of anyone until now. "Good morning, Deedee," he'd said, and she hugged him, and might have cried a river that second she'd relive into her eighties when everyone who'd played a part in the story had died save one. He'd passed the test. They gathered his stuff. He'd refused the wheelchair, walked out the door first, color in his face, a proud man, still. The hallway was lined end to end: custodians and day nurses, food handlers and janitors, other patients who'd seen him learn to use the crutches, up and down, up and down, window to window, that look like a heavy tree limb about to crash down any second, clean-shaven Coffin holding the elevator door, all clapping, not loudly, just enough to let him know. They were applauding him for living, how about that? "Going down," Coffin said, and just then the right crutch's rubber tip slipped through the crack between elevator and floor and he almost fell but didn't—by dent of will.

Everyone in the lobby was on their feet, some had taken their hats off and some were nodding, as if Weldon Stepwell was the right answer to some question they'd carefully considered and finally decided upon. A younger man in black glasses asked him for his autograph, and he'd said what for? Surely to God simply living wasn't enough for that.

"You're number ten," the kid said. "The Catch."

"Oh," Weldon'd said, and signed his name awkwardly in blue ink over the chest of the man he'd been when the Little John team photo was taken for the playbill. The last one, it occurred to him that second, that would ever be taken of him on two legs.

"Thanks," the kid said, and then came another.

Everyone standing.

And more outside, driven from Danville to join the entourage that would see him home. For the first time since he put his hand on the tree and pushed, Stepwell breathed sweet earth air and held it in his lungs. The breeze touched his face and he smelled the fresh cut lawn. There was birdsong and a trellis of roses blooming against the building, American beauties, scarlets, and miniature Fourth of Julys. The car was waiting, door open, a little line on either side for him to pass through. Perry's truck behind. And then the rest of them paraded around the circle drive. He got in the front seat, rolled down the window. Thinking get us the hell out of here, he didn't say it. Someone took a picture as Dee pushed the dash button to start the Ford, put her in gear and drove away, slowly at first, Highway 27 home. September 12, 1949, the war behind them, how they'd kicked Hitler's ass, come home and played some by god baseball, and now this. They'd got through it, too. Anything was possible. Anything at all.

In that way, with that sort of hope in his heart, Weldon Stepwell went home to the life he'd left and damned near lost on that other day, the details of which were only beginning to become clear. There was something about the leg that had to do with Jack Thorpe. Stegall'd given him blood. The rest of them. Three weeks had passed. There'd be a stack of bills a foot high. He'd have to set up rehab at the VA in Little Rock. As Honorable Discharge, he was benefits eligible.

They'd try to fit a prosthetic leg. No reason he couldn't walk again, young, strong as he was. There were programs for people like him. They'd talk about it, him and Dee. Eternally Yours could reopen. He could bother to learn the floral business for a change. With positivity, a lot could happen.

He saw his house from a mile away, read the WELCOME HOME DADDY sign his daughter'd hand lettered in the rainbow colors of her birthday crayons. Fresh mown grass. Somebody'd built a catywhomp handrail out of two-by-fours up the steep front steps. Raw lumber all hammer dented where the nails had been driven, bent, clawed out and renailed. Funniest thing you ever saw, that handrail. Earl's work.

WE LOVE YOU on grocery store butcher paper, the door.

October sky was azure blue and all the hickories up Danville Mountain went from olive to gold ochre, yellow orange to orange, just like they were supposed to. So when the sun got low and he'd swallowed yellow medicine for game one of the 1949 World Series, broadcast on live radio, and she had permission to listen with her father, and Earl was off sulking down the street and Mama was at the shop working late, all the trees caught fire like the crowd at Yankee Stadium after the National Anthem when the first pitch was about to be thrown by a little boy who'd survived polio. He wore braces, the announcer said, but they could not stop him from making that first pitch, into his wind up, the release, a perfect strike, though daddy made the sound that meant it was a crock of shit, the little polio boy throwing a perfect strike.

It was like this: they were set up in the front room with its wavy glass picture window looking out on the trees of fire, after a dinner of pinto beans and potatoes, cornbread and sliced tomato, from the back porch where they'd stored all the green ones because first frost was coming, maybe that very night. Mama'd gone in to make a funeral lay for the church lady. Josie'd done dishes, dried, put away. Earl'd run off. It was a school night, a Wednesday, October 5, and the Series was opening in New York City, where no Stepwell'd ever been, far as daddy knew. He was not a Yankees fan, daddy. He'd rather be a fence post in a Yell County cow pasture than play for the dirty bastards. That's what he said, *dirty bastards*, right after the little polio boy threw out the perfect strike first pitch.

And Brooklyn Dodgers had just beat their Cardinals with right fielder Stan Musial who'd hit .338 and was the best slugger in baseball. Daddy and Mama'd been to St. Louis. They'd ridden the elevator up in a silver arch tall as Mt. Nebo and they'd looked out the tinted windows at the Mississippi River, which was the biggest on earth, kicked the shit out of anything they had in Africa or South America, don't pay any attention to what Home Room Miss Redd said, but that Blue, she sure was a looker, or did he have them bass-ackwards again?

The wheelchair they'd brought him left little tracks on the linoleum when he went to the kitchen for the beer he'd got Mama to buy for this special occasion, game one of the 1949 World Series at Yankee Stadium in New York Goddamn City where everyone was either a Yankee or a Dodger.

The radio was the kind built into a wooden box, and when the static came on, Daddy'd slap it silly, get that smile on his face, and say something like *Ding Dong Daddy from Dumas* or *Humphrey the Camel*, or *I'll rip your rompers, Joe DiMaggio*. Josie didn't know who they were for, exactly, it was like they were against them both equally. Pitcher number one, this rookie named Newcome came out throwing smoke, can't nobody hit him, strikes out eleven, walks none.

The beer made daddy have to pee.

And when he had to pee, he had to get up on his crutches because the wheelchair wouldn't fit through the bathroom door, and she'd hear him cuss in there, sockless in the one shoe, a Hushpuppy, Mama'd hid the other in the closet, said he'd accidentally left it behind at the hospital. He'd need it for when they fitted a wooden leg, so he could walk and play ball and maybe they'd go fishing if her grades were good.

Pitcher number two, he was a Yankee, retired all the Dodgers in the top of the ninth. The beer was in little brown bottles. Earl said it looked like piss inside there, that he could open one up and pour the beer out, fill it with pee, how'd daddy like them apples. He was always saying stuff like that when everyone thought he'd quit talking.

The other medicine was in a glass vial. He kept that in the bedroom which the chair would fit through, little tire tracks there and back. The trees had all gone out, the fire. The slapped silly radio was too scared to make static. They could hear it fine.

A Yankee put one over the right field fence, bottom of the ninth. New York, 1 to 0. The announcer made a big deal out of it, winning game one at home. Even though the Dodgers were just across town, so it was kind of their home too. They had a Black man on their team fast as Gil Stegall. First one up from the Negro Leagues.

"He really give me blood, Josie?"

When Mama came home, they argued just a little. In the bedroom. She could hear them. Earl'd put a pillow under his sheet to make it look like he was in bed. His first-grade teacher, Mr. Pecker Head, Daddy called him, had sent home a note with a line for one of the parents to sign. Daddy'd asked for Indian red, drew a picture on it.

Guess what?

Game Two was the very next night, only Daddy was out of beer and Mama'd poured the whiskey out, and the Black man doubled, scored. Dodgers won, which meant Yankees lost— they won either way. And lost. The radio cabinet was hard wood, dark, little bulbs glowing and hissing inside. Listening to the game in the front room on a Thursday night, he'd go out on the front porch in his chair and smoke a cigarette. She wasn't supposed to open the door for him. It was important that he do it himself. She didn't know why. He'd always opened doors for her, for Mama, too. She caught a glimpse of white bandage through the pant leg while the pitchers went after each other for all of Game 3, New York's starter and reliever, and it was 1-1 in the ninth, when the runs came fast and furious, and he got excited, Daddy. Mama was doing something in the kitchen. The bills had been coming and coming. She kept a yellow notebook, the legal kind, and on it were lists, one side in black, the other in red. They had green tomatoes that night, fried.

Yankees knocked a runner on then another and another, bases loaded, then another hit, so 3-1, then Dodgers turn at bat. New York had a new pitcher, and Dodgers knocked Jesus out of him. Home run city. The catcher came to bat, Roy Campenella. The announcers talked about how he held his bat, hugged the right side of the plate. Daddy was a catcher, hardest position on the field, sort of the game's general, he'd explained, calling signs, one of which was for a bean ball to the head, closed fist and one. He'd just come in from smoking and Dodgers catcher was at the plate, 4-2, Yankees on top.

Two outs. Count full. Yankees crowd screaming. Trees on fire. Hit the goddamn ball," Daddy said. "Knock it to China."

His stump rose up and fell. She saw the stained bandage, color of a tongue, the fourth red in her box. He was bleeding still, Daddy. It hurt. That's why he took yellow medicine. Hit the goddamn ball, knock it to China, her mind the second after she saw the bandage.

Roy Campenella at the plate. Big Roy. Two outs. A man named Page on the mound for Yankees, a sign flashed in the dark beneath legs. Mama adding and subtracting in the kitchen. Earl who knows where, always run off, he'd peed in one of daddy's empty beer bottles, fitted the cap back on just so. It was the only one in there. He was waiting for Mama to give in and let him have another six-pack. I'd pushed it behind the milk, that one bottle.

"Does it hurt? Your leg?"

And that second, Campenella hit a blast over center field, into the second deck and farther, out of the stadium, on its way to China. So, she didn't hear if he said yes or no or anything at all. And Dodgers lost anyway, last batter frozen on the third strike.

Game 4. Friday night. No school mañana. Mrs. Redd spoke Spanish in class, hot today, chili tamale, Daddy said. No beer, yellow medicine. They'd talked at the dinner table about the stack of bills, options, selling Eternally Yours, the car, borrowing from Perry Wiseman's father over to the Bank & Trust. He was rolled up to the table in his chair, a little lower than us, than Mama. Daddy'd slapped the table with the palm of his hand, so the plates jumped up just a little, then settled back down. She'd baked fresh biscuits, Mama.

Yankees pitcher fanned the last ten batters. One game away now, Dodgers down 3-1.

Then it happened. China. The moon.

Trees on fire.

On the Saturday of Game 5 a hard rain came then passed, and behind it came the first chill of autumn, bourbon and cider weather, wood smoke mingling with burned pine needles through the open window. But he knew that wasn't an option, was it, like throwing gasoline on a fire, Doc Coffin'd said in no uncertain terms, absolutely out of the question. Not in the realm of possibility. What about beer, then? Well, what about it? She'd shaken our blankets out, Mama, made beds with fresh sheets with star-patterned quilts that smelled like the hands of church ladies who'd picked flowers in a fall rain, and the sun came out burnt sienna on a Saturday. She'd gone into their closet, Josephine had, not knowing what she was looking for until she came on it, the shelf where his catcher's mitt was folded around a white baseball, sweat-stained and smelling of pine rosin, sticky inside of the wristband, the same flourish on the S and L as came out of her own hand. Mama's dresses hung from hangers, her smell on them. In here, the both of them mixed, so it was them together instead of apart, out there in the kitchen arguing over a six-pack of beer from County Line, a hunk of baloney from Wiseman's Grocery, where she'd got the butcher paper for the WELCOME HOME DADDY sign. I LOVE YOU, the colors had all run with the rain.

Wasn't she them mixed together, Josephine?

All day long her hand smelled like the inside of the glove, the sticky resin welding her fingers together. It would be a part of the mix when the Star-Spangled Banner was being sung at Ebbets Field in Brooklyn, when Daddy cracked his first beer since Game 1 and touched it to his lips. The dark insides of the catcher's mitt would flow together with the smell of Earl's pee, even as her father spat and coughed and goddamned the world to hell. She wouldn't wash it, the right hand, not for as long as it took Earl to take his spank-a-butt and cry like he was dying though, of course, he wasn't. The musk of it would be with her in bed that night, in the protective chill of fresh sheets under the star quilt. If she could have bottled it up and kept it near for the rest of her life, that part of her father that lived on inside the glove whose webbing held the world they'd lost.

Yankees took the World Series in 5, their twelfth title. They'd win again next year, and the next and the next and the next. She'd come of age before they'd lose a Series. Goddamn Yankees.

On the nights when the morphine hadn't swallowed him whole, when he had some thin sinewy strip of skin still connected to the living world, Weldon woke screaming, always a shock to her, his sweat and blood and harsh voice screaming the name that he alone called her, and she could never tell if he was screaming for help from her or fear, that knife-gash between them on the headboard, you could see it in the dark, even, like a night light, only reversed. A darkness in the dark. You had to watch out because sometimes he'd wake up throwing elbows, jaw breakers that sometimes connected so she'd see stars and tell customers she'd run into a wall or slipped on a sidewalk, so people must think her the clumsiest woman on earth, twenty-nine-year-old Dee Stepwell.

Other times, like tonight, she'd touch his face with both hands, bring her lips close to his, and tell him it was okay, no one was coming after him, it was just a dream he was dreaming. They were with him. On his side. He could do this. He was bigger. Stronger. Inside and out. His family was with him. They'd stay no matter what. No matter. Turn loose of it, baby. Let it go. Tomorrow we'll drive out to Petit Jean, have a Sunday picnic. Him and Earl could bream fish with cane poles, catch enough for a fish fry, she'd make hushpuppies, they'd fry green tomatoes and okra and there'd be cobbler and ice cream, muscadine, and all this would lay down and let him be.

His breath'd be ragged, the sweat with that smell on it, that godawful yellow smell, and the new one from a sore that wouldn't heal, was it gangrene? Had it come back for more? It leaked on the sheets, his stump, and wouldn't come out with washing, no matter what.

Thank goodness the sister, Weldon's, had stayed away. Trouble with a capital T, Naleen, married to Chandler who'd graduated from the University of Arkansas and wore a gold ring with a red stone that said so, that he'd graduated and was now in Agriculture, a tomato grower which got Weldon's goat, because that's what he was good at, had been good at, growing two-fisted Big Boys, and now Sis was sending the ripe fruit to them by the bagful so she was sick to death of them, tomato sandwich, meatloaf, spaghetti sauce, juice, and if she ever ate tomato soup again, especially the cold kind, she'd gag. But at least she didn't darken the door herself, Sis.

He breathed, calmed down, asked for water, had to pee, could she bring the chamber pot, thunder mug he called it, was it there? Where it was supposed to be? Only it wasn't, she'd washed it, set it outside out back to dry. She heard it hit the floor, the splatter. And then he cried. She heard him hopping for a towel.

He never talked about it. Not about the dreams. None of it.

What he'd said to Earl about the rail up the front steps—the one he'd been so proud of building, same as Josie and her door sign she wouldn't let anyone help with. He'd measured and sawed and nailed it all together, used post hole diggers half again as tall as he was to set the braces. Sanded off the rough places and splinters, all he could think of to help his Daddy get up into the house, to come back home and be himself again, play ball, flash the signs. And Weldon had gone and said that, first thing.

The holidays were coming. Winter. She simply could not live on the wild game his teammates would no doubt leave daily on the front porch: squirrels, rabbit, duck and wild turkey, deer when season came, hard bits of lead shot between the teeth, the taste of blood, she'd never get that taste out of her mouth again.

And who was there to talk to? Not Mama and Daddy, at least not Daddy when Mama was around, him with his heart gone funny. Forget Hoyt, her brother, he'd just say told you so. Weldon's people off in Morrilton. The team? Coach? He'd bailed him out that one time. Perry?

The first reminder notices—she'd got the first one Friday.

He lay there breathing while she wiped it up.

"I'm sorry, Dee."

The windows were open, and the urine was cold, soaked the towel. She left it lay, retrieved the chamber pot, set it in place. Before long he'd be back asleep. Sometimes it only happened once in a night. She'd close her eyes and try to think of nothing, the earth a ball, orbiting another ball, the purest of silences, nothing but that.

He was telling the truth, she knew. He was sorry.

Was he ever.

9.

Stepwell cutting his leg off had knocked the whole team off its feet. Each of the Little Johns took a go at catcher, learning signs, one for fastball, two for curve, three for knuckle, and four for change. Five, dust off. Clenched fist, bean. He tried it himself, Jacky. Started a double-header down to Dogtown against North Little Rock Bulldogs, and he'd tried, he'd really tried. Jimmy Paterson on the mound. But it was no good. The truth was that it was hard to squat behind the plate, nobody knew it, but just to do that and stay balanced on the toes of both feet took superhuman strength—who'd guess. And then, to do it while a fist-size ball hauled ass straight at you upward of ninety-miles-an-hour, and you're supposed to catch the thing, because if you miss, runner rounds third next time scores, and before you know it the dogs have hopped the Johns, and there's nothing to do but drive the short bus home and unpack gear, go home and eat supper with playing ball over for another year and winter coming on, those late Ozark afternoons when the shadows snuck up on him before he ever reached Jimmy Simms's place and White Horse with his ringing neigh silver as First Methodist's church bell. The kicker, though, the hardest thing wasn't the squatting or hauling ass baseball or missing pitches so three goddamn runs scored before you knew what hit you, the damndest part of it was the man swinging a number thirty-three Louisville Slugger so you could hear it whiz past your ear, not a finger's width from your head, and you're supposed to be good with that?

They'd all given catch a try, so much for that—he'd rather eat dog turd.

Coach Stringham called a team meeting after the last shut out, October, the Series started already up in New York City. They'd either have to recruit a catcher, or Stepwell'd have to teach somebody to be one, and this last idea fed into Jacky's original vision of a Stepwell Benefit in spring to help pay off medical bills that were no doubt afflicting the family about now and set into motion whatever had to happen to get an artificial limb. That was the plan, the chief focus of the Little Johns' end of season team meeting after having their asses kicked in Dogtown, way down on the other side of the big river, the one Petit Jean had floated up with her beau who thought her a boy, though an unusually little one at that. Say five o'clock, straight up happy hour, though no one'd thought much about that since August, just wasn't the same without Stepwell and his bourbon and branches garnished with lemon juice from a yellow squeeze bottle. What they needed was a call to action, a summons to put their collective heads together for just a little bit of clean thinking toward a positive end, all of them sitting there, coming on a Friday night, grown men in their Little John uniforms the oil company had donated, Danville writ in red across their chests, in the outbuilding that doubled as a field house, the snow cone machine all shined up under plastic in the corner, ready for winter.

Coach was not a talker. He pretty much told you what he thought by the cast of an eye, chin point, the sign for stealing, right index against the nose, belly pat, left fist clenched then not. He'd driven the short bus back from Dogtown after the ass kicking, and just before they left one of the dogs had laughed out loud, said something with the word little in it.

Stepwell'd of cut his head off, stuck a carrot in its mouth

and rigged it in front of the bus, Dogtown hood ornament, he'd call it. He wouldn't really have done it, but that's what they talked about, Lew and Fay and Hicks and Jacky, best watch out who you flung pecker jokes at, might be someone on the listening end about to rip your rompers.

Coach chin pointed at Jacky, he was supposed to start the talking.

They all looked at him, October outside, nip in the air.

In attendance, the whole motley, seated in a half square on the dugout benches they'd drug in from outside. Left to right: Perry Wiseman, Jay Marcum, Jack, empty spot where Stepwell always sat, Jimmy Patterson and Bill Lordes. Lew Blanding and Horace Hicks, Baskin who everyone called Bastard. Lloyd George, Mathison, Elvin Moore, Coach.

"Fellows," Jacky said.

A pouch of chaw went around, Red Man, an empty corn can. The overhead light was on, one bare bulb with a string tied to it. Coach made the sign for swing, big palsy-spotted hand over his heart.

"I was thinking."

"Trouble," little George said. His daughter'd had the pox, spotted up her face, poor thing.

Jacky said, "Yea, I know."

Coach made the sign to hit away, send the runners, katy-bar-the-door. Miss and you'll run the fence line path outside and in, full uniform till the cows come home or coach gives the sign to stop.

"Stepwell's knee deep in doctor bills. Hospital and ambulance and medicine. Be a hard winter for him and Dee. The kids."

The last of the ruby-throated hummers hovered outside the one window, sucking sugar water from the feeder Coach kept filling till they all flew south, any day now.

80

"I know we all given blood. That helped. Traded off for his transfusions. But we ought to do more. Don't you think?"

"More than give our blood?" Bastard said.

Hold, Coach said. Take. Big farmer arms, Stringham'd hit the ball a mile, make you chase it down to the creek where copperheads sipped water with forked tongues. Once Jacky'd had to haul down and take a country shit and one had crawled right up on him, flicking its tongue, and he'd said "what do you want," and "go on now," and finally "kiss my ass," which the son of a bitch must've understood because it swam straight at him and he'd had a shit fit right then and there, damn snakes.

Swing away.

Bastard said, "Tell us that leg story."

Horace Hicks spat in the corn can. "Aint'a gonna hear it," he said.

Two or three of them nodded. Coach still as stone. Pay attention. Be alert. Now's the time. The impediment to action causes action. What gets in the way becomes the way. All of that out of his stone still body.

"What I'm saying. I swear. They in a boat load of trouble. Stepwell and Floradee. And I had this idea over to Jimmy Simms's place, dropping off the mail in that knocked down box."

Lew Blanding only had a thumb on his right hand, but could he ever throw the be-Jesus out of a slider, keep it coming with the change. That second he held the one thumb up so light shone on its nail, crooked just a little, three wrinkles on the knuckle.

"You ain't never told the whole thing. What happened to it."

"Aint'a gonna hear it."

Coach clench fisted.

"Shut up, Bastard."

Hit away.

"This spring I propose we throw him a benefit, Stepwell."

He re-envisioned the tin roof over to Simms's place, diamond shaped, the green field shimmering, out buildings right where the bases should be. How White Horse had neighed, and he'd neighed back, and it had come to him, the particulars.

How when the redbud bloomed and all the shining dogwoods revealed Christ crucified, they'd run a straight line from home down left and right, sift the lime to the fence in either direction, the tornado sirens would all be turned off and they'd throw him a by god Little John Baseball All You Can Eat Fish Fry and pack it to the gills. Hell, they'd throw in fireworks and a guitar fiddle band, have Miss Dardanelle over to sing the Star-Spangled Banner. Two dollars a pop, they'd make enough dough to pay off the whole nine yards, plus some. Be enough for that wooden leg, or whatever they made artificial out of now. They'd have him on his feet. Goddamnit, he'd be their catcher coach, and they'd kick shit out of Dogtown, turn that boy's sneer into a short bus hood ornament, so help him God.

Such was the gospel Jacky Thorpe preached to his people that long dark World Series evening in October 1949, when the Yankees were on their way to sweeping the Dodgers, despite that first Black player's prodigious base running, fucker stole home, didn't he?

Stepwell'd shit his pants, stealing home.

"Boys?"

Each one of the Little Johns nodded in turn, passed the chaw, the cup. Bastard shut up about the leg. Lew held up the one thumb, and little George got up and poured some more red-dye sugar water in the hummingbird feeder. It was agreed. They'd do it. They would.

Nodded, Coach. Chin pointed. Well done, son.

Each was given a part in bringing the thing about. Bastard was to find a worthy opponent for the game itself. Faye Mathison had contacts over to R'Ville for the fish-fry goods, and Lew'd once went on a date with Miss Dardanelle's first cousin Daylene. Hicks had people in hardware. They could build decent bleachers, make space for a crowd of Yell County folk, Pope and Washington, invite the State Rep up from Little Rock. And Perry Wiseman's daddy, Codger, ran the Bank & Trust. Wouldn't daddy Codger be willing to kick in for such an occasion? They went home that night to their wives with a sense of purpose that only those who've been robbed of something that mattered a whole lot in life and then figured out how to turn it into their favor have, of nothing less than making a wrong right. And it was decided that under no circumstances should Stepwell be allowed wind of his benefit. Not Dee, nor the kids, nor Sis nor the Subiaco Fankhausers should be told, lest the beauty of surprise be squandered and bad luck come upon one and all. They swore it to each other on that which was most holy to them, on their mother's graves, hope to die.

Coach went last.

Swing for the fence. For Stepwell.

The fence.

Normally, Perry Wiseman didn't darken the doors of the Bank & Trust. Not unless he had to. Dear old dad could hold down that fort and plenty more. He'd grown up with every kid in school living in a home his daddy owned or held the mortgage to, and a good many worked for him in some capacity to boot. The Fire Department's new truck, Codger Wiseman's doing, as were the uniforms and helmets fitted to each volunteer's head. School building, the new goal posts and cinderblock bathrooms—a Men's and Women's—Codger. The Mason's Lodge, pharmacy, his signature'd made them happen. For that matter, those light poles around Little John Field everybody thought was the bee's buzz, Daddy'd approved the loan and arrangements. For that goddamn matter, Codger Wiseman had himself flown off to a belfry foundry in Pittsburgh, shopped for and bought the very bell that clanged atop First Methodist, so not an hour struck in town that wasn't of the Bank & Trust's doing, of which Codger Wiseman was President, Chair of the Board and Chief Executive Officer.

Mama'd been a clerk.

She never heard the end of it. Perry himself had been a part-time teller, running the till on slow days, retrieving this and that from safety deposit boxes, wiring funds across state and county lines. Where he'd first met Floradee Fankhauser, that bright spring day way back when. She'd walked in fresh as new cut flowers, what her name put you in the mind of, the flowery double vowels. With one of her dad's paychecks, written out by Mr. Wayland Kep, their Volunteer Fire Chief, for carpentry work—twenty-five dollars, something like that. It was folded down the middle, the check, sweated through. Blue ink blurred.

He remembered. The smell of it. Unfolding what was no doubt a full week's pay for a grown man with a family of ten. 1939—ten years ago. He'd been eighteen, one summer away from Arkansas Polytech where he'd study Business, but girls mostly, finally Jeanine who played a silver flute for the Wonderboy Marching Band which was famous in Arkansas, Louisiana, Texas and Missouri. But he'd yet to meet his wife on that spring day, March 28 to be exact, he remembered because of what happened the very next day, and what life might have been like had those two days got mixed up, one happen instead of the other.

"Morning," he said. "Can I help you?"

"Or is it afternoon," she'd said. "Yes you can."

A Thursday, before the Friday everyone would remember forever and ever. Outside, nothing special, redbud, jonquil, Arkansas springtime. She'd walked—in those shoes. Her eyes put the twenty and five he passed her to shame. The green of growing things, life, everything that came first.

84

"You're a Fankhauser, aren't you?"

"If I wasn't, you shouldn't have cashed that check. Huh?"

That smile, the same one. And she was a feisty one, wasn't she?

She unsnapped a change purse, folded the money inside, snapped it shut again. Groceries—beans and potatoes, country food that his own mama despised, because she'd grown up on it herself. Squirrel. The odd duck. Liver tasting venison. She was probably hungry, Floradee, that very second. On her way to buy food. There at the tail end of March, exactly one day before the great Danville Tornado of 19 and 39, a honey babe that blew into the river valley, tore a gash in the Ozarks that you could still see today if you knew where to look. Tellers, customers, everybody'd locked themselves into Codger's vault, so that it was dark, and they were close enough to smell each other, to offer small comfort, breathe prayer together. Exactly the same time of afternoon, one day instead of the other.

How might it have been to have shared such violence in the vault's protective seal? Might they have talked, prayed in unison for the Lord to spare them, their people, this place that they loved? He would have comforted her. She, him.

But that's not the way it went, was it?

He moved off to Russellville and met Jeanine, got married, had little Perry, and started the Hardware and Grocery with Codger's backing, the Insurance, shares in the Bank & Trust if not a seat on the Board.

Stepwell'd come along and swept Dee off her feet. They had kids fast, managed a loan for the floral shop with its funny name. Eternally Yours, they called it. Now where had they come up with that?

Eternally Yours.

Had the ring of a curse to it if you asked Perry, that poem from freshmen English about the albatross.

And under ordinary circumstances, Perry steered clear of the bank, but not unlike the serendipity of that other time, he'd just happened to have business on the very day that Dee Stepwell had dropped in to have the talk with Codger that everyone knew was coming. To make the deal if she could win him over, sign the papers, whatever it took to get her family clear for a while. To save the house. Business. The fight for their lives.

In his right hand, a bank bag with the October-November take up through Thanksgiving, enough to cap off a good year, a red-letter year for him and his wife, little Perry. About to deposit the whole load into savings. A trip was in the works. A cruise. And he had just that second initiated the transaction with a pretty young teller named Daylene who sang on the third row of the First Methodist Choir when Floradee Stepwell walked through the glass double door, a shade whiter and leaner than the last time he'd seen her, that morning when he'd accompanied her to haul Stepwell home.

And still, that smile.

"Morning," he said, as she crossed the room for her appointment, long dreaded and put off, but inevitable, with the father who'd once intimated that he was no Weldon Stepwell, Perry.

"Or is it afternoon?" she said.

He thought to hand her the money, the bank bag with the last two months' receipts, enough cash to fix her wagon, more probably. Cruise money. Cash him and Jeanine didn't even need.

But of course, he couldn't do that, could he?

Thanksgiving next week, the three-day weekend hunt over to Hallowell, the hunt club daddy's money'd built, Chickalah Mountain, hired men'd been sent out to clean up, lay in firewood, do something with the infernal bucksaw, he pictured it gleaming under the first flakes of an early snow. Pushed like a tiller, plowing time. Whoever knocked down first meat on opening day got out of firewood duty for the whole year, had first dibs on the butterflied back strap fried in drippings, a wave of turnip or winter squash, the last of the tomatoes, salted on a plate set aside for first kill. Who had it been last year? Not Stepwell, who'd slow danced with the bucksaw. If Hicks be believed, gave it a look that'd turn blood to stone just after, there on the ground, the first scarlet bird wings of hemorrhage, then that scream, a bleat, a tear in the throat. Aint'a going back, said Horace. No damn shit.

Codger held the mortgage on Eternally Yours. The house. Car. It was entirely in his power to see them through, the Stepwells, but he'd want something in return. Assurance. And he'd brook no sass. Stepwell's freewheeling tongue.

He wasn't in a position to fight his way out of things, now was he?

Say?

The Little John Benefit, it'd help, but it wasn't the say all, end all Coach and Jacky envisioned. Word was he'd have to fly off to Boston, Massachusetts to get the new leg fitted, and if Jeanine's church lady friends had it straight, Stepwell'd got hooked on that horse medicine, mixed it with sour mash. He'd got mean, and then meaner. Windows had been busted, something about Dee having to visit Doc Jenkins herself. To get stitched up. A full-through laceration. He might have made it out of the woods, but their shadow still hung over his ass, Weldon Stepwell. And now they needed a loan. From the Bank & Trust. Daddy's signature and terms.

He was no Weldon Stepwell, Perry. He damn sure wasn't. Not by a hundred miles.

10.

If smell had color, so you could see it coming, run like hell out the front door and across the street, down past the pharmacy and hardware to the river bridge, jump right in and hide under a piling, breathe the wedge of clean air, hold it, then maybe you could put it back in the box, the one with the pansy-ass painter on front and little sharpener in back, put that box in the tackle box, and the tackle box in the well house and the well house in the shed, and not have to breathe it ever, not ever. It would be a shade of green going to black, with some of the reds mixed in, yellow in places, the worst. Black where it was deadest. Nothing came back from black, it was where the smell disappeared in fire that winter when she was nine in what she'd come to understand was a turning point in her life, when one thing ended and another began, Josephine Stepwell in 1949, the year her father cut his leg off and nearly died but didn't. They'd saved him, got him out of the woods. She herself had twisted the tourniquet. Loosen, tighten, loosen, tighten, Doc Jenkins had said, big rain falling through the hard sun, the devil beating his wife hill folk called it, before she knew that that's what they were, hill folk, every last one of them, herself included. People who'd never seen a passport or known someone who'd owned one for any reason other than wartime. Who had teachers named Redd and Blue, and mix those two together you get purple, and there was some of that color, too, in the smell that came from Daddy's room that winter.

The word for it was just as bad. She'd woven it every which way in her head, thrown it to the sky the way some spiders spew silk, so that the air catches them up into the jet stream and they're hauled across the world to Timbuktu, who knows where all they went, the flying spiders. The word is green, it twists and turns, walks through walls, is not capable of being lit by moonlight, can appear and disappear, be a cloud and rain and wind all at the same time. You gag on the word, it gets inside of you, gangrene, is always near, ready to pounce, eager, it knows your name and where you ran off to, sniffs you out under the river bridge, scolds you for hiding. It wouldn't be a man, but a thing, with a bleat for a voice, a gang of them whose breath was poison to your blood. Nag, rag, gag—the green word twisted through her dreams that November before she turned ten, Josephine, when daddy drank yellow medicine, chased it with Ancient Age, and the word was with him, and he was the word.

Even after they burned the sheets, it was there, at night, when the glass shattered, and his split knuckle took seven stitches, tight and black on his left index finger. The blisters that popped and oozed and the doctor'd laced them with fly larvae what made mama puke, so the maggots ate the dead flesh and grew fat and wriggling white before they scraped them off, burned them with another round of sheets, so there was a black spot out in the yard, and nothing'd ever grow there again, Earl peed on the spot, other things. Made fudge out of the dirt, fed it to the dog, said *eat*, goddamnit, *eat*.

Gangrene was their dinner guest for Thanksgiving that year, just walked on in and made itself at home, took a slug out of the buttermilk, let fly a belch that faded flowers clear across town at Eternally Yours, which was neither eternal nor yours anymore, was it? And if you said anything, anything at all, well Mr. G'd get all hissy-fit and turn green. Then came the yellow medicine and the whiskey, and the bleated scream that meant

89

he was having a charley horse in the cut-off leg, and the only thing on earth that would make it go away was to massage the stump, the exact spot where the severed nerve ending burned under blistered flesh. She'd do it, massage the stump in the exact spot, and his shrieking'd stop after a while, the invisible muscle'd release its grip on him, leave him be. Under her fingernails, between her fingers, like a web, like a color turning to the next color, like Mary's lamb, like your shadow, it was part of her. It was not a color. You could not lock it in a box. The smell said *jump*, she said *how high?*

Tell me.

Tell you what?

You know.

I love you.

Said, How can you?

How can I not?

Don't hate me.

I won't ever.

Already do.

It would be with her when she gave birth to her own son, when she'd hemorrhaged and both of them had passed through the valley of the shadow, when she'd wake up and they'd lay him on her chest. That smell, the green word with its gang, nag, rag and gag, they are and will be, always near. Walked right in the front door with its faded I LOVE YOU sign, no one had it in them to take it down, so the words just ran down to the floor, got walked over, the postman stood on them when he delivered the mail, the letters that made mama cry after everyone was asleep, except Mr. G., who got mean with the first snowfall, peed his yellow name in the front yard, so neighbors stood staring.

And before they could stop the septic infection, the blood sickness, more maggots to do their dirty work. Flesh after successive layer of flesh, green to blue to brilliant rose to black. Before the phantom charley horse and his twin brother in the thigh had oozed into memory and then the memory of a memory, when Mr. G still had a card up his sleeve and it came time to fish or cut bait, the word became flesh, the stench overwhelming and the fire of its anger burned into rage. Anger and rage, rage and anger, the yellow letters pissed crisp in the front yard, bright under the moonlight, *oh* black hole of her dream burnt clear into the dirt, blistered pus under her nails, the vowels of his screaming phantom unknowable goddamn misery boat ride through the morphine underworld till she wished, prayed, begged to be the little crippled daughter wheeling herself out to first base in his stead. Throw the perfect strike.

If smell had a color, she'd have seen it coming. All there in that name.

And run like hell.

He'd wanted to know where they got the name, Eternally Yours, what those words meant in the grand scheme of things between her and Weldon and the world they'd made for themselves and the kids. Standing there with that sack full of money, silly Perry Wiseman. Nothing like his father, nothing at all. He'd played basketball with Weldon, though never the sort to make a show, quiet, maybe a little stutter, maybe not. He looked at her, but not that hungry way, nor its opposite—something else in there, promise. Married at twenty, Josephine then Earl, now this, didn't life just get up on its hind legs and go to beat the band? Thanksgiving week, they both knew she'd come to make the loan her and Weldon had gone back and forth on. They were flat broke, nothing to put up but the floral shop he'd put everything he had into after they'd married. Eternally Yours, they'd named it, the phrase stamped into each piece of the silver set they'd registered for their wedding. Rogers Brothers sterling plate with 1847 and IS beneath three flowers in a bunch, they lay on red velvet in a wooden box under the bed with the butcher knife scar in its headboard, Weldon's side. Where he lay that second, stoned on morphine and whiskey, though the infection had passed, oh God let the infection be gone. They could not share the same house anymore.

"How is he?" Perry asked. "You?"

"Which?"

"Either," Perry said.

He had this way of nodding at you, sort of a facial Morse code that told you that whatever you were about to say was right as rain and somehow the solution to whatever problem was at hand. Some people are like that, aren't they?

"Oh, fine. How's Jeanine? Little Perry?"

"Pies. They're baking pies. Pecan and pumpkin. A chocolate cream."

Between them, the elevated counter for paperwork, black slate with blue ink pens strung on silver chains, deposit slips and scrap paper, a sheet for wire service withdrawals. A little bowl filled with peppermint candy. He'd started his already, a deposit, a whole lot of numbers. He'd carried Weldon up the front steps where Earl's walk rail was strong enough to lean into, if only.

A woman from First Methodist choir worked an adding machine behind the teller booth, her fingers bobbing, sewing the numbers together. At the far end, high up on a wall, a white clock face with black numbers, the first and second hands.

"I'm here to meet with Mr. Wiseman."

Outside, everything dead or dying. Not right against the blue sky.

Perry said, "I know."

"I guess everybody knows everything."

Perry nodded, she'd somehow solved a problem without

even trying. Maybe he could try the trick on Weldon, whose gargoyle stare could break rocks in two, your heart.

"I guess."

"What I've always wanted to know," Perry said, nodding himself toward it, "is where you came up with that name, Eternally Yours?"

Clickety-clack went the pretty clerk's nails on the keys.

She smiled, Dee. The first thing she'd heard all day that had any brightness to it, Josie and Early off at school, making turkeys out of traced hands, getting fed the load about how Squanto saved the day on first Thanksgiving, fed the poor starving pilgrims wild turkey and squash, venison and cornbread.

"You like it?" Dee asked.

Perry said, "It has a ring."

"Does?"

The choirgirl teller was looking at them, the president of the Bank and Trust's son and Mrs. Stepwell, who was very pretty for nearly thirty, what a horrible cup to drink from, hers. Perry was pink-faced, blushing, giving her something, the bank bag? Well what do you know. Maybe they had it planned, to meet here in public view and transact the exchange, this for that, but what did Mrs. Stepwell have to offer? They ran the floral, but the Trust held the deed, overdue. The Stepwells hailed from Morrilton, had once owned bottomland where the county seat was built, but they'd sold all that, the Stepwell bottoms. Maybe a scrap left here and there, the family cemetery in Lanty, up on the hillside overlooking a lightning struck tree, those who'd walked down from Henry County, Tennessee. A few doctors in there, a lawyer. Uncle Marlan'd been a sheriff who'd got famous for riding a donkey onto the floor of the Arkansas House of Representatives. Floradee's folks over to Subiaco, even the abbot monks were poor over that way. And Weldon? Codger liked him or was maybe afraid of him. Who knew the lowdown on the old man?

She had business with him, the old man, not Perry. She

was taken aback, Mrs. Stepwell, shaking her head, no, she couldn't accept whatever he offered in the blue bank bag he brought in every few months with the take from the hardware and pharmacy.

Yes, she would take it, she surely would. Codger'd make her swear her firstborn, worse. They'd lose their business, their house. Take it. There was more coming, Stepwell needed a state-of-the-art surgeon to fit the prosthesis. The Little Johns had a plan, a spring benefit, they had to count on each other, that's what this was all about. What happened to one, it happened to all of them. Take it. Pay it back when you can. That's it, Dee. Take it.

Her adding machine fell silent, and the big bank clock clicked into another minute. So witnessed the pretty teller who could hit the high notes, whose memory of those few moments before Mrs. Stepwell accepted the blue bank bag and buttoned it inside her coat proved keen. Pay it back when you can, she read her boss's son's lips, a grown man with a family himself. Surely this had not been planned, no it wasn't. There could be consequences. Thanksgiving next week. The holidays coming. New Years. A new decade. Still plenty of time to put Danville behind her back, the pretty teller. She'd always thought to see New York City, Rockefeller Center, Radio City Music Hall, the Rockettes, Sunday brunch at the Waldorf. There was a whole lot of world out there, if you could just get to it.

A whole lot of world.

She made the notes in long hand: blue bank bag, same one as always. Mrs. Stepwell, bright red lipstick, ten o'clock appointment with C.W. Papers in a manila folder. Blush. Surprise. Shakes her head. Can't take it. Yes, you can. Will. Pay back when you can. Wads up his deposit slip, Perry. Puts it in his pocket. Smart. Ten-o-two. Puts it inside her coat, a button up, teal. Crying. Or laughing. Afraid. Looked like she was stealing something. Forgot to cancel. He did it for her, Perry. Mrs. Stepwell just asked me to cancel her 10:15. With Daddy. She had to go home.

Daylene's days as a teller, the paper cuts and fingernail trimmings and smile till your cheeks ached, the ink spots and rubber thumb tip and numbers running altogether in her dreams, she saw light at the end of her tunnel.

Did.

There's an airport in Little Rock. A two-hour drive.

She pictured herself with the first-class seatbelt taut across her lap, this vast green hillbilly hootenanny disappearing in her rearview mirror until it was gone, the thrum of propellers up through her solar plexus. Would madam have a glass of champagne? A mimosa? Peach nectar or pineapple? Did madam prefer fresh-squeezed orange?

Esque tu a tojours si joli? Oui?

Six thousand, give or take. It was as if Perry'd handed the blue bank bag to her instead of the Stepwell woman, said take it, pay it back when you can, and now the money was burning a hole in her head, Daylene's.

She was a smart girl, top of her class. The Stepwell woman'd never even finished school, Weldon'd seen to that. She'd married him for his letter jacket, silly-willy. And she'd looked her straight in the face and not recognized who she was, how that other time she'd hauled off and thrown a butcher knife just a shade over the crown of her head, swish, swash, swish, what a sound it had made in the headboard. She didn't know. That much was for sure.

Now, all she had to do was figure out the right angle.

Perry?

Too dangerous. The old man's son.

Codger? He'd sure as hell be pissed to lose the chance of having a fistful of Weldon Stepwell's balls, much less Eternally Yours. What had once been the simple irony of the name, how

Butch'd visited her at her mother's house under the pretense of delivery, now seemed like a millstone tied around the neck of the Stepwell woman. Floradee, whose name sounded like a flower.

Floradee.

She was the way. They'd met eyes. For the first time.

And the guilt came on sharp as the idea unclouded, point by point. What a shit thing to think up, girl. But sometimes you just had to hold your nose, didn't you?

Blue ink was harder to forge—all the fountain pens on their silver chains, blue ink. It was written on the deposit slip in Perry Wiseman's front pocket the moment he turned to see if she'd been looking. But of course, she hadn't. Busy doing the math, just a choir girl who'd made it to junior teller.

Daylene, a name dumb as dishwater.

The first thing she'd have to do was gas the car and hope for small bills because Red Sam at the Texaco was a big mouth bozo, and for the next few hours it was critical to do things right. Gas the car, don't fill it. Drive the twenty-five minutes to Russellville. Start an account. Joint. It was best not to have all your eggs in one basket. To ensure accountability, that's what the Russellville account was for, why she'd chosen to go there with the balance of their loan. A bank book with checks. Weren't nearly all of their bills due to Russellville creditors?

She felt for the world like she'd robbed the Bank & Trust, and she'd forgot to cancel the appointment. Maybe they'd already dialed the neighbors asking about her. Was Mrs. Stepwell still planning to meet with President Wiseman, was there something wrong, did they need to reschedule? Had Mr. Stepwell had a change of heart about the Gift and Floral? Was one of the children sick? The flu'd been going around school. Had their dog got run over? Did he need more medicine, Weldon?

What on earth was Perry Wiseman thinking. Looking into the blue bank bag was like looking into a rattlesnake den. Like fangs about to bite her on the face.

She'd best get her story straight.

She'd best.

Over there was St. Mary's, the green grass of the front lawn dead now, trees going leafless, the room where she'd slept those first nights when it was anybody's guess what would happen. There. The exact spot she'd stood on when Weldon'd woke up and asked for water, he was thirsty, was he ever. And she'd held it to his mouth and refilled when the glass was empty. Where Perry'd stood when they arrived to take him home, the trash can where the right foot Hushpuppy lay untied. That split second of energy that passed between the two men when they first caught sight of each other, Dee between them. How he'd called her Deedee for the first time in front of another soul, and there was no shame. Perry'd half carried him into the house that morning. And now look at them.

Of course, she couldn't tell. Wouldn't. He'd make her take it back. Burn it in the backyard with the sheets. His pride, you couldn't saw that off. There'd be hell to pay. But she couldn't tell him. Should have never walked out that door.

Probably bank presidents all knew each other, called each other by first name and had the kids' birthdays written down, anniversaries, special occasions. Likely Codger'd get wind of her deposit, that's what she was thinking when she parked on the street outside River Valley B & T, turned the key, the car engine ticking.

Wouldn't it be easier just to come clean? Tell the truth? They were teammates for Christ's sake. And there'd been something Perry'd said about the Little Johns, a spring benefit, counting on each other.

How much was in there? She can feel it through the fabric, the heft of it, bills rubber banded together.

Don't let the plow get in front of the horse. Play it as it goes. What she'd always done, right? Don't look a gift horse in the mouth.

All that malarkey.

11.

In the dream, it's all about the fire.

Two choices, bury it in the cemetery, which would call for a funeral, maybe a special casket for a calf-length leg, and what sorts of songs or prayers or graveside words should be said over such a body part? Would the leg that remained miss the one that had departed the way one leg craves handling while the other is massaged? Would it go to heaven or hell? Wait somewhere in between? And what if it ended up in a different place than Stepwell, how would that go? What would the stone say? He'd gone with fire. It'd seen him coming from a mile away, him and the leg wrapped in his blue mail bag, special delivery, return to sender, the little finger pointing back and back. Surely he was the only man on earth ever climbed out of a mail truck to strap such a thing around his shoulders. Walk up to the incinerator door so the flame lit his face just a little, and the man inside gave him that funny look when he asked could he throw it in. Thrown the bag in with it, his own name stitched into the pouch by his good wife's hand, the stench of it, the stain, the spirit of the thing. Once he'd walked a railroad track through the bottoms, and it was no good, couldn't balance on the rail, and the steps between ties too short for his stride. Long gun over his shoulder, though it wasn't season, neither hot nor cold, in between. His nose told him he'd better stop walking, whatever he'd come up on wasn't going to be pretty. And in that split second while his olfactory bulb went off, he imagined it—his mind simply filled in the blank.

The dream-fire was like that, his mind filling in the blank. Only instead of Stepwell's leg, it was the red can of lawnmower gasoline in the shed with MOWER written on top, so Red Sam at Texaco called him Mr. Mower, and of course it wasn't the right thing to do, throwing a gas can in the incinerator, should have stuck with burial, "Pow'r in the Blood."

Another time it's a child, a loaf of bread, the bloated thing he walked up that day on the railroad track. He'd come to sweating, wonder if Stepwell dreamed of it, if it ever came back after him, the saw blade, the sound of it.

If Dee comforted him, so he woke to her saying, it's okay, it's okay, and it never was okay. The dream-fire, always there, a finger snap away.

Yes, what it said.

The note came out of nowhere. It was typed, said: *The blue bank bag, it's not all yours. You will place $1000 of it in hundreds where you are told. In three days. Enclose it in a 9 x 12 manila envelope. Put it where you're told on the morning of the third day. W. does not need to know.*

New Courier font, twelve point. Scrap paper, could have come from anywhere. Came in Scotch-taped to the front page of the Yell County Record. Lay right out there on top of Josephine's Welcome Home We Love You Daddy sign.

A rattlesnake sure enough. Staring at her from the black insides of that bag. She'd known it. Now this. All week long she'd been writing checks out of it. Had bought a black ledger book and set up accounts for St. Mary's and Doc Coffin. Anesthesia people and blood. Pharmacy and ambulance, skin people and bone—every kind of doctor under the sun seemed to have worked on Weldon and they'd all sent their bills. Thirteen inches of them stacked one on top of another. She'd met herself coming and going at the post office. And though it felt good, crawling out from under that stack, getting their heads just far enough above water to breathe again, there was something about the money, a taint to it, would bite her on the butt, she knew it would.

The morning of the third day had a church ring about it.

And you could read *W. does not need to know* to mean three different things all at the same time. The first way, it dawned on her, said that her husband did not need to know about the requested transaction, that it's not something he needs to be aware of. Read from the inside out, Weldon did not need to know that she had not actually met with Mr. Codger Wiseman and secured a loan for six-thousand two hundred and fifty dollars, that she'd made that part up, along with the need for the separate account at River Valley in Russellville. And the third way, the reading that sets her heart to beating, is that Weldon did not need to know that she'd taken the money from Perry Wiseman, who, out of the goodness of his heart had offered her a bank bag with six-thousand dollars in it, said pay it back when you can—the little exchange between them, is it morning or afternoon. The blushing. How Perry'd stepped between her and his father.

Somebody'd seen.

Who?

Someone who could type. Who knew that a manila envelope was 9 x 12, that the word had one l instead of two. Who wanted a share. Who felt entitled to Perry's earnings. She sniffed the paper, taped over a picture of the Fire Department posed in helmets in front of the town's first fire engine, a 1946 Ford La-France. A woman.

Not Jeanine, God no, she'd never go in for this. His money was her money. Someone who could type and spell, had access to Scotch tape and knew what a hundred-dollar bill was all about. The morning of the third day, when Mary returned to the tomb to find it empty, he'd risen, hallelujah Christ arose.

She heard the high notes, Floradee, saw the bright faces splashed with light fallen through stained glass, how it pooled at the pulpit before the groan and hiss of the pedal organ. A woman who went to church, who knew about her and Weldon, and that Perry'd given her the money bag out of the blue, that it hadn't been planned, couldn't have been, not ever. How he'd asked her about the name, Eternally Yours, where it had come from. And there was something else, something she wasn't quite remembering, like a word you can see but can't say. He'd handed her the bag. She'd buttoned it into her coat, left, scared, in tears.

Driven to Russellville, transferred the rubber-banded bills to her purse, walked in, made the deposit, requested temporary checks in a book, kept not a green back dollar of it, drove home, washed her hands, checked in on Weldon, still in bed at two in the afternoon.

"Did we get the loan?"

"Yes," she said.

"Good. I guess."

Someone who knew that he didn't need to know. What might happen if he did. The morning of the third day. First Monday of December. Last month of the year, the decade. *Decem*, it meant ten.

Winter coming. A hard time for finding flowers.

Rest in Peace, 1949.

At Subiaco there was a monastery where monks in dark robes raised chickens, made their own whiskey and cultivated the vine, got up out of bed at 3:10 a.m. every morning, walked outside to pray, got down on hands and knees and touched faces to the dewy earth, said thank you for this day, for life, for the water and light and goodness of homemade shine, how it brought them closer to the spirit from which all spirits came, that great shining for which there were no words. They went shaved-headed, the monks, bug-eyed from reading the Bible in Latin, from reciting the endless chants and liturgies and prayer vigils, the sheer focus on their vows of stability, conversion of morals, obedience, punctuated by the silence of manual labor, humble work that bled into evening vespers, the following of the rule of Saint Benedict of Nursia. Monk, the Greek word for solitary. Peace, pray, work, the ten-day fast sustained by nothing but stout brewed beer, the swirling visions, hawks in the hickories, entrails torn from barn rats and chickens, catfish noodled from submerged logs in the muddy river, skin from an alligator gar hung from an abbey nave, she'd grown up near to all this, Floradee Fankhauser, and had dreamed the monk life for herself, but of course it was the pursuit of men, and she'd thought to disguise herself as a boy, attend Subiaco Academy and swear the vows of St. Benedict of Nursia, run away from home—peace, prayer, work.

Five miles from the river, she knew the place. It was where her people, German Catholics, had been lured by the Little Rock-Fort Smith Railroad Company in 1886, the offer of dirt cheap land in Yell County offered to upright, decent folk that might somehow subdue the rowdy outlaw clans who'd populated that neck of the wood, James and Youngers and Jenkinses, the colorful Ozark hill folk who wore iron on the hip and over the shoulder, who'd conceived the Bowie Knife, Arkansas Toothpick, and whose feelings were hurt deep down by what had been forced on the stars and bars, the carpetbaggers and base treachery, and then poverty and starvation and sickness, so the only thing to do was rob some goddamn rich folk banks, hit some trains and pioneer parties, lynch some Mormons and steal their shit. Spread it around, hell with the Fed.

Her brother, Floradee's, the youngest, was named Howard after Mr. Jessie James's alias just over the line in Missouri. At the family cemetery in Scranton, Coleman Younger's daddy,

daddy's brother and mother were buried right amongst her people. The German Catholics were summoned to subdue the outlaws, but had instead become them, got married and buried with them, the outlaw Arkansas Travelers. Arkansawyers, they called themselves. That's what she was, Floradee, an Arkansawyer. From *Akansi*, an Indian name.

She'd seen the stained-glass pool on floors where the thin voices of men praying shimmied in the rafters, in the golden light from candles that glowed through the abbey windows at night. And she'd dreamed of the black monkhood, solitary in the work of obeying the rule—peace, work, prayer. And it revisited her on certain nights like the one before the morning of the third day, when Weldon had quit screaming long enough for her to fall into a deep enough sleep to dream, and it had come to her, the abbey with its light and prayer and good people meant to subdue the outlaw she'd made her bed with in sickness and in health.

The monk dream that was not for women, and she could have pretended to be a boy, like Petit Jean all those years ago, frightened by the guillotine that flashed that summer in the Champs Elyse, so she'd dressed as a ship's mate and run away from Paris with the lover who didn't even know she was a she.

December, the darkest night coming.

Subiaco, the abbey dream full on her, his breathing hoarse beside her, the children through the wall, Josie with her head full of colors, Earl's mood black as the monk's robe. Hawks tearing entrails in the hickories. Five miles from the river.

Candlelight quavering in the rafters.

Not a place for a woman.

And it was that moment, no moon to speak of outside, cold stars, that she saw the face of the pretty choirgirl who'd been teller that day, whose eyes had met hers, whose fingers had sewn the numbers together.

She was the one.

Floradee was sure of it as the heartbeat in both ears, smell of his sweat, the other. 3:10, the first prayer.

The high notes. From her bedroom, a woman's voice, a girl's.

A hard frost shining on the well house, reflecting the hunter, club raised to whomp the red-eyed bull, portal, Indians believed, to the spirit world. The two realizations resonated against one another.

Christmas soon, time to cut down the tree.

Daylene, her name was, the pretty choirgirl so good with numbers, a teller, what her husband Weldon didn't need to know, here on the morning of the third day. To extort her on her own front porch, same one she'd walked over on The Day. Same one she'd run out of white-faced, an eight-inch butcher nigh unto her young head. We'll see about that. We'll just by god see about that.

It was against the law, little huzzy.

Embezzlement, or was it extortion, blackmail? She could take it to Sheriff Kemp, make a full report, have the little floozy thrown in County, let her hit the high notes in there. Maybe she could be in the same cell Weldon had been in after that brawl she refused to bail him out of. And just about then, when it was all sinking in, Floradee Fankhauser Stepwell chose not to tremble in bed with that sniveling fear for another second, when the absurdity of the whole mess came clear, her heart said *No. I won't.* After all she'd been through, they'd been through. The kids. Mama and Daddy and Weldon's people, Sis and Leo, all those men who'd given their heart's blood so he'd live, Jane Ann who'd stripped off naked, the whole yardful of them waiting for one turn or the other. Poor Jacky Thorpe who'd had to drive out that godforsaken road and walk past the saw for the leg, what that must have done to him. Little Earl, the step rail, the fallen down WELCOME HOME DADDY sign tromped down on the front porch. The whole black truckload of bad luck that had visited itself up them since The Day, and if she had wished him dead, she took it back, because she'd never really meant it, not in her heart. The whole thing comes in a rush on her, a flood, she's the one breathing hard, could explode, take the whole house and city block with her, go on burning everything in her path like that far-off tornado, day after she'd first met Perry in the bank, when he'd blushed and cashed Daddy's paycheck so she could buy pinto beans and potatoes, what they lived on and he knew it. Now this bed, the blistered corpse of Weldon's leg that her own daughter has willed herself to touch, to massage the charley horses from a thing that's not even there, what that's doing to her, to them all. The smell of burned sheets on every breeze, surely her house must be some sort of godawful landmark tower to adultery and anger and bad mojo and morphine yellow medicine that pissed its name in the first snow. Good God how had all this happened? The leg laced up in its leather boot, the good one half gone as well, the tourniquet loosened and tightened, *goddamnit to hell, goddamnit to hell*, hadn't they had enough? Hadn't they? Jesus, Christ. Hadn't they?

And now this? Having to hide money given to them freely? To be cheated by the very floozy who'd have your husband in your own bed? For her to walk up on your front porch and lay down a note asking for money? After what you've been through?

Isn't that just really too much. Isn't it, really?

Just too damn much.

"What's wrong," Weldon moaned. "Was I screaming?"

"No," Dee said.

"Then what?"

He'd always been an early riser, Weldon. Their best talks had always been morning talks, the smell of coffee, weather on the radio, a warm front moving into the Ohio Valley, thunderstorms in the deep south. West wind for the Arkansas River Valley. It had always comforted her, up that early, smoking together, straight sober, lining out a day, their future. He would have shaven, first thing, and she would see in him her first love.

"The loan."

No moon, dark. He sat up, back to the headboard.

"You got it."

"From the Bank and Trust."

"How we're paying bills."

She knew the look on his face that second. Had felt its harsh gaze a thousand and one times, if ever. Her strength was what had kept him straight, her hardheadedness.

"Dee?"

"I'm here."

"You're writing the checks. I saw you."

He lit a cigarette, so the ember glowed in the eye that was turned on her, a red dot, a bullseye. Then he passed it to her, she drew long and hard. Smoke rose up between them like Indian prayer, like when the Lakota sing *Tunkasila, Wakan Tanka* and make prayer with the *canupa*. In the smoke, their prayers.

She could have told him the whole of it.

Until the first faint daylight came in through the bedroom window, sewed the story's parts into a whole, and when the Yell County Record hit the step on the morning of the third day, he would've known all, Weldon. And whether or not he saw it the way she did, it might have marked a turning point in their lives together, when she'd figured out what was what, and how things were going to be, or not be. He would get better, he by god would. He'd have to promise that. They'd all gone as far as they could. She would not go around telling people she'd run into a wall, or slipped on the porch, or the car door got her in the rain like she was the clumsiest woman on earth. The cover stick was trash. They'd pay Perry back. One way or another, they would. They'd have papers written up by the law clerk at the courthouse to make it official, make a plan they'd stick by. He'd go back to Eternally Yours, a day a week at first, for the holidays. She'd take over deliveries. She'd find a tree. They'd celebrate Christmas. Didn't they deserve that? Didn't they?

She could have come clean.

Brewed coffee.

Moved to the kitchen. Him in his chair. He'd lost a good fifty pounds, down from two hundred pounds of muscle. And how much did a leg weigh. How much?

Josephine stood in the hallway looking at them as if a dream of the world before, a hundred years ago, a thousand. She felt her brother at her side, that feral smell he'd come to have. They looked at their mother, their father, and waited for the shoe to fall, the words, the everlasting grief and suffering whiskey-breathed curses to rattle the walls. To walk out the door toward school and be happy in a way that only a child can be to put home behind their backs. But that didn't come, did it?

Daddy'd dressed, had on the blue shirt, buttoned. Mama'd scrambled eggs in butter and there was toast and jelly, orange wedges and apple. Hot chocolate had appeared out of nowhere. They sat at one table together for the first morning since who knew when. The radio was on—forecasts for the New River Valley, snow on Christmas, maybe, all clear for the New Year. No matter what happened after, whatever was coming already down the pike, they had their eggs that morning, their toast and jelly, their lives. Back from the bottomless pit, they gathered themselves to themselves, and it was something to hold onto in the account the heart makes against hard times to come.

No one could take that away.

Not anybody.

PART 2

12.

Boston, Massachusetts must have been the oddest place on earth for Weldon Stepwell, not yet thirty-two, to wake up sober, an amputee, and alone. The rehab facility overlooked Boston Bay, so he could hear the foghorns and whistles of vessels departing and returning from sea. Valentine's Day, there was weather to contend with on the other side of his window, cutthroat wind with snow in its teeth, the air heavy as if it did not want to be breathed. That strange sensation of waking in a place one doesn't know, how it comes back bit by bit, and you work it backwards to the blackout and beyond to the thing you've done for which there is no apologizing nor forgiveness. Her letter is on the table, too dark to read it yet, but he could smell her on it and that hurt. He was sober and could recall the day clearly. And beyond that to the day his daughter was born, how they'd let him hold her while they stitched Dee, and he'd hummed a song he had no words for and she'd quieted and he saw himself in her. Earl, that fire in his eyes. There'd been a family photo of the four of them. He ached for it, knew it would kill him to see it—that first morning in Boston, before light, clear as a bell.

Beside the letter, his wristwatch, cold to the touch, faint shine from the glass face. Breakfast was at six. There were other men here, he recalled, messed up from the war, mangled, missing legs and arms, hands and fingers, a nose and mouth, one of them. He'd met their gaze with his own yesterday at check in, the absurd clipboard of questions he was supposed to answer:

What do you want to be able to do with your prosthesis? What activities do you plan? Do you want to walk or run? Do you care about the way it looks? The prosthesis is an extension of your style—what will yours say about you? Learning to use a prosthesis is a tough job. You will need support. Your prosthetist will train you to don (put on) and doff (take off) the limb, and how to walk on uneven surfaces. Do you prefer crutches or a wheelchair for break time? Are you prepared to join and make friends in our limb-loss community?

Christ.

Last time he smelled saltwater was as a Marine out in California about a million years ago. Fish, there'd be fish out there. Boats to go get them. Whales north of here. Nantucket. Ahab country. Moby goddamn Dick.

Dear Weldon. The letters are small, her hand shaky at first. Perfume from her right wrist. All that empty space between them, the snow and sea. How one world ends, another begins, a lifetime becomes many lives. *I don't know how to begin this. I really don't. You're there now, reading this, and we're here. Josie says to say I love you. Early, too. Just know we're all pulling for you. Love you, me*

P.S., You'll know that's not true, about Earl. And I don't want to get started with a lie. The truth is you need to get straight. What happened was because of the morphine, and that was because you're hurting so bad, and that's because of the accident. I know. I understand. They'll fix you there if you let them. If you let them, they will. I love you with all my heart, we all do. I hope you know that. How much we love you.

On the bottom of the folded page, bright and red, a heart, the smell of crayon and the words: *get well daddy.*

Light was coming now. Stepwell was hungry.

What was the level of his pain? Did he sometimes wish that he had not survived? Had he been able to accept what had happened? Were there times when he could not quit thinking about it?

Had he thanked the ones who'd helped him through? Apologized to anyone he'd harmed along the way? Did he have faith in a higher power? Were there steps he needed to take to get back on his feet?

Was he ready to face himself?

Accept?

Boston must be the strangest place on earth to wake up sober, an amputee, alone, the sounds of the harbor, wind, snow in its teeth.

Was he feeling sorry for himself? If not him, who?

All the get well cards had said to have a speedy recovery. He was to get well soon. Hope you recover quickly. He was in their thoughts and prayers, Stepwell was. They were lifting him up in prayer. Wishing him a speedy recovery.

New Year's had come and gone. What had happened happened. A month of blood and broken glass. Someone singing that out of kilter song. Arrangements being made. The transfer of a substantial sum of money. Doc Coffin's instructions. He could get through this, he could. Flight. The troubled engine sound. Bumps. Cold glass. How the crutch rubbed him raw under the arms. Skin on his arms sagging. Goddamn charley horse. A fire. Smell of flesh burning. Hair. Josie with his catcher's mitt, calling the pitches, making the signs, fastball, curve, take him out.

Daylene. Wiseman. Two sides of the same coin. He'd thank them, he would. Truth was he needed to get straight, say he was sorry. Face himself. Have a speedy recovery.

1950—a new decade, midway point of the century. A clean slate. Time to move on.

Stepwell dressed, a clean shirt Dee'd pressed. He found the shaving kit inside the suitcase with what turned out to be a heart-shaped box of chocolate wedged under the zipper. A foghorn sounded, once, then three times hard.

Valentine's Day at the Boston Institute for Rehabilitation. Time to join the other cripples for the dance.

Years later, as an old man, he'd remember that it was snowing. When he'd parted the curtains and looked out over the catwalk that wrapped around the building where he'd learn to walk again. The flakes were falling, how that had always made him feel. Hopeful and new. How Mama'd wake him and Sis of a quiet morning, a gas burner going in the kitchen, bacon on cast-iron, the smell of biscuits, and the three of them'd run out in it barefoot, and it'd burn like fire. They'd girl-laugh, Mama and Sis, snow day, breakfast on, make cream of it later, time for Rook, the black trump.

He'd remember on a morning before daylight, when the glow of it had raised him from his bed, quiet, white wings flying from the hickories. He'd see his life then, the braids of it, light a candle, let it wash over the window between them.

Foghorn, snow, cardboard heart, how he'd thought to join the host of other cripples for the dance. Stepwell'd remember that first morning in Boston, when he woke up sober and alone and it was snowing.

People there'd be known for what they missed, Josephine guessed. Arms, legs, hands, fingers, toes, ears, maybe, what else? Wasn't that a song? Heads, shoulders, knees and toes. You could miss an eye, teeth, a boy named Terry Berry'd showed up first day of school bald headed, and it never grew back, like he was an old man already in third grade. Miss Redd had shushed them, treated the grandfather boy like nothing was wrong at all. There was a name for it, Mama said. She looked it up in her medicine book. The one she studied like it held the secrets of the universe, and maybe it did, could tell the future and unwind the past. It had a blue cover, the medicine book, a touch between cerulean and cobalt, was thicker than the Red-Letter Bible, and the words were about the same size, the letters. If there was a name for it, being a ten-year-old grandpa, well that made it real. Mama'd marked some of the words, circled them in red and blue and made big check marks beside them. Human Locomotion, Phantom Pain, Trigger Spots, Ischium, Suction Socket, Radiation. Sometimes she made notes too small to read, like she was hiding something there. Inspiration had *Please God* written after it in blue, underlined in red.

On the map she'd checked out from the school library, Boston looked like a bow tied on top of an elephant's head. About to jump into the ocean, the elephant. Could elephants swim? Would daddy be able to? At the airport, he hadn't even waved goodbye. He didn't want to go to Boston. It was a shithole. Yankees lived there. The Red Sox. *Encyclopedia Britannica* said Plymouth Rock was there, where the Pilgrims landed in the Mayflower, and Squanto and the Indians gave them wild turkey and squash so they didn't starve to death that first winter. The elephant's trunk, the part that curled upward, was Cape Cod National Seashore and you could see whales from there, pods of them swimming in the Bay. Daddy'd like the whales, how they blew spouts of shining breath out their blow holes. They fished for them there, Massachusetts, the whole whaling industry run by Quakers on Nantucket Island. How they'd sail these big empty ships out into the North Atlantic, then head south down the mid-Atlantic Ridge where they'd begin to sight whales, Greys and Humpbacks, send men out in dinghies with a spear man who'd throw deep into the whale's blubber, let the rope uncoil, and what a ride then for the men in the little boat. Out in the big blue ocean, dragged by a whale, *whoa nelly*. After, they'd tie it from the sail masts and skin it, carve off and boil the blubber into oil in the huge hole below deck. They'd sail their way down the length of South America and back up on the other side until the hold was full, out for two years sometimes, before sailing home to Nantucket, flying the flags that meant success and I love you and coming home. So the wives and the sons and the daughters would stand on the highest spot and search the sea for their men to come sailing with the colored flags unfurled and whipping in the wind, and such joy as cannot be put into words or songs or poetry, even, would be with them when they reunited, walked home together, through the door of the house where they lived and their lives would be whole again—please Jesus let it be.

The streetlights of London burned on oil from Nantucket. The light of the world was there. The American Revolution. Paul Revere. The British are coming. All of that.

Her prayer on the morning of Valentine's Day, 1950, when her father had flown off to Boston to be rehabilitated and fitted for a prosthetic leg, after so much had shifted in the small family's world that no one would ever believe it, not with a gun to their heads, was simple. She asked nothing for herself. As she never would for the days of her life. She prayed for forgiveness, for Mama to forgive Daddy what he'd done. For the family to stay together. For Earl to stop his meanness. For spring to come. That they might plant tomatoes. For Mama's head to quit hurting. For Daddy to get well. For them to meet him on the day he returned under colored flags, so the light of the world would shine on them. That they might be happy. And begin again.

Earl stared from his place in the room. He'd quit talking. Who could say what went through his head? Half through first grade, he should be singing his ABCs, playing bitty basketball with the Little Little Johns, reading Dick and Jane, seeing Spot go.

Her brother just stared, thinking who knows what. Brown eyes like Daddy's, same color hair. Who knew what was in front of them? A world with bucksaws in it, yellow medicine and peanut butter jars, cracked open heads and a whole lot of blood. Every color in the box.

She knew the language now.

She was fluent, Josephine Stepwell, in the language of blood.

Mr. Stepwell had chosen the very best time in human history to lose a leg. Never before had such opportunities been made available to the amputee, Dr. Staggers explained that first cold afternoon in Boston—administering the ACID Evaluation to new admissions, testing them into the proper prosthetic unit. It was a new era for amputees, and Doc Staggers was responsible for proctoring the first test battery that would determine if Stepwell was an appropriate candidate for prosthetics, if his mind was right, if he was ready to proceed into a new life. The longer the period between amputation and fitting corresponded directly to the feeling of emptiness Stepwell was no doubt struggling with, the anger and addiction, the tendency toward violence that so many of them suffered. It had reared its ugly head already, had it not? There was the conflict between himself in this new state and his former as a whole self. No? His notion of self must be revised, Staggers said from behind the desk, behind which was a window, and through that the blister of harbor Stepwell wished to swim through to some place where he would not have to hear that voice ever again in his life.

"To be honest, Mr. Stepwell," the doctor said, "this is your hour. The moment when you find out what you stand for."

On the wall to the left of where he sat, bold black letters about the size of a hand said:

A—get ATTENTION
C—arouse CURIOSITY
I—get the INTEREST
D—awaken the DESIRE

"Mr. Stepwell. Do I have your attention?"

117

Acid. He was to start his brand-new day, the moment when he was to find out what he stood for, with Acid. He'd once got battery acid in an eye, jumping off Lew Blanding's flat block Chevy. Burned like a motherfucker, the acid.

"Yes sir," he said, met Staggers' eye.

There were birds flapping up a storm behind doc's back, seagulls he guessed, pecking each other's eyeballs out, looked like. Through the gauze-white drape, you could hear them, the demon birds.

"That voice," doctor said. "Texas?"

"Arkansas," Stepwell said. Sometimes the stump had a mind of its own, would bounce and jiggle, trigger points tingling to life so he could feel his little toe on the missing leg, like somebody was banging it with a framing hammer.

"So it says," doc said, ruffling some papers. "And you're a ball player."

"Was," Weldon said.

On the wall opposite the ACID test, not the least bit crooked or askew, a framed diploma, with another one just like it underneath, Doc's full given name, Raymond Thomason Staggers. He'd once met an ear doctor named Error, just too goddamn much.

"Losing the leg makes you not a ballplayer?"

The smell of strange food cooking, something with cabbage in it. His stomach turned, made that sound. There was a name for it. Dee'd found it in her medicine book, the stomach sound.

"Say, Mr. Stepwell?"

Sudden heat in his face, the desire to slap Staggers silly. The little toe curling in on itself, swelling, surely broken now. "Never seen no one-legged catcher."

Staggers turned the face of a pretty little girl toward him, framed behind clean glass, Josephine's age, maybe, went through him like a spear.

"Her name is Letitia. She was born without legs. She can ride a bike and skate backwards. Any time a unilateral amputee comes in here feeling sorry for himself, I show him this picture. Usually shuts them up."

The birds are all gone now, their work done on each other. He didn't know, Stepwell, but it was high tide, the harbor filled to its deepest, mid-February snow falling faintly on the decks of fishermen who'd long since gutted their hauls. It was Valentine's Day back in Danville, and the kids will have taped up little red hearts to the refrigerator. A Tuesday, maybe pork chops and mashed potatoes, a mess of beans. Dee's gravy. Peanut butter fudge for dessert. Would she ever make it again? Would he be able to eat it?

His family seemed a million miles away, and that hurt, and the fear was on him of a sudden that he'd never see them again. That he'd lost it all, everything.

"Your curiosity, Mr. Stepwell. Interest?"

She'd never forgive him, Deedee. She'd meet another man. Already had, maybe. What was he to her now?

"Desire?"

13.

If numbers were flowers—which they surely the shit were not—they'd wilt outright by the light of this day, the godawful mess she'd made of things. "You'll not see a red cent," the Stepwell woman'd said, and she hadn't, had she? Hadn't mama told her she'd amount to such, that she'd never be fit to walk in cousin Darla's shoes, Miss Dardanelle, waving from the hood of a blood red Hudson in the Adkins Pickle Parade? It wasn't her fault, she would not accept the blame, Daylene, for what happened. And she hadn't asked for much, a measly thousand, a grand, was that worth a busted skull, a full-through laceration. And now everybody knew. They knew and knew and knew. Daylene, dumb as dishwater. Why couldn't she be a Kathy or a Susan or a Mary Elizabeth? Shelly or Brenda. Colleen, even. She had to be Daylene, now, for all the days of her life. Daylene Dishwater from Danville, not fit to be named with Ms. Floral Floradee Stepwell. If flowers were numbers, how many would it take to cover the smell she'd made? How many?

Codger would find out. Little Perry'd make sure of that. So she'd lose her job at the Bank & Trust, that was bound to happen any day. Mama'd left the coffee on the stove. She could smell it, scorching.

Weldon would have found out anyway. He wasn't stupid. Not really. Six thousand buckaroos didn't just grow on trees, did it? What was Perry thinking, giving away that kind of moolah? It was his fault as much as anyone else's. And it's not like she could be prosecuted in a court of law, could she? For one thing, the note could not be traced to her. Anybody could have typed it and put it there on the Stepwell's front porch. Couldn't they have?

It was all in the Stepwell woman's head that Daylene had anything to do with it. How she'd glared in church that Sunday. Her and Weldon side to side, his first Sunday—the Christmas Day service with the big bell ding-donging up in the steeple. For her to walk in and sit down and glare that way. From the choir loft she'd felt the white-hot heat. But not from him. Silly-willy. He didn't know, couldn't have, not yet. And hadn't she been clear in the note, clear as a beer: W. does not need to know.

And he didn't. That much she was right about.

Reverend Day's service had been all about the birth of Jesus, how love was made incarnate in his issue. "And Mary said, Behold the handmaid of the Lord; be it unto me according to thy word," the Reverend said, and she could feel the green-eyed heat, on her alone.

"Glory to God in the highest, and on earth peace, good will toward men," they sang it and it was in their hearts.

Mary and Joseph and the babe, lying in a manger. To give light to them that sit in darkness and in the shadow of death, to guide our feet into the way of peace.

Christmas goddamn day. It had to happen on Christmas.

She never closed her eyes during the prayers. Like she and the Stepwell woman were connected to each other alone then, during the prayers, when Weldon's healing by the hand of God the merciful inspired some in the congregation to cry out thank you, Jesus, so it was like that afternoon on the hospital lawn again, the energy. And the whole time she stared her through, the two kids there with heads bowed, his crutches on the floor between them.

She remembered the sound of the knife. How it whistled

past her head. The terrible sound of it cutting headboard flesh. Like they were the only two people ever lived on earth, her and Floradee Stepwell, open-eyed during the too long prayer. The woman wanted her dead. For sure. No doubt about it. And on Christmas, in the church. Like daylight, like tomorrow, like a house on fire, those eyes.

And after, lined up at the double doors with Reverend Day, the four of them with their hands held out for the shake. It was some already knew about the first thing, her and Butch, that's what he wanted her to call him, Butch. Danville's Danville. Darla wouldn't throw herself at a married man. Darla had the good sense to steer clear of Floradee Stepwell. Darla this, Darla that. Cuz Darla could go jump in the lake. Couldn't she?

She could have gone out the back door, on home to unwrap presents under the scrawny cedar tree nailed to crisscrossed two-by-fours with a tin foil angle. A Sunday, the Bank & Trust tomorrow, eight hours on her feet behind the teller booth. A slice of Christmas ham at noontime, canned peaches. Mama'd actually stuck a hunk of charcoal in her stocking, "takes one to know one," Daylene'd backsassed.

And that's when she'd slapped her, Mama.

Like everyone else, she shook their hands, the Stepwells. A lot of people saying Merry Christmas and Thank the Lord, you're in our prayers, you sho' growed up little girl.

"You'll not see one red cent."

She could have been talking to anyone, the Stepwell woman. That Christmas morning on the front steps of the Methodist Church. Her husband, Daylene's lover, on one side, sad-eyed kids on the other.

He was afraid of the knife, Butch.

Round yon virgin, mother and child. Whatever the hell that was supposed to mean. You shouldn't go giving dirty looks to somebody you don't know. Not on Christmas. In the house of the Lord. Not ever. People should watch out. Watch their asses. Be more careful. You never know what's coming down the road.

Do you?

The ability to feel pain is God's gift to humans and certain blessed species of the animal kingdom. Without it we would not know to pull our hand back from the hot oven as children, or that sharp objects were dangerous because they hurt. Self-preservation was the fruit of sensing pain and understanding such required of the residents of Boston Institute of Rehabilitation a monumental shift in thinking. The mind was the palace of pain, but also reason. The two walked hand in hand. Understanding oneself physically, emotionally, mentally and—yes—spiritually was the task of rehabilitation. They should not underestimate the import of self-understanding. They were more, much, much more than blood and bone. Rehabilitating the body meant rehabilitating the mind, in all its various colors. Man reacts to the loss of a limb in ways far beyond that loss alone. There could appear deep psychological disorders, wherein one must come to terms with one's sense of not being whole. One must learn to live in spite of one's incompleteness. To do so necessitated coercing the regal mind to stand on its own two feet again, so to speak. Baby steps must follow. Patience would be required and the understanding that to fail, and to do so often and with great vigor, was critical to their success. One must risk making a fool of oneself as often as possible. As Blake said, "If the fool would persist in his folly, he would become wise."

Staggers had almost started to believe the whole boatload himself, so often had he had to tell the uplifting lie that what these men faced was a mere battle of mind over matter. That was, of course, not true, never had been, never would be. Truth was, if you could make somebody believe they were getting better, they got better.

The ends justified the means. Whatever it took.

Out before him in the lecture hall, the afflicted of all shapes and sizes. She was right, the little girl who'd sent the colorful letter that had arrived with her daddy's bags only last week; they were known, though they should not have been, by what they missed. Sitting right out there right of center, looking at the floor, big Arkie. Above the knee amputation of the right leg, history of skin disorder on the stump, pressure points, lack of adaptation to skeletal change. A point of support transition from ischium to hip joint right side at time of fitting. Note to prosthetist—a tendency toward anger, history of assault, consumed alcohol while prescribed morphine at time of violence. Perpetrated against the wife. She had not filed charges. Arrangements were made by the local court and law enforcement to disallow jail time in lieu of rehab. The funds were mailed in advance—he was paid in full, sitting out there with that pathetic look on his face. The family'd seen it happen. A mess. Could they help him? He'd been a ball player, the paperwork said. Refused to speak at entry interview. Undergoing effects of detox. Dreams. Heightened heart rate. Delirium tremens. Thirty-two years of age. White male. 5'11", 177. 207 before the accident. Wood cutting. Some kind of band saw. Hemorrhage. Out by the skin of his teeth. Comatose beyond the 48th hour. No sign of brain damage. Gangrene. A second bilateral amputation. Skin flap redrawn and successfully attached. Released to the spouse. Domestic altercation. A strong candidate for rehabilitation and fitting for prosthetic. High muscle-to-fat ratio. Good stump dynamic.

Phantom pain.

Severe. Incapacitating. The little toe of the right foot.

On the stage of the human body, the phantom pantomimes

the melodrama of the ages, the central mystery manifest in all religions and mystic practices, the singularity of all that could not be seen but must be believed, what was not but most certainly was. A ghost in the electricity of neural receptors. How on earth to fight what could not be seen nor calibrated nor extirpated with blade nor saw nor *pharmakon?* When the phantom arrived at the opera of the body, you could take all the goody-two-shoes inspiration in his opening lecture for newly admitted amputees and throw it out the door. Fight fire with fire.

"Spinal Cord Responses to Sensory Nerve Impulse," words from the mouth of a warlock celebrating black Sabbath, Young Goodman Brown losing Faith in the night of the deep dark wood. Ghosts cross-firing in the fabric of the nerve.

"What kind of name is Staggers for a doctor supposed to teach me to walk?" he'd asked him at entry. The only thing he'd said, Big Arkie. Out there with the rest of them afloat on a sea of self-pity. He had gall, Arkansas. And that's what it took, wasn't it, a shitload of gall.

He'd looked the man in the face, a full minute of silence pregnant between them until the other lifted eyes from the floor, met his gaze. The entry interview was over; it was time to move on.

"What kind of name is Stepwell for a lame man?"

He hadn't expected that. Had he?

The sad thing about it being Christmas is that it keeps on being Christmas all goddamn day long. After you've hauled out the wrapping paper to the trash bin and stored the bows and ribbons along with the leftover name tags from last year and the year before and the year before in a paper sack in the root cellar, when you've stacked and carried to your room whatever gifts Mama'd wrapped for you, and the big one Santa'd left—a black purse this year with a roll of dimes in it, not even paper

125

money—and put away dishes from the Sunday Roaster—what kind of people eat yard bird for the holiday? And it's about to be a whole new decade, and you're twenty-four in Danville, your daddy driven to who knows where by his wife, your mother, and the afternoon comes and the light fades and the stockings grow dark on the mantle with its sad little piddly-ass fire beneath because the wood was green still, and the tree'd wilted and the tin foil angel taken on the semblance of a snake, and it's just you and mama and no one else. The toilet seat's ice cold when you go and there's the smell of Pine Sol and urine because you'd cut yourself last night with the razor dulled by endless leg shavings, under the arm, and for who (or was it whom?) and the afternoon turned to dusk, and it just went on being Christmas Sunday with the last light the poet said had the heft of a cathedral tune, Christmas, Christmas, Christmas.

"What was it Missus Stepwell said to you this morning?"

Mama'd lit her cigarette from the stove burner in the kitchen, carried an ashtray into the living room where no lights were on save the red bulbs on the runt Christmas tree, a couple of which were out and blinked off and on without warning, about to burn the house down.

She sat in her chair, the foam dented to fit her just right. Made that sound, like she could smell the dirt on Daylene, how she'd gone and done something that Miss Dardanelle Darla Diamond'd never do in a million years. She'd got wind of it.

That sound again. Christmas, Christmas, Christmas.

"I like my purse, Mama. Thank you."

The butane smell mixed with her smoke and baked chicken. Pine Sol and pee. She was twenty-four, Daylene, a Goodno on her daddy's side. No good, Mama called him, she'd scared him to Timbuktu.

"Say, honey. Missus Stepwell had words with you'ins."

Mama tapped her cigarette in the beanbag ashtray, tap tap,

tap. She was twenty when she had Daylene. Over to R'Ville, St. Mary's where they'd taken Weldon that far-off afternoon. Mama's family lived there, well not far off. In Morrilton, a white wood frame with a big front porch overlooking the river valley. They'd churn ice cream there sometimes in summer, slice in bruised peaches. Harvest catalpa worms in spring for crappie fishing.

"The usual. Thank you for your prayers."

The house made sounds she'd grown up to, a rental just off Highway 10, the Petit Jean River bridge just uphill. She'd come of age listening to logging trucks dropping gears to the hilltop. She'd never lived in a house her people owned. Daylene had run away three times, but always came skulking home. Sometimes Mama'd pretend not to be home, let her sit out there in the rusted-through shellback chair, same one Daddy'd smoked in, the coffee can for his butts still half full.

"Malarkey," mama said. "That's not what I heard."

He'd said she could go with him, daddy, way back when the world had that sheen to it still, when she hadn't fallen for yellow roses delivered to their mailbox, the silly red flag folded up so she could see. His sign, folding the red flag up. Darla'd never fall for that, sell yourself out for six yellow roses, offer up the fine hair of her head to a spinning butcher knife. She was too old to live with mama. It made her crazy.

"Mama, I've decided to move. I can't stay here anymore."

There was pie in the kitchen. Someone had sent divinity. Not a drop to drink in the house since daddy left. Mr. No Good. Good Riddance. She could have had a good girl like Darla, hadn't been for his no good blood.

"Sounded like she said something about one red cent. What's at s'posed to mean?"

"When I leave, I want us to stay friends."

"Why'd she tell you that? One red cent?"

She'd been pretty once, mama. A looker, Butch had said

127

when he ran into her that first time at the drug store where she'd worked her first job as cashier that hot summer. "What's your name?" he'd asked her, and when she answered he'd said he knew her mama, that she was a looker.

"When you get a phone, I'll call you up and we'll talk."

"It's your daddy in you makes the devil come." She put out her cigarette, cupped the beanbag ashtray in the palm of her left hand. Tomorrow was a workday, breakfast shift at Codgers. She'd be gone by daylight.

"Don't think I can't see through you."

"I'm leaving tomorrow, Mama."

"Him in you."

"Tonight."

Her mother regarded her the way she'd looked at Daddy when it was clear to Daylene—even at fourteen—that there was not one iota of love for him in her heart. None. That's how she looked at her now. Despite the dark Daylene knows it, and for a second she wished it wasn't so, that her and mama could be friends and love each other and call each other up on afternoons when the rains came and honeysuckle bloomed and neither of them had ever heard anything at all about one red cent.

Consider the prosthesis. What is it, exactly?

Some of them have notebooks and pencils, the ones they were issued upon admittance, encouraged to record their feelings and visualize outcomes, to make a plan for the future beyond BIR. If you can get a man to write just one true thing, just one true thing, to lance the boil of his psychopathy, before you know it you've got a gusher, they'll ask for another notebook, and another. He used to read them, the men's notebooks, but not anymore. Staggers' seen enough, what he'd really like was his afternoon highball, neat, no ice in this weather, the devil's own wind out in the harbor.

Silence.

No one answers.

It's not a trick question. What is a prosthesis?

A man raised his hand, Size 4, Caucasian, fingers splayed, bent 45 degrees at the middle knuckle, wedding ring, gold, on the second finger. "An artificial limb," he said, Number 4.

Excellent. Let's look at that. What the gentleman just said. *Artificial*. Where do we get that word?

This morning he'd found cougar tracks outside his study, right up to the backyard gate, big as a hand, the nails showing, had tracked her to the road, where she'd peed in the snow. He'd read a book by a folklorist from Arkansas titled *Pissing in The Snow*. Strange what you think of, standing in front of an audience, thick as bricks, deliberating over something simple as *artificial*.

If you'll involve them, they'll remember what you say.

Somebody said, "Art." Texas. Arkansas.

Who said art?

The hand, big knuckled and raw, sewn with hair black as the lobe of the cougar track in this morning's snow, raised slowly. Stepwell.

Staggers said, "Mr. Stepwell. You say art?"

The other men looked at him, Stepwell. Bull-chested after it all, a catcher for the Danville Little John minor league baseball, Dixie Association Leagues, men who'd come home fresh from the war to play ball. Why not?

"Yea."

"So a prosthesis is a work of art?"

"I guess."

"You guess?"

"I guess."

"Fine. And just for our purposes, what exactly is Art?"

129

Here's where things got tricky. Fight fire with fire. When it got down to it, he had faith, Staggers, had to. One of them would always make the leap for him. They'd never let him down, crippled men with little notebooks on their laps, that look on their faces, the light flickering somewhere overhead, him craving whiskey, wind like a knife blade outside, the cougars coming down from New Hampshire, Maine, maybe, blood of ancient Ice Age cats in their veins, meat eaters, carnivores deluxe, works of art, *what immortal hand or eye, dare frame thy fearful symmetry?*

"One thing stands for another."

Stepwell. Again. The brawler. Throw a man out just like that, story went. A surprise, these Southern boys. They all of them write it, some borrowing paper from their brothers, tracking down an ink pen, a spare nub of pencil. Sniffing a world beyond guilt and sorrow. As if they'd caught the shining secret of the universe there in that stinking sad room, a host of the afflicted whose heartbeats had stirred.

One thing = Another.

The pee had been bright yellow. He smelled it before he saw it, out under the parade of stars, throwing down spears, yes. Through him, just then. They'd never let him down, had they?

The afflicted. His teammates called him Butch.

The tracks led home.

Always, always home.

Did he who made the lamb make thee?

14.

She could have told him all, Weldon, laced baby's breath around the parts to heighten its innocence, make the arrangement mean nothing more and nothing less than simple kindness. Whatever Perry Wiseman stood for in this life, however he'd explained it to Jeanine—and yes, Codger, even, if the old man got a whiff—his motives were clean, only the best. They'd grown up together, all of them. Stepwells and Wisemans and Fankhausers and Thorpes, there were of a kind, had seen it through hard times before and knew that they were in this together. Second youngest of eight, she'd both given and received. Christmases when the shave-headed monks at Subiaco Academy wrapped and delivered gifts for the kids, strange elves in their somber cloaks, never talking or hardly ever, they'd taken the oath of silence, Daddy'd said. He'd go out walking in the morning, looking for work and sometimes he'd find some, sometimes not. A carpenter, farmer, millwright, mechanic, and blacksmith, if something broke, Daddy'd fix it. He was a lawman, finally, and carried a .32 caliber Colt revolver in his pocket at all times. How they sit with their hands in their hands, her in back of the photo, tucked in behind Arthur's shoulder, smiling, showing teeth. Mama with that look that'd back any man down. Fierce and beautiful, a Jenkins, which made her kin to the Jameses and Youngers and Clays and Deans, the outlaws whose blood ran sure in Floradee's veins, though she didn't know it then, or maybe she did.

She could have told him about the bank bag with six thousand dollars in it, the one Perry handed to her that morning at the Bank & Trust while the little floozy watched them on the sly. Had the thought come to her immediately? Had she seen the way Perry decided on the spot, how it wasn't something they'd planned? And that he hadn't expected anything in return. He hadn't, had he? It all happened so fast. And this after all that had happened since August. How her heart at once leapt like a fawn and shuddered. "Take it, Deedee," he'd said. "You need it more than me."

Deedee. The word. What Weldon alone had ever called her. Had she heard that, the little choir girl with her oh so high notes on the morning of the day? And she knew Weldon had a jealous streak cut with a sudden temper. She would have known both of those things, wouldn't she, little tart. W. doesn't need to know, she'd typed on a machine right there in the bank, a threat.

Had she forgot the butcher knife?

Had the gall to reach for her hand at the Christmas Morning Service? Had she already planned it out, extort her with the threat of tattle-tailing to Weldon who she knew was capable of violence? How would she have sweetened the story to her ends? *Well, I don't think there's any hanky panky going on between them, who would I be to know that? Judge not lest ye be judged.*

The morning of the third day. The nerve of it. Leave a thousand of what had come from Perry's blue bank bag. In hundreds. Where you are told. In a 9 x 12 manila envelope. W. does not need to know.

Well, well, well.

We'll just see about that. Won't we.

It was a wedding gift from her mother Idell, a Jenkins on her mama's side, a Clay on her father's, the butcher. German steel, ice-hardened, bluish in the light, it held an edge. He was afraid of the knife, Weldon. Always had been. She'd held it against him twice, so far, thrown it once.

It would come back to bite her in the butt, not telling. She'd prayed the prayer promising God the Father everything, if he'd pull Weldon out of the woods, she'd give everything under the sun. She'd needed, *desperately* needed, her family back, and he'd given her that, hadn't he?

"Darla'd never blackmail her lover's wife," last thing Mama said.

Monday morning, day after Christmas, on her way to wait tables at Codgers, where everybody that walked in and ordered two eggs over-easy, grits and toast knew and knew and knew. They knew how Mama'd run Daddy off, and where he went. That she'd had a fling with this one and the other, and that the wives had found out. About Reverend Day over to First Methodist, the choir loft and the baptismal. About Butch before the accident. That Floradee'd been livid. Looking down their noses, calling each other up on their phones and telling it over the party line, the snickers and self-righteousness, like theirs's didn't stink.

Darla was an idiot. Mama didn't know it, but she was. She couldn't spell her own last name, Titsworth, enough to make you fall down laughing just to hear her say it: *Hi. I'm Darla Titsworth. All my mama's sisters are named for gemstones. There's Aunt Ruby, and Aunt Turquoise, Aunt Topaz and Aunt Emerald and my own mama Sapphire—she's the brightest of the bunch. And my middle name's Diamond. Darla Diamond.*

She'd been a Bulldog cheerleader, Darla Diamond. One whole wall of her bedroom was for bows to tie in her straight yellow hair. She'd been Homecoming Queen, waved at Daylene from the hood of a red car in the Miss Pickle Parade. Now she was Miss Dardanelle and had a little boy from her first husband, who'd left her high and dry. Now she was the pen pal to a famous writer who'd read from his new novel in R'Ville and fallen for her and promised to move her to New York City and marry her soon as he could divorce his other wife and get the children.

This wasn't about Darla Diamond. It was about her. Daylene. Dumber-than-dishwater Daylene No Good. Who was blackmailing the Stepwell woman. Who'd got onto her. Who wasn't going to give her one red cent. Who knew she worked at the Bank & Trust, and might just walk in that very second. The thought came to Daylene just after opening her register for the day, filling the trays with bills: one crisp hundred, nobody'd touch it all day long; two fifties; eight twenties and ten tens; twenty fives; and she was counting out the slick green ones, fifty of them, FIFO bills, first in first out, when you know who walked through the double glass front door, just like she had the other time, only different.

Eight o'clock sharp. Come walking in just like that.

Floradee Stepwell. Green eyes flashing.

A beeline for teller station number one, Daylene Goodno, open for business. Monday morning, first thing—Darla'd never blackmail her lover's wife.

"Good morning, Mrs. Stepwell."

"Good morning. Miss Goodno."

"Can I help you?"

She smiled serenely, could smell the money in the drawer, the eight crisp twenties, the one hundred. She'd spritzed herself with White Shoulders, the other, lips bright red, the little rubber tips on her right thumb and index finger. The big black hands on the wall clock had not moved. Seen from above, from where Codger Wiseman sometimes gazed down approvingly at the floor of the Bank & Trust he'd built with his own will and fortitude, this morning on the cusp of a new half century could not have been brighter. The pretty teller and Floradee Stepwell about to do business. An easy week before New Year's, a country ham ready to roll out, depression and war and hostilities done. It would be a red-letter year, wouldn't it? Surely it would be.

"Why you surely can. Miss Goodno. Daylene, I believe."

Daylene said, "Bingo," and immediately regretted it.

The kids were off from school today, Early and Jo. Home with Weldon, who'd made a good turn these last few weeks. He was optimistic, had got his faith in himself and the world back in line. There'd be a benefit for him in the spring, when he was ready. The boys would play baseball again, and he could sign on to help coach. Earl would come out of his funk, he would. Josie was the apple of her daddy's eyes—she'd help. Maybe they'd visit the lake, make picnics under a shade tree and plan it all out. The life in front of them.

"I'd like to start an account. Can I do that this morning?"

It was the same blue bank bag she'd brought, appeared from the fold of a nice coat that swallowed her, Codger thought from on high. He'd seen that bank bag before, or its twin. Perry's, no?

They were being watched, the transaction. The other morning teller was counting bills, making ready for a day that was sure to be slow, the Christmas decorations old now, snowflakes scissored out by Miss Redd's third grade class, a strand of popcorn and cranberries, a bunch of mistletoe one of the men had shot out of a tree up to Chickalah Ridge, poisonous, somebody'd said.

"Why yes, Mrs. Stepwell. Will that be checking or savings?"

"Both," she said. "And what else is there?"

Their voices rang through the empty room, quiet, smelling of carbon copy paper from checkbooks stored in the safe with land grant and house titles, car loans and disposition documents, safety deposit boxes and cash on hand. Where they'd hidden during the great tornado back before she was married, the tellers.

Certificates of Deposit. United States Savings Bonds. Life Securities. There were mortgage and property accounts, common stocks and bonds, a buy-in to Bank & Trust annuities. More ways to make money than poor folk could shake a stick at right there at Danville B & C.

"What is a Life Security? Miss Goodno, how does that work? Do we need to sit down for this?"

She'd unzipped the blue bank bag. From inside the nicely manicured hands drew a thin stack of bills rubber banded together over Ben Franklin's ten green faces, In God We Trust on the backside, a drawing of Independence Hall, big clock on a steeple with a little bitty man sitting on a little bitty horse,

"It's for when somebody dies," Daylene said. "The funds help the family with preparations and such. That's how I understand it, Mrs. Stepwell."

It was a whole lot of green, in her hands.

There was the need for proper paperwork, carbon copies and receipts on security. Who in their right mind walks around with that kind of money? She must have run an end around, gone to R'Ville for a mortgage loan on the business, the house, both of them peanuts. From where Codger sat, something was amiss. He could call down but didn't. The sight of two pretty women exchanging money held his attention, their hands, the color of their nails, the crisp stiffness of the bills. And ever after, when what would come to pass had come to pass, he thought about it, how he could have somehow circumvented what happened, but chose not to. For whatever reason, that's what he'd done.

She turned her knife-green eyes on the other.

"To help my family?" she said. "Is that what you say?"

There was a button just under the drawer that she was supposed to push at the first sign of danger, a little alarm that rang up to Codger's office and made a little red-light flash in the break room. She'd never pushed it, the little button, Daylene.

"Yes. Mrs. Stepwell."

"Don't call me that." She took the rubber band off the money, put it around her right wrist. Clear nail polish, cuticles pushed just right.

"What do I call you? Mrs. Stepwell?"

"Three hundred in checking. Three hundred in savings. Deedee, Daylene, you can call me Deedee."

8:03. They were talking too much, the two women. Floradee with a bank bag he was sure once belonged to the B&T. Maybe it came from River Valley over to R'Ville. He'd been in Church day before, Christmas Day Service, Stepwell. Had taken a turn for the better. Might just get out of the woods after all. But the bills, good God the bills. Lucky such never happened to any of his own, might just have been better for him to have stayed in the wood. Easier. For the family.

"Four hundred in a Life Security."

"In what name, Mrs. Stepwell?" She should have eaten breakfast, Daylene, her stomach was turning on her.

"Deedee."

"Deedee."

Mrs. Stepwell smiled. "Daylene Goodno. How about you write it in her name."

She touched the button, but didn't push, not yet.

"And if you ever threaten me or mine again, I'll see you dead."

He was no lip reader, Codger, but looked like the Stepwell woman'd come to do business, set up books again with the B&C. She'd brought cash, zipped up in that blue bag. Well, well, well. She was still a looker, Floradee, her flowers the prettiest in town. Maybe he'd order a New Year's bouquet for the bank? He made a note in his little book, right below the number from the church take yesterday: floor bouquet Eternally Yours. Next time he read the words, they'd take on another hue, like somebody else had written them.

She pushed ten crisp bills across the hardwood, printed her name and the P.O. Box she'd secured in blue ink from a pen on a silver chain. Three temporary checks were issued. The book would be mailed parcel post. It would arrive in five business days. Here were two ledgers, the one for savings was blue, the one for checking was red. She could switch the colors if she liked. She pushed four bills back.

"Of course, I can't do that."

Would there be anything else?

"No," Mrs. Stepwell said.

Well thank you, have a good day.

All day long, it rolled around inside her head. She thought it this way and the other, backwards and forwards, upwards and downwards, and the seventh direction when the idea scathed inward. Truth be told, she vomited up the leftover chicken sandwich into the break room toilet and had to brush her teeth with soap from the little dispenser to get the bits out. That's what she'd remember from fifteen hundred miles and thirty-some years away, the afternoon when she had to brush her teeth with bathroom soap to get the goddamn Christmas chicken out from between her teeth. On the day Butch died in the Little Rock VA, after they'd botched his back surgery and he'd hemorrhaged himself into a second week-long coma, Daylene would remember the afternoon when she decided their fates. Though God had long ago forgiven her for it, and there was no use living in the world of guilt and sorrow, the heft of it never went away.

I'll see you dead, the woman had said.

"You wished it on him," she said to her back. "That saw. Didn't you."

"Maybe I did," she said, Mrs. Stepwell, without ever turning back. Like she'd seen the question coming with eyes in the back of her head.

15.

Part of the deal was that when they were clean and sober, when the DTs had eased off and the vividness of the dreams, when they'd gathered themselves back to themselves enough to know who they were, each of the men was to write a letter to every person they'd ever harmed physically or emotionally, apologizing and asking for forgiveness.

That way the ball was in their court, they could forgive you or not, the weight was off the men who desired recovery. And you had to desire it, didn't you? ATTENTION, CURIOSITY, INTEREST, DESIRE, what it said on Staggers' wall, and the man seemed to know his business, whatever else. He'd played ball once, knew the Red Sox roster by heart, and could even tell you the salary for each of the players, their height and weight and number, if they'd been traded and why. Knew that Birdie Tibbetts had started seventy-four games in 1949 at catcher, that he was thirty-seven years old, a grandpa twice over already, and that his back up, Buddy Rosar, was only three years younger, which put the average age of Sox catchers at thirty-six, oldest in the American League East, and that's a hard goddamn row to hoe, isn't it, squatting down to catch a whole game at thirty seven, seventy-five games year in year out, those wild pitches like the one Walt Masterson would throw against the Yankees harder and harder to dig up. Shit fire, what they needed was some young blood. Did Stepwell know any catchers down in

Dixie, somebody that could take on a full-grown man throwing spikes at the plate? Was there anyone down there like that who'd take twelve thousand a year to play at Fenway with Ted Williams and Bobby Doerr?

"I was catch," Stepwell said. March 4th, a Saturday, new moon, the day to begin new endeavors, he'd been told.

"So you were," Staggers said.

Behind his desk the same old window, seagulls going apeshit at each other outside, not so cold, spring coming, a light rain rippling the glass. A few of them would be home from Florida next weekend. Maybe they'd drop by for a visit like they had last year, the Sox, good for morale all the way around. Wouldn't he like that, Stepwell. Maybe old Birdie Tibbetts himself would pay a visit, sign autographs, talk shop.

"He was a bomber in the war, Williams."

Staggers had started in already, not yet three o'clock. Stepwell could smell it from ten miles off, the whiskey, good Scotch, something from a named creek over in the Highlands.

"Best goddamn hitter ever swing a bat. Don't you think, Butch?"

A good persuader knows that there are no rules to persuasion—the end always justified the means. And what Staggers was selling was that long list of letters to everyone and their mother, and maybe their daddy, too. He knew baseball, give him that. Might even be telling the truth about some of the Sox dropping in to say hi, feeling sorry for the houseful of cripples. He was clear as a bell, Stepwell. That's what he'd written Deedee. I'm clear as a bell, honey. And I'm sorry. I'm so, so sorry.

There were other letters, ones he'd already written and others that were rolling down the pike. To Josie. Little Early, who'd not spoken a word since Stepwell'd said what he said about that two-by-four rail his son had built onto the front porch. One to his mama and papa Stepwell, Lord what he'd put them through. Dee's people. Jacky Thorpe who'd had to drive up to Hallowell and get the thing. The team. Coach. It'd take forever to track down every soul he'd ever wronged and say he was sorry. But that's what he was supposed to do, what Staggers was asking of him if he desired to be whole again.

Sooner or later, he'd have to write to Daylene Goodno.

He'd have to. Wouldn't he?

And what about himself?

Stepwell.

How do you go about writing a letter saying I'm sorry to yourself? How do you forgive the dumbass walks right into a bucksaw—wham, bam thank you, ma'am? Somebody like the man Staggers looked at now, that funny look in his eye, Southerners with their violence and tendency toward drama, dragging a boatload of guilt and Jesus bullshit, don't you call my mama that, where I'm from, the whole load. The Laphroaig in his file cabinet smells strongly of peat, no doubt Stepwell's got a whiff and is judging whether to tell or not. An afternoon knock is not entirely against the rules, is it? Working at a place like this, you carry the men's heavy limbless grief and emotional paralysis home with you nightly, couldn't outrun it to save your life. Is that what he'd signed up for all those years back? Sit here in a room smelling a man's stump flap, expected to fit the prosthesis and be the prosthesis for his mind? Was that it? Their crutch? Their walking stick? How did you say you were sorry to a man like yourself?

Say?

It's what the cougar had come stalking, his pathetic need to say he was sorry—to his wife, his son, the men, God, if there was a god, which he was pretty sure there wasn't, at least not in Boston, he'd moved on somewhere else, as far away from the blue blood as he could get. The mountain lion's claws were unsheathed, she was on the hunt. Stepwell was hungry for forgiveness, maybe he'd understand.

"I'll fit you tomorrow," Staggers said. "You'll have to take me to your duck woods when this is all done."

"You know why I'm here, don't you? You got the papers on me."

He must have been a truly handsome man, Stepwell, before being mauled. Get more than you could shake a stick at. Isn't that what they said down there, more than you can shake a stick at?

"You're here for the same reason as everybody else."

He stood to his full height, the one-legged man. Fitted the crutches under his armpits, the right pant leg held up with a clothespin. He said he'd best get on with his letters, there was a lot he needed to say his piece to.

Soon as he was out the door, Staggers would knock back one whap, then another. Then he'd call for the next man out in the waiting room wallowing in self-pity. It was all of them had to forgive themselves.

For one kind of assault, or the other.

It burned like hell, the whiskey.

New Year's Day, 1950, half a century behind them and another half shining nascent and clean, and if she'd wished the saw on her husband, that was all behind them now, had been a mistake, how their little world shone like a brand-new day, a Sunday morning in Danville, Arkansas, Yell County, she'd be thirty in four days. There was the ham to get on with, black-eyed peas for luck, collards for money. Throw in scalloped potatoes for sustenance and a skillet of cornbread—butter drizzled—they'd get it right this year, no messing around. Weldon had turned the corner, thank God. They'd got out from under the crushing bills. Earl'd showed signs of overcoming his funk, and Josie at twelve seemed a confidante, a sister rather than a daughter. Cold and clear, a good day to make fudge, the peanut butter kind Mama'd taught her on a day just like this one, a hopeful moment that flared for a minute before the worst of it.

She took the jar from the pantry, set it on the kitchen table, was retrieving a pan from under the stove when he crutched in and there was the flash of light, searing pain, then nothing.

When she came to, it'd all been cleaned up, the glass, peanut butter, most of the blood. He'd got her to bed, somehow he had. Josie and Earl'd gone to the neighbors. It was bad, the cut, what Doc Jenkins would later diagnose as a full-through laceration of the skull, encephalitis a real possibility. Did she have to let him kill her? he'd ask, a cousin on her mother's side, a woman who could back a man down, why wasn't she more like her mother? She could file charges down at county. What on earth had happened to cause this—what'd gone on between them? He'd have to tell. He couldn't keep quiet on this, it was against his oath. What had happened. Did she have to let him kill her?

She'd have to drive herself. Would she tell? What would she say happened?

How he'd thrown it at her head, the peanut butter jar.

He didn't mean to.

Years later, when they wanted to cow her, grind the second wife's name off the stone and have her buried there in Solgahatchia beside him, they'd send one in the mail, Sis would, Weldon's younger sister, who on earth would do such a thing after something like that? What was wrong with the Stepwells?

Would she tell?

Why on earth?

He was sorry. God was he sorry. It had hit him wrong, Perry giving her all that money. Why had he done that, given her that much money. And what did he want in return? How would they pay him back? Why hadn't she told him? About the money? He hadn't been thinking. The yellow medicine, it still had him by the hair of his head. He was sorry. He loved her so much. Josie and Earl. They meant the world to him. He didn't mean it. God, if he could only take it back. Forgive him, Deedee, please God forgive him.

But she'd have to drive herself over to Doc Jenkins. What would she say? No one had seen it happen. She could have slipped. There was some glass. In her head. Could have been a window. Slipped into a window.

What kind of person slipped into a window, Weldon? What kind? Of course she'd tell, he was already onto them, Doc Jenkins. Do you have to let him kill you? he'd ask. He'd have to report it this time. This time he would. He'd be saying this while sewing the fourteen stitches, seven on the inside, seven out. She'd need an antibiotic. Amphenicol, Neomycin, Tetracycline. How was the pain?

For the rest of her life she'd feel it when least expected, the moment the pastor of Faith Unlimited led her into the shallow end of the pool for baptism, when their grandson, Joey, graduated from college, and the speaker'd been a stutterer, while auditing the superintendent of Lonoke High School who'd end up in Tucker, before certain storms, she'd see the flash, then searing pain, and it would all be there again. How the tips of three fingers could fit inside. The smell of her own blood. The shame of letting it happen. It had been her fault, hadn't it, taking the money, starting those accounts. She must have known it'd provoke him. The betrayal. Hadn't she known?

The little bitch. She'd told.

Well of course she had.

She'd see her dead.

When she least expected it her head would act up. Could she forgive him? How do you forgive that? Would she? He was so sorry. So, so sorry. It had hit him the wrong way, Perry giving her all that money.

What would she say?

He kept on saying that. What would she say?

What was wrong with the truth? Perry'd given her six thousand dollars. To pay off the hospital bills from him losing his leg. There'd been blood transfusions, the second amputation brought on by gangrene. The medicine. The time in the hospital. The ambulance. Everything. He'd almost died. Could have died. Then where'd they be? Something had to give. Perry'd stepped in. He never said not to tell. That was her idea. Her fault. She'd made a mistake. She should have told. Shouldn't she have. Of course. The little bitch had told him. Hadn't she?

Weldon had found out and lost his temper. He'd been through the ringer. He wasn't himself. Anybody could understand that. Couldn't they? What they were talking about. It happened. No one could take it back.

Do you have to let him kill you, Dee?

No.

No.

No.

No.

She didn't.

He'd have to get better. He'd have to get straight. She could not stay with him like this. Wouldn't let him kill her. She knew he was sorry. How he was so so sorry. She could not go on with him like this. She couldn't. It wasn't right for the kids. It would mess them up.

It would never happen again.

He'd promised. Before. Before, he'd promised.

She told Doc Jenkins as he sewed the fourteen stitches, he promised it would never happen again. That was so much bullshit, what he'd said. He'd promised. And promised. And promised. And God was he sorry. He really was. You can't fake it. Being sorry like that. They were his life, her and the kids. He couldn't make it without them. She knew he couldn't.

In the nursing home room she'd die in, when her grandson

had only known her by the one green eye, in springtime when the daffodils bloomed and the redbud shone out, and it was her last springtime on earth, nearly her ninetieth, it would flash through her, and there she was, four days from thirty, leaning down to get the pan to make the peanut butter fudge, and he'd crutch in, the flash of light, the searing pain.

He'd have to get himself right. There was enough left. There'd been talk of the rehab facility in Boston, a prominent prosthetist at the Boston Institute of Rehabilitation. They could fill out the paperwork, get the referral. He was a veteran, Weldon, they were actively seeking veterans.

He'd sprinkled sage and cedar in the four corners of the room, the grandson. Sending home the spirits. Making it ready for her to die. He'd picked the yellow daffodils, what his mother Josie had called jonquils, brought them aglow into the room, and her great granddaughter had played "For All We Know We May Never Meet Again" and she'd felt it coming, that flare before the worst of it. And then she turned loose, and it was gone.

He'd have to get himself better. Of course he would.

He was sorry. It hurt. It wouldn't happen again. He loved her. He did.

The New Year in front of them. Hopeful, still. Spring coming. They'd rehabilitate him. Give him a chance. Didn't he at least deserve that.

After all.

Didn't he?

He was fitted. Flesh color, Caucasian #8, size eleven foot, inseam of the leg entirely right at thirty-four inches. The abdominal belt, thirty-six inches, securing a unilateral suction socket limb, engineered by the Northrop Rocket folks out in California, same outfit made airplanes and guided missiles. How about them apples? Other skin colors of note to choose from: Mexican, Oriental, light Negroid, medium Negroid, dark Negroid, Chinese and American Indian. Albino. There was a new bracing system, stainless steel, it'd never rust. Took three hours to get it right, before the first attempt at ambulation, which Staggers witnessed, no one to holler walk, the way he imagined faith healers would way down in the sticks where big Arky'd lost his leg.

People who earn the money for their prosthesis treat them better than those who don't. Had Stepwell earned his money? If not, how did he intend to pay it back? There was work to be done. Daily trainings would take place, graduating to the catwalk outside the facility where the men could breathe fresh sea air, and have a look at the harbor while they practiced the various gates, uneven surfaces and stairs. They could walk with the vision of fishing boats returning with their catch and know it was very much possible for them to do the same one day, the sky was the limit, nothing to hold them back but themselves. What was a prosthesis, anyway, if not a mere device allowing what mother nature had denied? An airplane, flight prosthetic. Telescope, vision prosthetic. Shotgun, hunting and gathering prosthetic. Think of it like that, Stepwell was instructed, as an extension of his natural self.

A lovely gait might not be the most effective. It varied man to man. The trick was to find the way of ambulating that required the least energy. That's what it came down to, finally, energy.

The first time he rolled the beige sock onto his stump and laced on the limb, buckled the belt around his waist, and stood, was a Sunday. Why did everything seem to always happen on a Sunday?

There was a shoe on it. A brand-new Hushpuppy, just like the one he'd laced on his left foot, the new scar there below the knee thick as a thumb. Thank God he didn't lose them both like the big Swede who thump-thumped down the hall that morning.

The foot had an arch built into it. Spring action. He was to swing the leg forward with hip muscles. Stepwell was fit. He should get this in quick time. He'd fallen down the first time. No one was allowed to pick him up but himself.

Goddamnit to hell. Josie said that on the day. Pictured Deedee, wished she was there. Because, you see, until you've had to go off and leave your family under such circumstances, you just didn't know, couldn't guess, the effort it took not to go under, walk out on that catwalk and jump off. Would the son of a bitch float, the leg? Drag him under? Should he write his name on it, a number, would there be a backup in case the house caught fire?

The fifth of March, right at New Moon, a good day for planting, stepping out into the plowed dirt in his backyard and sewing collard seed, peas, radish and turnip. Spring onions and strawberries for Dee, what she liked best, fresh strawberries and cream, shortcake. That first Sunday morning, that's what he was thinking, wishing he could walk out into his own backyard and plant strawberries for Floradee. A Sunday, boats and shadows slipping across the harbor. He'd shaved and the fresh air—the first he'd felt since he'd been there at the Boston Institute of Rehabilitation under the care of Dr. Raymond Thomason Staggers, head of Orthotics and Prosthetics, whose 70th birthday was that very day, only he hadn't told Stepwell, of course, this was his day—felt good and real on his face, Stepwell's.

He fell, sure.

But there was a handrail, and his upper body strength was still good, it hadn't failed him. He'd pulled himself up and went at it again, and he could smell the saltwater and feel sunlight on his skin, and it wasn't as hard as he'd thought it would be, this walking. There on the catwalk around the wooden facility, replete with stairs, rises and falls, a thing made of wood, so it was solid and real, a place to learn again before asking the earth to suffer your footfall a second time. Many a time down the road he'd see himself as he was then, and sometimes it would move his heart to think that that man had been him, who'd strapped the device on and stood into the brisk moment. It had been him there, that Sunday in March, two weeks before spring, who'd swung the leg forward, pushed the stump deep into the socket and let it support his full weight, an instant of faith such as he'd never had, and it had held him, the leg, supported his full weight. He'd picture how he walked the full length of the walk on the harbor side and made ready for the turn into shadow where the sun hadn't yet shone, because it was morning, and it was still low in the sky, the ecliptic on the rise, but not yet equinox.

Anyone who'd ever loved him would have been moved by the moment, who he was then. Who'd made it through the hemorrhage and coma by the skin of his teeth, who'd been hooked on godawful morphine to within an inch of his life and had run up a bill that put them in the poorhouse from here to who knows where, who'd done a thing beyond words to the one person on this earth who'd helped him most, and it was her who saved him from himself. For it was right then, at that moment before the turn into shadow that his heart lifted, and he knew for the first time that he could make it, that it would be okay, that he would live and know the sweet things of this world again.

When he asked forgiveness for all, and meant it, with his heart.

He'd fucked up. More than anybody he'd ever know, he'd fucked up. And he was sorry. That moment with the bright sky over one shoulder, and a shadow with cutthroat wind in its teeth that would lift him off his one foot and the other, he made words for the thought.

Before he turned the corner and the cold gust waylaid him and the shadow seemed to suck him to its dark core, Stepwell said out loud to no one at all save himself, *I'm sorry.*

And he meant it.

He did.

16.

You wouldn't think it, but between fall and spring the house mice can chew the finish off a first baseman's mitt, leave it looking like a cur dog splotched with mange. Not something at all you'd want to stick your left hand into, limber up for the day draweth nigh, the redbud blooming to beat the band, tulip, daffodil, every yard of barbed wire fence from here to Jimmy Simm's blown over with blackberry bloom, and the by god Little John All You Can Eat Fish Fry Baseball Benefit for Weldon Stepwell had made it past the planning stage and commenced toward operation. Coach Stringham had head nodded Jacky to take the lead, set up subcommittees necessary to pull the thing off. Baskin, who everybody still called Bastard, even in front of his wife, which would make her Betsy Bastard if the thinking held, he was in charge of finding a worthy opponent for the baseball end of the deal. He'd sniffed around England where Gil Stegall played shortstop, Black as a King James Bible and fast as Jackie Robinson, what people said. He'd give blood for Stepwell, Stegall had. That made them sort of brothers, didn't it. Lew Blanding had dated Daylene Goodno, who was first cousin to Darla Titsworth, who could come as Miss Dardanelle to officiate the event, sing the Star Spangled Banner and Great Speckled Bird like she had for talent in the pageant last year— Stepwell'd like that, he had an eye, used to. Hicks had people in hardware who'd agreed to donate building supplies for new bleachers at Little John Field, and Sheriff Kemp'd agreed to turn loose some inmates from Yell County to help with the building. Faye Mathison'd made the call to his daddy who ran a catfish farm over to Humnoke, ponds where you could call the fuckers from a little pier with a bell built on it—ring a ding ding the suckers up thick as thieves. Think it was feed time, dip net a hundred pounds in a finger snap. The fish was a done deal. And Mr. Perry Wiseman, who'd acted peculiar of late, what could he talk out of Daddy Codger for such an occasion? What would the old man be willing to kick in for town and team?

White Horse stood shining on yonder hill, just as he ever had. One true thing. The silver neigh where the idea'd first come from. His new mail bag was stiff for the loading, a boatload of the flyers printed on sky-blue paper, Jane Ann's idea, to get folks' attention, get them thinking on springtime and baseball, all you can eat fish fry for the Stepwells. A buck fifty a ticket, they'd raffle off one of Clyde Billingsly's donkeys, a couple bicycles and a Remington Woodsmaster .30-ought six, a pair of Red Wings and a full weekend at the Arlington Hotel Spa over to Hot Springs. Coach Stringham knew the mandolin player for the Yell County Yellers who'd agreed to play a set or two, first Saturday in May, here she comes.

But that was a ways off, wasn't it. Best not to let the horses get in front of the buggy. There was the mail to attend to, tornado season on them, coaching little Jacky's Teeny League team, the Little Smokies, and a half dozen other things he wasn't thinking of. Jane Ann wanted a rose trellis and some stone laid. Time to plant peas.

And the house mice had eat the finish off his first baseman's mitt because he'd somehow forgot to season it with linseed oil and wrap it for fall, all that Stepwell business had turned him sideways. He still sees the leg in his sleep, how it trots itself into his dreams, the heft of it, ablaze in ten-foot-tall tongues of flame.

Jesus.

He shakes the sign off, stuffs a flyer and the other business into Jimmy Simm's box. White Horse trots up nostrils flared. He wants his apple. Gimme my goddamn apple. What he likes.

Not a cloud in the sky one minute, God's own thunderhead sailing east the next. Nothing good ever comes out of the east. Maybe three in the afternoon when the light starts to go high yellow. That smell from the bitterweed.

"How you doin', hoss?"

"Who you callin' hoss?" White Horse nickers, nods his head. Shows big stained horsey teeth. He's having a fine day, and it'll be a little finer once brother man gid him his gotdamn apple.

Tossed a Granny Smith from the market, right out the truck window from the driver's seat, a storm rising out there, sure as shit. White Horse snatched the apple from the air, *glomp-glomped* it half in two.

And that's when Jacky Thorpe had his second idea, one that opened all sorts of possibilities for the fish fry benefit. He could catch it every time, White Horse. Jacky sat there idling as it blew over him through the windows drenching his flyers before he could roll them up. What might such an exhibition look like, the game of catch? Simms might play his sousaphone, Miss Dardanelle yodel, ain't nothing going to top White Horse catching the low-do knuckle. Dust his ass off boy, ho-down.

All through the rest of his route he plays with it, pitching to the horse, how to involve signs and throw outs. His Cherokee ancestors had united man with beast in their games of old.

Would Stepwell think it funny, White Horse catching?

He'd ask Jane Ann—she was good at knowing what people could accept and tolerate, part of being a nurse. And it was still a million miles away, the Stepwell Benefit. He imagines Gil Stegall stealing home on White Horse, the blaze of black on white. A bunch of horseshit, he decides. What on earth made him think up such things? The storm lay down and he finished what he started. How was Stepwell? Dee and the kids? There'd been a trouble in January. Another emergency room visit, Dee this time. They'd flown Butch to Boston, though where they got the beans for that who knows. Word was he'd be back before Easter, which gave them a good three weeks to set the stage.

Just then, the sun came out, a silver glow with a batter of rain shining down, devil beating his wife, just like that other day.

The relationship between a man and his prosthetic is no different than that of another man and the guided missile he is directing to a specific strategic point in space and time. Both require the practitioner's desire for an intended outcome related to the various directions possible at any given moment. Up, down, on either side, in front and in back, and the holiest of all cardinal points—inside. Because what's inside a man is critical to the outcome. All the rest is simply wires and pieces of this and that, conjured together in a way so as to respond to the former's will. And what a man wills is directly proportionate to what a man is capable of believing about himself at any given moment. The variations from individual to individual were beyond quantification: there exists at present no way of discerning the difference between what a man believes himself capable of, and what he actually is capable of. Clearly, belief cannot be underestimated, nor should the lack of such.

Consider Stepwell this second, through the many-paned window that looks out on the blue harbor this day, how he'd just turned the corner, the fitting all done, the training in gait, hip thrust and ankle spring, how to feel through the foot, the socket suctioned to the stump, the works all done save the mind and heart, the seventh direction. How he struggles. With himself.

When the wind takes him off his feet. The moment of truth.

Get up.

What can one man, even a trained over-educated Scotch-infused goddamn M.D. of a man, do for another? Make him get up? Some will. Some won't. You can lift a man's body off the ground. But you can't lift his mind. He has to be willing. The same way you will an airplane to its landing, part motor skills and an equal part belief. What the folks over at Rockwell Aeronautics have understood all along—you've got the maverick human mind and the rest is wires and knick-knacks, preferably light ones with good tinsel strength, materials that retain their shape after manipulation, titanium, certain plastics, wires the width of a human hair.

Get up.

The war had brought them home in droves. Pearl Harbor alone had accounted for thousands, men missing arms and legs who the state would have to support under the Veterans of War Act, and what a whopping goddamn expense that was going to be, and that just in support of their physical bodies. What of the maimed minds? The percentage of the populace that could give two country shits for government assistance. Who'd beat their wives and assault their children and generally be of no use whatsoever because they'd lost all, or thought they had. And ten years ago, there were some understood that, who'd had the vision to see that the men needed prosthetic devices that worked and could be paid for, and they needed to get their minds right. So they could be useful, work again, dance with the wife, drive a car, fly an airplane, maybe. And if you could get that man to believe in himself again, after he'd lost all, then you had him back as a citizen, a voter and taxpayer and father and husband. You had to get the son of a bitch to get up and make him think it was his idea.

And that's where Staggers came in, part of the first critical wave of M.D.s to be trained in the science of the psyche, to master body and mind, harness the unified self to the aircraft-engineered advances in prosthetics. They were surely in the golden era of all time for such. Weren't they? It was a good year to be an amputee, 1950. A red-letter year to have a leg fitted at the Boston Institute of Rehabilitation Center for Veterans of the late war who'd kicked the living shit out of Hitler and his Huns, and now they had to reach to brothers and sisters so that all were lifted up and all manner of things would be well.

He was talking to himself out there, Stepwell, having it out.

A good sign, when they got there. The inside opening itself to the out. Becoming one, the magic of daylight and salt air and sucking a breath into the lungs that pushed oxygen to a beating heart. Let the man know he was alive.

And you have to live while you're alive, don't you.

That's it.

Stepwell.

That's it.

Staggers lifted his glass to the man, thought not for the first time today of the diamond of bases at Fenway, how they shine in the red dirt, the bags white as new-fallen snow: first, second, seen from his four block of seats above third, right there where Jackie boy'd stolen home on a summer night not so long ago. Down the line in deep Left, the wall, thirty-seven feet tall, a monster some called it, snatch your ass so you never make it home. His own father, a big-fisted dock man who drank his whiskey without a splash, a man who smelled of fish and sawdust, and the tang of saltwater dried into his sleeves, he'd bought two tickets for the first game ever there, April 20, 1912, a by god Saturday night. He'd walked from the station with his old man, up Jersey Street to Kenmore Square, a jewel box, they called it, Fenway. He was ten, Staggers, a second baseman for Our Lady of Lourdes, and he'd peed his pants the summer before, waiting out a long inning. Daddy'd thrown a shoe at him when they got home, called him pisser. Twenty-four thousand of them there that afternoon, first pitch at 3:10, everybody a little shell-shocked because the Titanic had sunk that Monday and in all the newspapers it was Titanic this and Titanic that, how a monster iceberg had snatched thirteen hundred souls from this earth in one foul morning. The mayor'd thrown the first pitch, there'd been a moment of silence. Eleven innings under the bright lights, the Red Sox won 7-6 when short missed a blast and the winning run scored. All twenty-four thousand went crazy into the streets—he remembers what that was like, with his father, long dead now. The first game at Fenway Park, a jewel box, in a week when the unsinkable Titanic sunk.

Stepwell was on his feet.

He'd turned the corner, had his mind right. He'd seen it happen a time or two, that moment in between, when all hung in the balance. He'd beat his wife, Stepwell. Fractured her skull. The kids had seen. Christians, their world of guilt and sorrow. Man's got to hit bottom before he gets up. Staggers pours two more fingers, a child's portion. She hadn't filed charges, the wife. They'd scraped enough together to send him here; he was a veteran, there'd been a spot for him, they always saved a secret spot, just in case the right man came along, someone for whom rehab would either make or break.

Stepwell would make.

He'd hit bottom and got up. Another week or so. He had the muscle mass and an athlete's body. Piece of cake. Staggers would sign off on Weldon Stepwell and do him the favor of assigning a technician in Little Rock to oversee the device's wear and tear. He'd make it home. There'd be monsters along the way. Of course there would be. A man like that. Maimed in his prime. Took getting used to, and everyone in the field of play best pay attention. Don't go pissing in his face, this one, he'd do for a tussle.

Sunday, the Lord's day, too early to be drunk.

On the way home from the game, his old man had stopped in for one near the station and the train that would take them home to his mother and brother and two sisters. There was singing inside, they had their Irish up. Tacked above the big cash register was a picture of the Titanic as it sunk, a drawing that looked so real that young Staggers was alarmed for a moment, Daddy taking it straight, the ship at a forty-five-degree angle, a whole living throng of men and women and little rich children, even, on the upward end screaming to God. The people on the sinking ship, you could see their faces, they were screaming and crying.

Lord help us all.

Perry had a pet peeve about being made out to be the bad guy when he'd committed no fault, had in fact acted out of the sort of profound kindness and communal sense of giving that warranted the high praise of his fellows, rather than their scorn. It burned him up, really, the unfairness of the accusation. What people wanted was a scapegoat, somebody to hang this trouble around their neck and get run out to the field for pigs and vultures. He'd always been pushed to the margins, hadn't he? Growing up with Codger as his father, always the sidelong glances and forced invitations to birthday parties, the picking of teams and membership in the hunt club. Dates and dances and a place in the church choir, he'd just about had it being son of the Bank & Trust president, everybody and their mother beholden to him and resenting it. Depression years, foreclosures and failed mortgages, Perry'd grown up not able to look them straight in the eye, town folk, and then he'd gone off to ArkaTech and got educated, met and courted pretty Jeanine, first flutist for the marching Wonderboys, wasn't he just something, that Perry Wiseman, come back from college and build up a brand-new Hardware & Grocery, name it Wiseman's like his shit didn't stink. The endless eye rolls, giggles when he wasn't looking. Bull chested Stepwell in the fore, with his letter sweater and pretty Floradee on his shoulder. Who'd helped bring the son of a bitch home? Who'd bothered to lift a hand with those bills? Persuaded Codger to go easy on Eternally Yours, to hold off on closing till they were back on their feet, cut them a break, the Stepwells.

To tell the truth, it was just too damn much.

All that morning he'd replayed the event that had initiated the trouble. A bright day, the whole of November's take and most of October's in the blue bank bag with Wiseman's written on it in Jeanine's flowing hand. Thanksgiving coming, the holidays, they'd talked about a cruise, maybe a steamer down to the Gulf. New Orleans, the French Quarter. Beignets and Café au Lait over to Café DuMonde. Stay at the Monteleone, you only live once. Everything winding down for the year. And it had been a good one, for business it had. The half-grocery, half-hardware plan he'd developed at ArkaTech as his Senior Project had reached fruition. Perry running the hardware side, Jeanine the grocery, suppliers up from Little Rock twice a week with deliveries, it was working. They'd make do. Run weekly accounts for them that couldn't pay, work it off unloading trucks, mop the floors, make produce signs for what needed selling before it spoiled.

Six thousand smackeroos, out of which he'd already written supply side checks, paid his weekend manager. A good haul. Buy little Perry a pony, throw him a big-ass birthday party. Roast a ham and bake a cake big as a wheelbarrow, they'd joked, him and Jeanine. She'd put on some, his wife, but hadn't they all?

Floradee Stepwell, her smell and bright demeanor. He hadn't expected to see her that November morning not so unlike the first day he met her, week before the big tornado, when she'd come in walking in fresh as May with her daddy's paycheck for Perry to cash. Flash that smile—like she was somebody and knew it.

About to sell her soul to Codger, she was about to. They were that far under, her and Stepwell. In the poor house, living under it. Wasn't right. She was made for better than that. A blind man could see. Her smell and bright demeanor.

How was she doing.

Fine.

Weldon?

Better.

Kids?

Tracing hand turkeys for Thanksgiving. That smile.

The Goodno girl Daddy'd hired with her long nose into everybody's business, teller one.

Up to no good.

The impulse that led to the act. What followed. How on earth was he responsible for that? How on earth? Who could predict that a man would do such a thing, kids watching? It wasn't possible. He'd meant no harm. It was the right thing to do. The Christian thing. He played it through, putting the bag in her hand, pay it back when you can. She hadn't told him, Weldon. Had kept it from him. Just as he had from Jeanine. He wasn't the bad guy, quite the opposite. Phooey on all that. They could all go jump in the lake, especially Coach whose look at yesterday's Benefit Planning and Opening of the Little John Ball Shed had said it all. And now he was supposed to suck up to Codger and beg money for the event. After what he'd been through, Perry. It was too much. Really. Too damn much.

What was it they said? No good deed goes unpunished.

No shit.

We'll just see about that.

17.

Though she had not walked with the four of five Little John graduates of 1938, and, in fact, had not technically graduated high school at all, Dee—how she'd introduce herself to the world beyond Yell County—had attended and been certified by The Memphis School of Floristry, where she'd ever so briefly fallen in love with a man of great wealth and charm. Picture if you will the Peabody Hotel where William Faulkner drank his whiskey late of the afternoon on a tall chair under which was a little bronze plaque with his name on it, and the title of one of his books, the one about the dead woman being a fish. The lobby was bright and fragrant with the bouquet of cut roses and nosegay, posies, tussies and cascades of every hue. They'd rolled out the red carpet for the ducks, and when the elevator dinged open, a white-gloved attendant snapped to attention and out waddled these hilarious mallards with black bow ties around their skinny green necks. Single file, they duck-walked to the fountain pool with its gleaming statue of Cupid and Venus, silver coins glittering in the basin, where they jumped right in, quack-quacking. And there stood Lyle Lewis across the lobby, hat in hand, gazing into her green eyes as if stricken.

Their spring affair had stretched into summer.

Lyle was a banker and had money, which he wasn't shy about spending. He'd given her a jewelry box and promised to fill it with a queen's ransom one day. Her name—Floradee

Fankhauser—was engraved on its face, and, when opened, the box played "For All We Know We May Never Meet Again," a tune that was popular that spring.

This was the seam of time between her girlhood in Scranton near Subiaco with its dour-faced monks raising chickens and brewing beer, and Weldon Stepwell, who'd swoop her off her feet and have her with child by twenty, with the idea to run a floristry, since that's what she studied those months when she'd taken a bus to Memphis and learned the principles and elements of design. She was second youngest, next to Hoyt, and the schooling was a splurge from her father who'd got on as Yell County Officer of the Peace and had a regular paycheck. She'd been shown the brochure for Memphis School of Floristry by the monk who grew the flowers she sold and delivered to three Baptist churches and one Methodist time to time for marryings and buryings and Sunday morning Devotional. He'd taken a vow of silence, the monk, just handed the thing to her, nodded. Inside was a bulleted list of what it entailed to be a florist, the rewards of such, including partaking in an immediate way of this lifetime's highest emotional events. With every season came a different palette of occasions. Sister Hallie helped her fill out the application, and she was accepted straight away. Daddy kicked the tuition in as a late birthday gift and, despite her angry mother's entreaty to the contrary, she found herself at eighteen on a bus to Memphis where awaited a world she'd never known but guessed, which included Lyle Lewis, and all he was to come to stand for.

Beale Street might as well have been the moon.

Try to imagine.

What it might have been like for the second youngest child of eight, fresh from Yell County on the Arkansas, to cross the river bridge into the city named for the Egyptian Capitol on the Nile, at sunset on a Saturday night in early springtime, 1938. Alone as anyone has ever been, she beheld the bright lights as if from a dream. There was music and men in top hats. Juke joints where walked women dressed for the night. Cars with chrome that reflected neon from the storefronts where pale-face mannequins in fur coats smiled coldly, their hair combed just so, gazing straight through the plate glass into Dee's soul. As if they knew her and could smell the country on her, and she checked into her hotel, was shown her quarters, and smoked her very first cigarette, a menthol.

She studied design, Dee.

Balance, dominance, contrast. How the visible elements of creating arrangements were the same as other art forms. She'd quilted with mother and her sisters, setting the shapes into motion, mixing the colors so they made something more than themselves, sewing the pieces tight so they'd hold together through weather and storm. How the human eye was a predator's eye, and every last one of them viewed a quilt or a flower arrangement through the locked-in gaze of a hunter. She'd never killed a thing in her life, maybe a housefly sometimes, grubs, a spider big as a half dollar under Hoyt's bed, a snake with a garden rake, a wharf rat in the compost, not much. A difference between hunting and killing, she understood.

Take purple and yellow. An example of complementary colors.

Primary colors could be mixed with secondary.

There were warm colors and cool colors. Tertiary hues located between primary and secondary. Colors to end and colors to begin. Those that stimulated hunger and others that put it down. Shades for birth and death. What color would Dee be if she was a color?

According to her text, there were eight elements of Design—light, color, space, form, pattern, texture, line and size. The florist was not unlike God—mama'd go crazy to see this underlined on page 102—able to mix and match from these to create what was needed. She had in her toolbox balance and rhythm, proportion, scale and contrast. Dominance.

She learned the language, Dee. On those spring mornings when the dust motes danced between her and the windows that looked out on the school gardens, she soaked it in with the others.

Juxtapose meant to dash unlike things together. Like her in Memphis, juxtaposed.

Penetration of Space meant to thrust one dominant characteristic against another.

Scale was all about size, like drawing ears that fit the face.

Weight was how important something was—like how shiny surfaces have more weight than dull ones. Enclosed space is heavier than wide open.

Rhythm could be created by color, form, contrast or line.

Space could be limitless or bounded. It could be negative or positive or somewhere in between. If space was missing, calm was present. Lines could be static or dynamic. There was form and depth and pattern. Texture, like the feel of Lyle Lewis's face of the afternoon when clouds sailed overhead as silvery as wings and she dreamed of never ever going back to Subiaco where Mama and Daddy and all the rest had planned a little party for her return that June, and Lyle had persuaded her not to go, though he hadn't proposed. Everything but.

He was married, Lyle Lewis. Of course he was. One of the girls at school had spilled the beans when Dee had described the most wonderful gentleman, who'd taken her for brunch at the Peabody and dancing on Beale Street, and on a car ride across the river to West Helena, where he owned a shack off River Road with cotton growing right up to the front door.

Why that sounds just like Mr. Lewis, Dee's schoolmate said. He's married, don't you know? He's always after one of us. The old silly.

Contrast of texture is good for design. Patterns should be of different kinds—bold, complicated, dense, simple.

Unpredictable.

Intensity was the boldness or dullness of color.

The lobby where she was to meet Lyle was bright and fragrant, and they'd rolled out the red carpet for the ducks. Mallards with black bow ties around skinny green necks, waddling single file, hilarious. And there stood Mr. Lyle Lewis, just across the Peabody lobby, the note she'd left for him at the front desk in his left hand where sure enough there was the imprint of a ring on his second finger, there was.

And until last night's dream, uneasy and sore afraid of Weldon's return, of driving to Little Rock with the kids to meet him at the airport with his new leg and everything that came along with it, Floradee had not thought on that chapter of her life for a long, long time. The rough, course texture of moss. An empty box with her name engraved on the brassy face.

Lyle Lewis across the Peabody lobby, hat in hand, gazing into her green eyes as if stricken.

Hushpuppies are suede, so instead of shining the shoes, Weldon Stepwell raised the nap with a wire brush until it was clean and even on the one he'd laced onto his left foot and the right. He'd adjust the brown laces until they were the same length, spit on the heel and wipe the sole until it shone black. A Monday, 20th of March, first day of spring, his sixth week away from home and family and everything that had heretofore been his life. He could walk on the device. Staggers said he had a lovely gait. When he fell down, he got up, had the upper-body strength despite all. His mind was clear. The shakes had let him be. The sense of guilt for the violence he'd perpetrated on his family was severe, the very worst of it knowing that they were the ones who loved him most, who'd seen him through the accident and beyond. He was sorry, had asked forgiveness of everyone save one he could ever think of having transgressed against. He was registered with the VA in Little Rock, had a support staff member there ready to take up where Staggers left off. Up before light, foghorns made the sounds he'd grown accustomed to since his arrival about a thousand years ago. Stepwell was fully rehabilitated, Staggers said, the whiskey on his breath no longer a surprise nor temptation. He was himself again, Stepwell. He'd cleaned his shoes, was ready, he believed, to walk away.

The flight was four hours, nearly. He'd pass over Tennessee where there'd been tornadoes, radio said. Seven killed that very week. The storm would have passed over Yell County, woke Deedee in the middle of the night, scared her there in bed by herself. He'd let her down. Terribly. He'd make it up, God help him he would.

The worst of it for paratroopers, he'd heard, was when they were short, the last few jumps before going stateside. And it was even worse if they had a woman waiting on them, who they believed faithful. Could downright torture you, Stepwell'd heard, remembering her smell, how the sunlight fell on her eyes, her voice, her touch, the arch of her foot, her hair. All the times he'd taken her for granted, been a dumbass, said words he couldn't take back. The way other men looked at her when they walked down the sidewalk outside the drugstore on Main. How she'd not meet their eyes, and the men would look at the concrete and he'd think to punch them through the plate glass window. How they'd cross the street and hope he didn't follow, and that he'd go off to war soon and start jumping the hundred jumps out of airplanes over France or somewhere, yelling Geronimo and falling into the weeds. So she'd be alone because for these men there were never kids. She'd be alone and lonely and in need of some kindness. He'd know to tell her about how concerned he's been, how he knows what it feels like to make dinner for yourself, get to the point where it's just not worth the effort. Go hungry until even that went away. To be on your last legs. To need somebody.

And in the meantime, the paratrooper, this Marine who'd been sent off to war, he'd jumped out of an airplane, fifty, sixty times by now, was on the short side, ready for it to be over, what a brick head he'd been to enlist. And so it'd be give or take, could go either way. No one could wait forever, could they? It was a fact that he'd sniffed around here and there, there was the business with the Goodno girl, Daylene, that'd come back to bite him on the butt. Hadn't it. What had happened. Who could blame her, Deedee.

In bed by herself.

Storm overhead, thunder then lightning, the kids scared. Little Earl all bottled up, how he'd pissed in a beer bottle, screwed the cap back on and put it with the rest back in the refrigerator. What it had taken to do that. Josie with her box full of Crayolas—the sign on the front door butcher paper: WELCOME HOME DADDY. Probably another one up now just like the other. Earl's rickety handrail, sixteen penny nails bent trying to toenail. The windows cleaned with vinegar and water, newspaper, they'd be shining. He'd practiced stairs, could get up if he fell. One last jump. Across Tornado Alley, home.

One last jump and he was going home. And that scared the shit out of him, Weldon Stepwell.

The stump sock fit halfway up his thigh. They'd issued a clean one for release, which was sort of the reverse of his entry, only he was straight now, had some sense of the moment's gravity. He had spoken with her exactly twice, Dee. The first was at the halfway point before the breakthrough on the catwalk, he'd been defensive, as he ever was—she'd no doubt heard that edge. Had hesitated before saying I love you, and he'd felt it, the doubt.

The guilt. Other people see you just the way you see yourself, what Staggers had said, can't nobody forgive you but yourself. A prosthesis was nothing but a technology to gain what nature had withheld: airplane, flight prosthesis. Telescope, sight prosthetic. Electric calculator, brain prosthesis. It was all of us were disabled some way or another.

The second call was a Friday, in Staggers' office, which happened to be St. Patrick's Day, no big deal back in Danville, but bigger than Christmas, Easter and Fourth of July to these Boston folk, so they'd gone apeshit, threw this parade where drunk men dressed up as beer barrels and painted their faces green. The noise of it had got through Staggers' window, the hoopla.

"What's going on there?" she'd asked.

"St. Patrick's Day."

"Yes?"

"He drove the snakes out of Ireland. Where are you?"

"Snakes. At the Wisemans'. I'm using their phone."

Staggers had left him alone in the room, let him sit at the desk. A half pint of Johnny Walker shone in the desk drawer when he opened it, a letter opener, some stamps.

"You're at Perry Wiseman's house?"

He'd been inside once, dark furniture, wood, a big square table. Smelled like something he couldn't put his finger on. Money. A casket.

"Jeanine invited us. Me and the kids."

"Oh."

She'd had the car checked at the station. It was good. The three of them were driving down to Little Rock Municipal on Monday. The flight was still on. He'd be there, wouldn't he? A den of iniquity, outside, everything he'd come to get away from.

"Weldon?"

He shut the drawer, passed the test. "I'll be there, Deedee. Can't wait to see you. And the kids."

She said, "We love you."

He held the receiver to his ear listening to the dial tone, until the Yankee operator came on and told him to hang up. *We*—he was thinking. Who was *we*? It was Perry'd give her the money. But they'd been through all that, hadn't they?

When he'd turned the corner, that first day walking, the wind had taken him off his feet. Just like that, cutthroat, laid him low. Out of nowhere. He hadn't seen it coming, none of it. Life rocketing at you ninety-miles an hour, spikes thrown up and flashing. How it was. Was going to be. Get up or stay down. Like a dog. No in between. He was going home, on a Monday, first day of spring. Time to plant peas, collards, radish and onion.

Pulled the stump sock up tight, Stepwell. Fitted the leather harness around it and let his weight settle into the suction socket. Then he laced the thing together and tied it tight as he could, remembered that he'd forgot to have the pants on it already, and had to start all over again. Stump sock, socket, shoelace, who would have ever thought that one Monday far out in his life, a day he was going home to wife and children clear as a bell, Staggers said, he'd think to put these words together, as he would every day for the rest of his life.

Stump sock, socket, shoelace.

Stump sock, socket, shoelace.

It had a ring to it, those words. Maybe he could make it into a song for Josie to sing during happy hours, get little Earl a Sears & Roebuck guitar, Floradee on spoons. Wouldn't that be something. Wouldn't it?

Staggers had the picture of a girl who rode a bicycle and skated backwards, another of a one-legged man on top of a ladder painting the underside of an eave. One man could run low hurdles. Another flew airplanes with hook hands.

A—get ATTENTION
C—arouse CURIOSITY
I—get the INTEREST
D—awaken DESIRE

Daylight, almost, his last morning in Boston, strangest place on earth to wake up sober, alone, an amputee for life. First day of spring, 1950, a clean slate, time to plant, spread the shit.

We love you, she'd said.

Perry Wiseman standing there listening. He'd heard her say it, hadn't he? Poor Weldon off in Boston getting sober, learning to walk again, make it to the pisser without going on the floor. Maybe he'd be able to paint his own house, ride a bike, skate goddamn backward.

How about that?

Maybe he could show Floradee the kindness she so deserved, after all she'd been through. Maybe he could.

On the other side of the door, Staggers. "You ready in there, Stepwell?"

"Yeah," he said.

"Well good."

The old man coughed. He could hear it on his breath already. He'd have the car drive past Fenway on the way to the airport, a warehouse looking place. Say there was a wildcat stalking his house for the fortieth time. He'd seen the prints, big as dinner plates. The claws unfurled. Hunting. Would he take him to the duck woods in Stuttgart next season, be boatman in the flooded bottoms? Arrange decoys, blow the feed call?

They'd shake briefly in parting, Stepwell and Staggers.

18.

She'd have a thing for amputees for the rest of her life. Would seek them out high and low, and even drive up on a boy with her son's same first name, just after he'd been run over by a freight train north of Jacksonville and lay there bleeding to death. He'd have died inside five minutes, surely, had not Josephine and Floradee driven up on him at the railroad trestle, one leg gone at the knee, same as Weldon's. The boy was from a broken home—who wasn't?—and after his release she'd asked him to move into their ramshackle house trailer out on the county line, not far from the authentic Trail of Tears with its bullet ridden sign of an Indian on horseback, so the boy'd wondered if they had horses, and she'd had to tell him not anymore, but she used to, back in Danville, that fine clover-green springtime when Daddy came home clear as a bell and able to walk again, and he'd bought her a Shetland pony for Easter. He'd been home two weeks by then, and mama'd cleaned and cleaned and cleaned again, as if there'd been a plague visited on them before. The windows shone, the doorknobs. She'd waxed the floor and done the oven. Burned the blood and pus-stained sheets and bought all new. Lampshades and curtains, recovered the couch, that first Easter Sunday after Daddy came home from Boston, with his new leg and clear brown eyes. Mahogany laced with Burnt Sienna. And the house was clean, clean, clean when they awakened to Easter baskets at the foot of their beds, her and Earl.

Easter Sunday, 1950, when she was ten and about to pass third grade.

And he'd bought her a Shetland pony, Daddy had. Hid it behind the shed where he'd once hid the whiskey she'd poured out. Had her egg hunt her way out, a yellow one in the fork of a dogwood, a pink beneath a gorgeously red tulip, green at the foot of the Chinaberry, turned the corner and there it was looking her straight in the eye like it knew her and what this moment meant, and how she'd recount it so many years down the road for a boy with her son's own first name who'd been run over by an eastbound freight, lost the leg at the knee, just like daddy.

"What's his name?" she'd asked.

Tawny brown with a lighter colored mane, one white hoof and fetlock, a pile of manure steaming on the green grass. Daddy'd dressed, a blue button down that was good with his eyes, the fresh hushpuppies, pressed pants. Earl had found a living yellow duck in his basket, had made a mess of the jellybeans.

He smiled, Daddy.

And there was Mama, a look on her face that could go either way. Before breakfast yet, the smell of bacon and biscuits. Church in a while, "Up from the Ground He Arose!" they'd be singing.

"What do *you* think his name should be, honey?"

It made her stomach hurt, thinking how they could lose everything again. She'd taken a cold bath which was good luck, said her prayer, just talked out loud the night before in bed, asked God and Jesus and Holy Ghost to help her family, to help Daddy, and Mama. Earl.

"How about turd knocker?"

Earl laughed out loud, the little yellow duck wriggling in his front pocket. Almost two weeks, the dust had settled, no hard words yet, no yellow medicine, daddy was clear as a bell.

"Weldon," Mama said. But she smiled, touched his big bear

arm with the hand that wore the ring. And they looked in each other's eyes, and everything was alright, wasn't it?

"Our poo poo pony, laid you some golden eggs."

He'd stood to his full height, Daddy had, clean-shaven, he barely limped, you could hardly tell, and even that small halt in his gait would soon disappear, so that in later life no one would know who didn't already know. Before all who have ever seen this disappear, it might never have happened, daddy's accident and what came after. How he'd become a man who refused to limp, and what that would mean for all of them. But not yet, his homecoming fresh, still, Easter, the pink and white dogwoods in full bloom with the new sun just shining down.

She'd always wanted a pony, Josephine had.

"Sugarfoot," she said.

Her horse's name was Sugarfoot, she'd tell the run over boy with her own son's first name, and he could lay down and hold his breath, Sugar, and when she said hop up, up he'd jump, so she'd play the trick on everyone who'd watch make the pony lay down, shut its eyes, hold its breath even, waiting for the word from her mouth to leap back to life.

"Where will we keep it?" Mama asked.

But before answering he'd hoisted her up on the thing's back, untied the lead rope and walked her around the house, a big fistful of mane in each hand, him taking big strides aside the pony. "Do you want to trot?" he asked.

Mama was back there behind us. Earl. Everything else.

"Say the word, we'll trot."

Bastard had succeeded in scheduling Gil Stegall's England Lions for the Stepwell All You Can Eat Fish Fry Benefit, though Lew Blanding had no luck at all with the Goodno girl talking cousin Darla Diamond into officiating the event, the girl having run off to New York City or some such. Might as well jump in the lake as go to New York City, aint'a going there, no way Jacky wasn't, the thing nearly on them now, Stepwell's benefit. Perry Wiseman'd gotten old Codger to cough up, and the lumber mill had kicked in a scotch of two-by-sixes for new bleachers. The Yell County Yellers had said sure thing to playing some bluegrass between innings, and Sheriff Kemp had an inmate who'd been a clown for Barnum and Bailey before getting caught whupping shit out of an elephant with a logging chain and throwed into the pokey for cruelty—he'd be there in full-regalia for the kids. Faye Mathison had scored the catfish, and Coach Stringham had got his hands on an industrial-sized fryer, invited Hallowell camp cook Lucian Skinner who was a wizard with puppies and fries, creamy cole slaw and bring on the tartar sauce. It was all coming together, wasn't it. First Saturday in May, come she will.

The sickness arrived out of the blue. Some kind of flu.

And then the earthquake.

Who'd ever heard of an earthquake in Yell County? The drugstore fire. It was as if a scourge had been set upon the land for a while there between Easter Sunday and beginning of May. Jane Ann claimed it was the Goodno girl put the hex on them. Preacher Day said God was trying to send them a message Sunday after the earthquake, a real shaker. The rope fell down from the cast iron bell atop First Methodist, and the same week the drugstore caught fire.

Why oh why?

A call went out—no more killing of spiders nor frogs. Lay off on moths and let woodpeckers be. Jimmy Simms had got bloody milk from three different Holsteins on a Sunday that threatened a storm that'd never come. Fever went round. Some were appointed to round up a black snake or two to hang from certain tree limbs, summon the cleansing rain. No defecating on rabbit trails. May Day was on a Sunday, so Preacher Day said uh huh to dancing the Maypole, though some did it anyway, the white cloth moist against the skin, colorful ribbons snapping in a stiff breeze, a fresh rain coming, black snakes doing their business.

So far they'd been able to keep it all from Stepwell. He'd busied himself of late with Eternally Yours, taking orders through summer, figuring bills, rising early to take and make deliveries. Sheriff Kemp had seen that he got a special handicapped driver's license, so he could drive, and that was good, having wheels again. Or so Jacky thought. To tell the truth, today was to be the first day he'd seen the man since. And it had give him the willies, replaying it all the sleepless night. The road to the hunt club, red eyes in the ditches, the one cigarette before the wood, wicked gleam on the saw tooth.

Smell of it mixed with the honest smell of mail, letters sent long distance from sons to worried fathers, bills being paid, Sears & Roebuck catalogues with glossy pictures of Zebco 202s, 6-string guitars and Daisy BB-guns handmade right over to Rogers. How the fire took it in the grave's stead. Would he be okay with that, fire in the grave's stead?

Because they were meeting for breakfast, first thing this morning, right over to Codgers here on the day after May Day of the month after God had sent his flaming wrath against Yell County, taken the rope from the black bell and burned down the drugstore.

Hadn't seen him since, Jacky hadn't.

Talked on the phone the once, and now Coach'd given him the sign to bait Stepwell out, to find a pretense for getting him away for the Saturday morning while they got things ready. And the first thing ole Jacky'd thought of was how now was when the bream were bedding over to Fourche LaFave, which coincided with the emergence of red wigglers in the leaf pile out back of his garden, kick a bucket lid's worth and it was worm city, feisty little s.o.b.s full of piss and vinegar. Dig yourself a bucketful and pack up the cane poles, head on over to the shallows off Redwing boat ramp. Go to town on the bluegill, maybe knock a couple back late of the afternoon, the cool night baiting lines across the channel, shoulder hooking the hand-size bluegill and sinking them deep, for the true monsters that lived in the holes, the way his daddy'd taught him to trotline, which was better than noodling, slick-skinned Flathead bedded down in sunk logs with the cottonmouth and bullfrog. You could have that. What Jacky was proposing to Stepwell was to go fishing, run some lines, spend a night out like they did before.

Monday morning, sweet rain overnight so the air tasted of flowers which put him in mind of Floradee, how she'd seen this through thick and thin, they all owed this to her, to pull it off.

He'd brought folding money for breakfast, Jane Ann conked out after the all-night shift at St. Mary's, little Jacky eating a bowl of oatmeal sprinkled with cinnamon and brown sugar just like he did every school day. The school year about over now, summer right butt up against them.

From the passenger side, Jacky shuts the mail truck door with his right hand, starts it with his left, column shifts into first and drives out past the sugar snaps spangled in white bloom, pink some of them, into the new day. Driving into town to meet Weldon Stepwell for breakfast, to ask the man if he could take him fishing, order up some grits and eggs over-easy. Ribbons skipping and dancing on the Maypole sapling Miss Sally Redd had erected in a clearing secreted under a gnarled evergreen, maybe wash away whatever curse had come down on them all April. Maybe so.

It was the sort of day you could get your teeth into, wasn't it? He'd been wrong to have a troubled sleep. Replaying the dead and gone past. Let it go. Time for a fresh start.

Today was the day.

He was better, Stepwell was. Staggers had got that much right. The leg wasn't so hard to use, felt like lifting a concrete block with his thigh muscle at first, but that was better now, no cut-throat wind off a Yankee harbor to take him off his feet, no. Kids seemed alright, dog recognized him straight away, it was a good dog, Suzi Q. Easter'd come and gone—the horse was a good idea, Sugarfoot, Josie called it, thing shit all over itself first thing, should have named the little gelding Shitfit. Boys be practicing soon, that's what this was about, Jacky Thorpe asking him to breakfast. He'd so much not as touched a baseball since, though he'd thought on it. Didn't even know where the mitt was, in the closet? Had Josie messed with it? Certainly not Early. That kid. Dee'd spoiled him, what he needed was a good spanka-butt. He loved his family. And he was better. Mostly, he was better.

Jacky'd beat him to Codgers. Old Chevy with the bass-ackwards steering wheel parked in front, see him at a table looking out the window, then at the floor when their eyes met. People did that, you know. Look down when they see you, pretend not to see how he got along on the leg, if the metal brace showed through, oh to get a look at that skin-colored paint—were little hairs painted on it? Did the foot have toes? Even the kids looked down. Dee, too. Best not to stare, make the cripple self-conscious. Staggers had warned him. He had. Be patient. Don't expect too much out of people, especially his people. They'd be curious, give them some rein, buy the little girl a pony, do something to show he was for real, but stay patient, don't take it personal.

Truth was, every soul within eyeshot was waiting for him to get out the Ford's door, walk into the diner on two legs and order hashbrowns and grits, some coffee, hold it on the cream. People needed closure, and a new goddamn catcher to bat clean up.

Everybody pretending not to notice him, three plate glass windows big as sheets. He smelled biscuits, bacon, coffee. His ears were ringing. Mayday, Mayday—signal for distress. He'd passed up the offer to be a radio operator back at Basic, not the first dumb choice he'd ever made, but one that seemed to have kicked a whole lot of others into gear.

Basic had been in California, San Diego, though it might as well have been the Moon for the Marines there, *yessir, nosir. Kiss my ass.* He'd said it to a platoon leader who'd assigned him to the first radio squadron. Stepwell'd wanted to be a gunner, it was in his blood, put his ass in the ball turret and see what happened. He'd have those Krauts gutted and skinned before they ever knew what hit them. He was a gun man, enlisted or no. The platoon leader called him Arkansas, first thing, soon as he heard the first yessir.

He'd said, "That's not my name."

"Not your name?" the man'd said, fake accent loud for the hearing. "Your name be whatever I say it is, Arkansas. Hear?"

In the brig, he wished he hadn't said it. Kiss my ass.

People in this neck of the woods—a thing the dumbfuck platoon leader would say in slander— were too polite to quit talking when he stepped through the door and walked without visible limp to the table where Jacky-Boy Thorpe had stood up and extended his big first baseman's right hand.

Both men gripped hard enough to hurt.

"Morning, Butch," Jacky said.

"Morning."

"How you been?"

Here, the moment of collective silence caught fire for a second, no more, and it was the sort of deep quiet as might have been heard on earth's first morning before all hell broke loose.

"Kiss my ass," Stepwell said, grinned. "I'm fine."

Then everyone in the place breathed and breathed again while down the road Miss Redd's third grade class made ready to dance the Maypole, the boys in the outer circle and girls in the inner, the pink and blue ribbons snapping in a breeze that blew down from Danville Mountain where the first of the year's blackberries had bloomed all up the barbed wire fences, to Holloway Hunt Club, where the ancestral bucks had grown felt over their horn tines and were crazy in rut for does in estrus who were themselves willing to accept the attentions of their randy suitors, and even the old bucksaw had a strand of wild rose grown through its gears so that just for a little while all manner of things seemed right in the River Valley where Petit Jean had once lived unknown in the company of her betrothed, while back in France the beheadings had begun, and already the world was spinning out of control, but what was there to do on a day like this, still on the threshold of May, but dance the by god Maypole, order eggs over-easy with sausage and grits, lay on the butter and pour honey deep into buttermilk biscuits, talk of bream fishing and trotlining on the Fourche LaFave where the whiskered Flathead hid in holes where their daddies had once hid, and the mamas and daddies before them, waiting for something good to come swimming by for supper, just one more time, let it be that way for us one and all.

Ruby Goodno took their orders, Jack's and Stepwell's, and she knew what to do with them, boy didn't she. For the first time in a long time, Stepwell was hungry, like he'd starved for a long, long time, living on Yankee cabbage and fry bread. What he wanted was some hashbrowns slathered in country gravy, sausage on the side, the food his mama'd made when he was a boy and could out eat everyone at the table, so it became a running joke—better fill your plate before Bigalow gets here. Open wide for Chunky.

He never knew why they called him that, Bigalow. Chunky.

Or why he thought of it then, on that spring morning of the very week of the Benefit he did not yet suspect nor have wind of nor any reason on this earth not to get knee deep into breakfast, sop gravy with one hand, knock back cheese grits with the other. Take seconds, thirds, had to shit, finally, find a splice of apple cobbler when he returned, a scoop of vanilla melting on the doughy lattice. Yes, he would go fish Fourche LaFave with Jack Thorpe, and Friday afternoon and night was as good of time as any. Yes, Floradee would be okay with it, and it sure wouldn't be any problem if they knocked back a few like back in the day.

It had been a hard year. A ball buster. They'd suffered. It was time to turn all that loose and live again. Can you pass me that biscuit basket? I could eat a dozen of those.

And just like that Ruby was there with a dozen fresh, a new plate of sweet cream butter and orange blossom honey from down in Florida where she had people that her daughter'd flown off to live with, though everybody thought she'd gone to New York City, but no, the Sunshine State was to be her refuge, and mama was to see that Butch Stepwell got that very jar, because he liked sweet things, and was anything on earth sweeter than orange blossom—anything at all?

By the time it was all said and done, he'd had to unbuckle his belt, Stepwell, undo the top button, good food coursing through his veins and bowels, giving him strength, making him strong.

It was whole 'nother man drove home to his family that day.

19.

Until he left, she couldn't hear herself think. There was so much to do, so much to think of that might not go right. A smolder behind his eyes, slow burn, she saw it at the airport that first day, and though he'd stood to his full height—the first time she'd seen him that way since the day he'd walked out the door, said he was going to the hunt club, and it'd been a Saturday, hot already, the sound the screen door made, she'd felt it for a long time coming, the knife blade of it spinning toward them. Yes. That day. When it happened. He'd held it against her. That she'd caught them. Him and the girl who'd laughed that day she'd walked home for a cigarette, August of another lifetime. At first, she'd intuited that something would happen to her, she'd get sick with Spanish flu or whooping cough, and the kids would be left motherless. A sadness out there waiting for its time. A photo of her and Weldon before the shadow came on them, they'd never talked of it, not once, what had happened on The Day. And maybe that was the problem, her catching her husband in bed with that girl and letting the knife—its threat— do her talking. The scar from it still there where they'd slept last night, just right of center, a mar in the hardwood, it wasn't going away, not ever. Was it? She wanted it there for him to see, didn't she? They'd hugged at the airport. He'd missed them terribly. He was better. He'd make it up. Promise.

Friday, not yet noon on the fifth of May, Jacky Thorpe was

taking him fishing, and Floradee'd opened a Coke, sat on the front porch step Weldon had now mastered, and tried to hear herself think.

A sunny morning, good weather, it was supposed to hold. Her moon had come, three days ago, she'd forgotten about it—isn't that strange. You can think a million things about that benefit that everyone's holding their breath over, or at least it felt that way, and forget there was such a thing as your moon. Josie'd shown her, the spotting.

School's out next week. There's altar arrangements to get done, and Alameda Hicks' wedding package themed on the color purple, the hue of royalty cut with white, iris, in full glorious bloom right now, the heat not yet on them. The kids will be home. They'll all be together. They've got to find a place to stable that pony, a thing he'd gone off and done without asking, buying it with her money. The pest had chomped down the last of the tulips, made a mess out of anywhere they staked it, grass bit down to dirt, one big pile where it went. Good for tomatoes, Weldon'd said, then baked her buttermilk biscuits last Sunday, the first thing he'd cooked since.

She pictured him setting camp out on Fourche LaFave, how he'd eyeball a flat spot for the tent, designate head from foot, which she always got backwards, so he'd say that all the blood would run to their heads and make them have nightmares. The stove went there, the folding table to face that way toward water, the gleam of which was called *seiche*, he knew for some reason, and would expound upon at happy hour—any time after 2:10—while he puffed his pipe. He wanted a woman who'd camp with him.

Of course they'd use the benefit money, whatever came from it, to pay Perry back. It'd been him that saved their butts. Not that they were in the clear or anything. Boston had not been cheap. Nor the fitted prosthesis.

She could smell it, the pony. She'd grown up disliking them.

They'd bite you in a second, stomp on your foot. The only one she'd ever ridden had reared and busted her bottom lip. "I could have got a goat," Weldon said, as if that made ponies better.

How would he take it? Watching a benefit baseball game in his honor from the bleachers, his team, the one he'd been catcher for? She'd always sat in the same spot with the kids. He'd nod to her sometimes from behind home plate, wink. She couldn't imagine him sitting there with her in a million years, the kids off at the playground, riding the seesaw.

Who'd catch. He hated hillbilly music. What were they all thinking?

A letter'd come from her mother saying daddy wasn't doing good, that she ought to drive over to Scranton to see him. They wouldn't make the benefit, but hoped it went okay. They'd be there in spirit. It was his heart, he'd had an episode.

Birdsong rang from the honeysuckle growing through the trellis on the south side of the house where the light was good. A male singing up a storm.

The Little Johns—all of them save Jacky and Weldon—they were up at the ball field practicing, decorating the bleachers, checking lights, issuing jerseys with DANVILLE in a curved red arc across the chests. There were cleats to dig out and gloves to tie, rosin for the bats. How many baseballs in the shed? All that mess. Caps with a Big D riding above the bills. They'd asked to use his Rawlings bull hide catcher's mitt and she'd said yes without telling him. Horace Hicks had picked it up—poor man, it'd shaken him, what happened up on the mountain. "I aint'a going back," he'd said. Dee didn't blame him. She wouldn't care to walk that piece of earth, not ever again.

Pony nickered out of nowhere.

What was he thinking, tying a horse in their yard? People didn't do that. Pick your fights, what daddy always said. Mama wouldn't let him be, that crazy James and Younger blood colliding in her, the Jenkins thrown in the mix. Earl had a touch of it in him, too, with Weldon's heat. One of these days that boy'd explode, and someone'd suffer consequences, talking potty talk already. Some years just roll on you like the plague. Plan was for Jacky to keep him out all night fishing, running the lines in the dark, surely a dangerous thing to be doing at night, the hand over fist with all those hooks sharp as razors. Bring him home and let him nap, surprise him with the benefit game. In his honor. England Lions. Gil Stegall coming.

The Coke's warm.

A dread she doesn't understand comes of a sudden.

She should have her hair done, make an appointment.

Perry will be there in Weldon's old position knowing and knowing what this was all about, paying him his six grand, Jeanine in the bleachers, her and her husband, the kids. She'd come out here to hear herself think. What? Something was wrong with Daddy, he'd had an episode. She should go see him. He'd asked her questions about what she'd learned in Memphis, listened with that look on his face, nodding, when she said that the best way to keep them fresh was a jigger of vodka in the vase water, believe it or don't. How a florist was always in a track meet race with time, trying to outrun wilt, stretching life far as it would go.

"Apples," she told him.

"Apples?"

She'd never seen him shirtless. He was the most decent, kind man she'd ever met, and she was his youngest girl.

"Apples are the secret to stretch life?"

She laughed at him, the silly. He had a way of turning his head and looking at you that she'd one day see in her grandson, a million miles away from that day before the benefit when her moon had come, and she needed to have her hair done, and the benefit for Weldon was tomorrow and there was every bit of a chance that he wasn't going to like it, not one bit. But maybe he would. Maybe.

"There's a gas in them that makes flowers wilt," she'd told him, and he'd said, "Oh, Floradee," the name he'd passed to her from his own mother. She'd take him some iris left over from the Hicks girl's wedding. He liked purple, the color of royalty.

Josie'd forgot again to feed the pony, Sugarfoot, she called it. Probably needed water, too. Tied out there to a stake.

The day was getting away from her—so much left to do.

She heard herself think it. Through the warped rainbow remembering makes, springtime in Danville, redbud blooming, her prayers were answered, her family hers again. Enough. She was hopeful and scared and sensed something not quite perceptible out of the corner or her eye.

They ran the lines at midnight, and again at sunrise. Nylon braid stretched bank to bank, sunk deep in the channel of slow-moving water with rocks looped to the heavy leader. The sun rose straight in Stepwell's face, and he felt it out there, crazed and alone. For all the days and slough-dark nights of its life, the fish had never known a live bluegill to bite back, but this one by god sure did, let me tell you. The silver hook's snell through the lower jawbone, she'd lay still on the bottom until light shone down in streaks, felt his hand take the line, lift. Telegraphed through the hundred feet of trotline, her to him and him to her, that knowing beyond words.

Northern tip of the Ouachita Mountains, the Fourche LaFave River ran west to east clear to the Arkansas. Named by that far off French expedition to which belonged the famed Petit Jean and her lover captain, in it swam living *poisson* that had over the slow accruement of millennia worked their collective way up from the Gulf into the Mississippi River Delta through New Iberia and the swamp wood forests wherein hammered the Ivory-billed for whom it was not uncommon for men to shout LORD JESUS in whatever tongue was given them. Migrated the river's bowels and meanders up through what would be named Natchez Trace and Vicksburg to that stretch of river where they'd sunk the body of Hernando DeSoto in a suit of Incan silver so the Akansi Indians would not know him as a mortal man but go on believing him to be a son of the living god, and therefore continue in their subjugation by the Spanish Conquistadors, who came after the French, and far, far through the depths of time after the slow creep of living beings who'd once known oceans and now swam the Arkansas's mouth into the Fourche LaFave which sliced the natural state into halves. Where swam the ancient species that knew no enemies until the Indian's stone-shafted spear and wooden traps, hands reached noodling into sunken logs for the white fleshed Flathead with a face full of whiskers, so they gave it the name they used for cat, *el gato*, the bottom feeder said to live three hundred years, more, grow man-sized and swallow ducks, rats, whole rabbits, could live on blood the oldest stories said. Whose fathers' fathers' fathers had swum the Mississippi before the Akansi, the Quapaw, Caddo. And now resided in a hole where the river channel cut deepest into the slough, and light fell as shafts or not at all, and she hunted by smell and sense of touch, fat with what the flow brought her, mollusks and freshwater snail, crawdad, her own spawn if they swam too near, and the blue-gill who lay in beds near the shallows at the edge of the deep. This one with the flash of fire laced through its shoulder, for she had known fire, the great burnings right down to the river's edge, windblown embers flung over the deep.

It was Staggers told him he'd felt the mountain lion before he ever saw it. The way the thing had held him in its eyes, a pull, maybe, or push. Gravity. It passed through the fingers of his right hand, up his arm and elbow into his chest, the jolt.

"Son of a bitch," Stepwell said.

Jacky said, "What?"

187

Bow to stern, his flat bottom was twelve feet, an Evinrude 3-horse, just right for the show. He'd cut the motor, let Butch take hold of the line tied to a Cyprus grown right up out of the water. He skulled black water with the boat paddle. "Something on?"

The boat bounced side to side.

"Shit," Jacky said.

Stepwell hauled them toward it, hand over hand, big-ball knocking forearms bulging this way and that as he arm wrestled whatever it was down there. From each of his fists the line jimmied down.

You could smell the water, it burned the throat.

Many years later, when he called the grandson up on the phone, he'd try to recapture the moment, and not be able. Like tomorrow when it's today.

He'd passed over two nice blue channels, a long-snout gar. The hold tree was a man who danced the hoochecoo.

He said be careful, boys. You never know.

Skulled the boat straight, Jacky. Close now, twenty feet. Not a cloud in the sky, pure-sweet May. A swirl roiled the water, flash of belly white, a tail? Surely to Jesus that weren't no tail.

"You want the dip net, Butch?"

He was holding onto it, not giving any quarter. A tree stump looked like a man stared at them from the other side. He hadn't noticed it, yesterday, Jacky. That it looked like a man.

"You can throw the goddamn dip net in the river," Stepwell said.

And he was right. For the thing they drew nigh unto would require a block and tackle, two crazy Arkies at the height of their strength.

What do you do, hooked up to such a thing?

She saw him clearly, the hooked nose, eyes mud-colored, how he was off balance in the boat's bow, something wrong and her weight hard on his hands, the line burning stripes on both palms, the next leader with its naked silver hook, snake it through a palm and take him down to the deep hole and let his air make the scream that leaks to the surface and is quiet. He couldn't lift her, take her from the water. So what will it be? You or me, Butchy boy? Year of the rat, or was it monkey? Say. Be careful what you wish for, boy. You wanted me. Called me. Well, here I am. My name is tomorrow. Tomorrow. And tomorrow. My lover is a fat brown god. Come say fellow. Let us greet in a good way. Throw the goddamn dip net in the river—that's a good one. Something to remember you by. She'd eaten a dog once, fell out of a canoe. Part of a seat cushion. A quart of 30 weight motor oil. A man's gold filling. A glass eye. Never a jet-manufactured Boston-fitted leg.

This was something new on heaven and earth.

Was.

The two beheld one another. Desire. Fear. The Other. He took her. Or did she give herself?

The one photograph, a Polaroid, with Scotch tape sticky-stained around the white borders, Stepwell'd strip it down from the wall of the middle bedroom of the silver Airstream, hand it to the kid, Josie's son, down to the lake for a week of summer. He'd look at it as if working a puzzle, his grandpa sitting on a five-gallon bucket in the bed of a truck, both feet on the lowered tailgate. Behind him a shovel, marine gas tank, the white top of a cooler. The truck framed by a metal rack, the kind carpenters use for hauling wood, two-by-twelves and framing lumber. And tied to this so it hung down over his right leg, the enormous, white-bellied fish whose tail spread the entire width of tailgate beside Stepwell's right foot, the leg bent not quite like the other. Looking straight into the camera with the heat in his eyes, silver wristwatch on the hand touching the fish's belly. Razorback hog on the visible square of cab window. The truck bed dirty, worn, beat.

Short sleeves, maybe cut off. A slight smile. The new planted tomatoes a foot high in the backyard, the wood frame trellis for his purple hulls, they'd grow eight feet up and eight down, violet blooms studding green foliage. The compost where he dumped coffee grounds and table scrap before anyone used the word compost. Man and fish embraced in front of the garden plot, strewn with quartz crystal, where the boy'd make his first five dollars running the old man's tiller. Gravel where they'd put bedsprings into a formed-up frame to pour the boatshed slab, the carport on which he'd break his front tooth, the grown boy, trying to show the old man how he could bench press a hundred pounds fifteen times, only he'd load the weights crooked and the bar'd break a tooth. The opening before the tall trees took the sky. How they'd hugged each other in this place where he'd come of age. Truck, gas can, shovel, Big Boy tomato plants. Hummingbird feeder, sugar water red, invisible to the right. Man, fish, truck, the old man gazing straight into his grandson's face when he himself was nearly sixty, newly diagnosed with prostate cancer, three months into the pandemic that would rage the planet, have them quarantined under the Shelter at Home Law newly imposed. And it would snow on the morning that marked the thirty-ninth year of Weldon Stepwell's passing, and the boy who'd grown into an old man would go barefoot in the backyard with his daughter, just as he'd seen his maternal great grandmother do. His mother, and the old man himself who'd hop one-footed, the prints size eleven, just like his. A people who'd run barefoot in the snow—hadn't the old man talked the boy into his first outing in a January storm before duck club? And the boy'd cried, said "This is crazy."

He'd see it for the first time that snowy morning in March when he was newly diagnosed and it didn't feel real yet, how the plague had hit them like a ton of bricks. The man and fish, embraced before the garden, had been photographed in the place he knew, and though he'd puzzled over the picture a thousand times, he'd never got that before. The earth beneath man and fish, he'd stood on the very spot, had broken a tooth trying to show how strong he was, that he was capable of standing in the old man's shoes.

And then it would all make a strange sense—the earthquakes and sickness, cancer, the missed prostatectomy because there were no more ventilators nor surgical masks, nor soap to wash your hands with, even. How the aftershocks would roil the water they kept in the bathtub for drinking, flushing the toilet, cooking during Shelter In Place.

On the morning when it snowed and they'd run barefoot in the backyard and he'd taken it out for some reason the photograph of his grandfather, eighty-seven-pound Flathead catfish draped over his right leg, and he'd recognized for the first time what he'd never discerned before.

When the last Little John was dead and gone and the world had morphed into a different place than the one they'd inhabited, Joey Stepwell'd coerce his twenty-two year old daughter, sent home from school because you couldn't go to school anymore, to the snow dance and see in the photograph the part of himself he'd neither known nor guessed, and it would become his story then, theirs. Before all who have ever seen this disappear.

The tree stump that had the other end of their trotline tied in a blood knot to its base, he wasn't going anywhere. It manstared the trio bound to boat and water, could stand there waiting for a thousand years if they wanted it to. Stepwell ran the line through a D-ring, tied it off on the steel grommet at his feet.

"Cut the cord, Jacky," he said. "Cut your end."

And that's what he did, cut his end, just below the D-ring. Let the fish drag the boat upriver and down, hooked between man-tree and boat as the sun rose higher, and higher then into the new day's sky.

20.

He'd have to use the mitt, Stepwell's, Perry would. Horace Hicks had picked it up from Floradee that very day. Sure it's okay, you just don't worry, she'd said. Weldon's out on Fourche LaFave trotlining with Jacky Thorpe, and he didn't have an inkling about any of it. So take the glove and don't think anything of it. She was sure Weldon would want them to use it, first game of the season. Who was catching? Perry, oh Perry. Tell him not to think twice—it was a team glove, wasn't it? And you didn't find Rawlings Full-Grain Bullhide Pro-Grade mitts growing on trees, did you? Don't think twice, she'd told Horace—beat the Lions. Perry wasn't so sure now that he had the thing, had practiced the once with Jimmy Paterson at pitch. Deep pocketed with his number 10 stenciled on its thumb, leather laced through the wrist strap grommets and around the entirety of the perimeter, it swallowed his hand, Stepwell's mitt. He'd heard stories of men who'd run into the burning houses to retrieve their gloves, who'd crawled through broken clubhouse windows after earthquakes for their gamers. It smelled of Stepwell, his sweat and blood, the linseed oil he'd rubbed into the heel well. As far as anyone knew, it was the only catcher's mitt in Yell County, and Coach had appointed him to catch, Wiseman. Floradee had told him that it would be okay, so that was that. He'd catch Jimmy Patterson for the Stepwell Benefit, use his broken in gamer. Not to mention the pads and steel-framed mask. This close to game time, he couldn't worry about it anymore. Perry had other fish to fry.

There's some days you wake up and can just feel it in your blood that something's up and nothing you can do's going to make any difference. Drink your coffee black or with cream, no matter. They'd shut down the hardware and grocery for the afternoon, him and Jeanine. Little Perry's over to the neighbors playing Cowhide Johnson or whatever else they play over there. Jeanine's gone over to First Methodist where the wives are commandeering the kitchen to make the world's largest mess of coleslaw. Banana pudding. Nearly noon, he's been left alone to get himself mentally prepared for the first ever game as Little John catch.

There's the signs to worry about. One for curve, two for fast, three for slider and four for bean. Or was it one for fast and two for curve? It was—one for fast, two for curve. And could he really make the sign for a man to be hit? Not just a dust off. A bean ball?

Squatting was hard, real, real hard. Try it.

And what about a man swinging a number thirty-three Louisville Slugger a mitt's width from your head? Was he out of his mind, Perry? What was Coach thinking, asking him to catch?

In front of Stepwell.

As if to underline how much the team missed him, having to resort to Perry. All that throwing runners out at second, blocking home with nothing but his body making the sign to bean the batter in the head. Jeanine had said he was making too much of it. It was just a game. They were frying fish. It was a benefit for the Stepwells. Don't overthink it like everything else, Perry. Maybe they'd get some of the six thousand back— wouldn't that be nice? Hmmm, Perry. Mister Generosity.

It had been partly her money, too. And they'd not gone on the vacation they'd been planning, the cruise in the Gulf, but it wasn't because of money, it had nothing to do with that.

They had everything they needed. Plus some. It was a sore spot between them, the loan to Floradee Stepwell. So be it. Maybe after today they could get over it. Maybe.

Game time was set for 3, which made pregame at 2, which meant he'd better have his ducks in a row, get on over to the field for the team meeting with Coach Stringham. He always forgot something, Perry. Cup, mouthpiece, his glove more than once, hat sometimes, always something. Maybe his mind this time. Maybe this time Perry'd forget his mind.

One for fast, two for curve, three for slider.

Four for bean.

Rawlings, St. Louis. Number stenciled onto the thumb.

Cup, mouthpiece, mind.

He'd played left last time they beat the Lions, whose short-stop, Gil Stegall, was the fastest high school hundred-yard dash man in Arkansas, Texas, Louisiana, and Missouri. Perry'd been a low hurdler for the Little Johns, just fast enough in the 180 to place in District and so get invited to State, in Hot Springs that year, this wild-ass town with gambling and horse racing, bars and casinos, Al Capone's own mafia buddies walking the street in three-piece suits and pistols bulging from their belts. Since it was just Perry, and he was representing the Little Johns, and Codger knew people in Hot Springs—didn't the old man always know people? —they'd put him up in the Arlington Hotel just off Bathhouse Row which, if not as grand as it had been in the days when Capone and Pretty Boy Floyd owned their own suites, was the nicest place Perry'd ever set foot in. Where he first tasted sour mash whiskey on the night of the finals in the Arkansas State Track Meet, 1942.

Outside lane on the cinder track, he'd been knocked out of the 180 lows in the prelims, so much for representing Yell County and the LJs. But he was there, what the hay, might as well spectate, watch the pole vaulters and high jumpers, Gil

Stegall line up to the starting blocks in the finals of the hundred. This in a day when no Black boy was allowed to run against a white, much less be invited to lace on spikes at State, but somehow it happened, that year it did—Perry's sure, he was there, on the infield near the finish where he could see the whole thing. Little Rock Central and Hall High sprinters, Larry Gunn up from Wabbaseka, one of the Henry boys from Sheridan, whose father was a Grand Wizard, they lined up on a May afternoon not so unlike this one, took places in the blocks, as the starter hollered: *To your marks. Set. Go.*

After, Perry'd walked back to the hotel in his sweats, replaying it, the starter's pistol, the way it echoed off the far bleachers. Stegall in lane three, the stunned silence. How he'd flinched at the sound of the gun, a time not far away when they'd hunt his kind in the field, came out low and burned the first forty. Had ten yards on the field at seventy-five. Broke ten flat by half a second, third fastest time in the world. The looks on the white boy's faces. How he kept on going past the finish line and right on out of the stadium gate, to who knows where. It was said Gil Stegall could stand flat-footed and jump onto the roof of a Volkswagen, maybe he went out Volkswagen jumping, or back to England where he'd come from. The record, of course, did not count, nor the third fastest time in the world. This was 1942, a scant six years since Jesse Owens put it to Hitler's boys over in Berlin, walked away with four gold medals and world records in the 100, 220, Long Jump and 440 Relay, but this was Arkansas, and there was the Elaine Riot mess that had gone down, Faubus on his way, Central High and the National Guard called into the integration. They weren't ready to be bettered by colored folk, not yet.

But he'd seen it, Perry had. And on the way back to the hotel, just outside Buckstead Bathhouse, this woman in a white car pulled over, waved him to her window. Wasn't he a pretty thing. Did he want to join her table for a drink. Why at the

Arlington, of course. She put him in mind of somebody, the green-eyed lady.

"Sure," he said, but he didn't have a taste for it, turned out. Liquor.

He'd had a spell, Daddy. She should go see him, Mama said. The drive to Scranton was a good hour, driving fast. Noon already, they'd be home soon, Jacky and Weldon. Josephine could get things ready—she could make it there and back, just by the skin of her teeth. If she left that second, she could. Thirty minutes to spare before the game started. It was enough to go see Daddy. She should have had her hair done, made the pick-up for the Hicks girl's bridal bouquet, the purple iris with its bloom gossamer thin, like lace, and Daddy liked it, purple iris. She could have taken him a vase full, good medicine, she was his youngest girl, his favorite, though he'd never in a million years say so for fear of hurting the others' feelings. And though he never intimated as much, it hurt him, the whole thing with Weldon, the full-through laceration her cousin Doc Jenkins had sewed up, and no doubt passed on the details. The two'd never got along, though Daddy's manners kept him polite. Mama'd threatened castration with a carving knife right at the dinner table. I'll cut it off, she'd said, the Younger in her. Maybe it had got into Floradee, maybe that's what it was. Maybe that's what Weldon saw in her, the wildcat?

The Ford was of course low on gas. Truth was, she'd never filled the tank full since they got it, save the one-time to the hospital. No one who'd lived through '29 filled their tank full, did they? Nor bought four new tires at once.

Less than half a tank. She could chance it. The needle went past empty some. She could take a siphon hose in case, a piece of bread to chew on if gas got in her mouth.

What she wasn't going to do was stop at the stoplight Texaco and let Joe Carl Brucker fiddle with the oil stick and windshield wipers, check the air in every tire.

Floradee, she couldn't hear herself think again. Call in Josephine, have her get Early ready, tell daddy Mama'd had to run an errand, she'd be back by 2:30, a quarter to three at the latest. She had a surprise for him. He should put on the blue shirt, the one she'd pressed. Don't let on, she told her daughter, it was a surprise. Feed and water pony. Don't step in the mess with her good shoes. Tell Earl. Be ready.

She was on her way to Scranton, to see Daddy. He'd had a heart spell, barely enough time, but time. Started the car, lit a cigarette, one of Weldon's, from the lighter, felt the heat from the orange eye. Half a tank, a little less. It was enough. Turned onto their street, the one printed on her checks, their two names, both of them. Little mailbox with its silly red flag. Josie looking out the front door window in her rearview, her life.

She drove away and onto Highway 10 through town, stopped at the stoplight. Little John Field over there, its light poles taller than anything else in Danville, bet you could see forever from up there.

Joe Carl waved out the Texaco door.

The light turned green.

She let off the brake, pressed the gas. She could promise to bring him flowers next time, make it a special arrangement with baby's breath and ribbon. It wouldn't matter. He just needed to see her. Have a hug. That was enough.

She met them at the cutoff to Chickalah Mountain and Highway 27. Jacky waved, honk honked. Weldon made a sign for her to stop. What she did. Put it in park. Killed it. Waited for the truck to double back. The flurry of excitement that followed. From fifty years off she'd recall the moment for her grandson who had his nose.

What was she doing?

Making a delivery.

Look what they had, him and Jacky-boy. In back of the trunk. He had the color about him, whiskey. In his face, something like that.

Look at what they caught. Can you believe it. They were driving to the gas station to weigh it. Deedee, can you believe it?

May 6, 1950, she'd be seeing the date for the rest of her days. How lucky it was that they'd run into each other. They could have their picture taken together with it. One with the kids. Follow them back to town. *I love you, sweetie*, he said out of the blue, Weldon had.

It was hideous, still breathing.

She followed, watched them weigh, a few confused onlookers gawking at her with the question in their eyes—wasn't today the day? Had they got it wrong? Why was Stepwell at the Texaco after noon on the day of his benefit? They'd bought tickets and skipped breakfast for the sake of the fish fry. Was this thing they wrestled in the back of Jacky's pick-up fit for the fryer? Fish that big, wouldn't it have worms or some such? Did they want their picture taken with it—eighty-seven-pound flathead catfish trotlined up from Fourche LaFave?

She never said a word, Floradee.

Followed them to the house, asked Jacky on the sly if he could speed up the dressing. Brought butcher paper and tape for freezing and weren't they going to have a by god fish fry, and that called for cold beer and cornmeal, a tub of lard and sweet onion. His fryer was in the shed, hadn't had any call to touch it since. Since what, the before and after? From that day on, it would always be before he cut his leg off, and after he caught the fish. The gap in between would evaporate, the gangrene and yellow medicine, stump on fire with the phantom charley horse Josie'd massaged out with her own hands, the World Series of 1949, Staggers and Boston Harbor and the sound of the foghorns before light, what got him there, for a long time it would all evaporate. There would be a Before.

And there would be an After.

She never said a word about how she'd been on the way to Scranton to see Daddy, that he'd had a heart spell and was of a mind to see her. How she'd planned on taking him purple iris only she hadn't been able to hear herself think for so long now, that she hesitated, she'd dropped the ball. The tank had only half of what she needed and in her haste, she'd driven off without a siphon hose or chunk of white bread in case gas got in her mouth.

What the day would come to represent for her.

Jacky managed to talk Weldon into icing the fish in the horse trough they'd bought for Sugarfoot. Laid it on top of it a good foot of chunk ice, covered it with as much. You could see its shape all gauzy down there underneath, the fish. There was something they wanted to show him, Weldon. They'd see to the meat after while.

Born on the cusp of the great flu outbreak of 1918 which roared to life during the Great War and could only be reported on from Spain, because they were neutral, and the Huns weren't about to admit a goddamn thing, when one of every three got sick and died and it seemed the end was at hand, whose first decade was punctuated with the crash of '29, and nobody had a job, nobody, when the soup line stretched from the kitchen of First Methodist clear to the stoplight before there was a stoplight, the generation of men who made up the Danville Little John semi-professional team in the Dixie League had fought a World War. They'd come home to rejoin their lives, play some by god ball because life was short, they'd learned that much. Give it your best shot. Make hay when you could. They were carpenters and volunteer firemen, worked for Arkansas Power & Light, were school aldermen, a justice of the peace, delivered the mail and sold hardware. One would be a State Senator, another a guitar player who'd bust it out on Louisiana Hayride. They owned businesses, some of them, would give blood and a limb for one another. More. They were not bad men who gathered at Little John Field on that May Saturday, to break bread with kith and kin, and try to put a little whoop ass on England Lions for the season opener, a benefit game for one of their own, Mr. Weldon Stepwell, who'd lost a leg in a woodcutting accident up to Hallowell Hunt Club, whose family had suffered in mind and body and spirit.

To a man they'd live their lives so that their obituary writers would not have to lie so much as usual, and they'd maintain that thread of fame of having worn the uniform way back when on the day when things got out of hand, and it had all started with the goddamn fish, they shouldn't have taken her from the dark waters of Fourche LaFave, they shouldn't have.

But they did.

And though they could not know it, Weldon nor Jacky-boy Thorpe, the After time had started the moment the great fish gills stopped their work under the foot of chunk ice in a horse trough in Stepwell's backyard. What good was such a thing? Not for eating surely, might as well carve up a refrigerator box and deep fry it, a little lemon on the side, tartar and cocktail. A trophy? It's not like anyone performed taxidermy on flathead catfish, did they? Bragging rights for a big-ass cat, maybe a state record, but of course it wasn't, not for a peckerwood trotline. Not good to eat, unmountable, and inferior to the record books, what was it, exactly, that drove Butch and Jacky to so risk life and limb on the banks of Fourche LaFave in 1950, opening day, morning of the Danville Little John All You Can Eat Baseball Benefit for Weldon Stepwell and his family at a buck fifty a pop, say?

Jacky'd cut his end, then dropped the knife, an Uncle Henry, into black water, never to be seen again. Fired up the Evinrude and cut it to the far bank where the Man Tree stared at the spectacle, got out of the boat onto dry land, laid hands to the line and pulled. Every three feet a razor-sharp treble threatened, and who's ever tried to haul in dam near a hundred pounds of living tornado with nothing but bare hands, hooks or no? Clearly it was as long as they were tall, and it would make runs where they'd be reduced to turning loose, goddamning the world to hell and starting again from the beginning, which was really the end.

Not a lot of talking. And it was the first heavy lifting Stepwell had done as an amputee. He couldn't get his legs underneath him the way he once could, and more than once the fish threw them on their faces. He'd peed his pants, Jacky. They struggled alone, no one was around. Under the blue sky with crazed sun rising. Time got squirrely, seemed to go backward then forward then stop altogether. A treble caught Stepwell in the forearm, and Jacky'd had to retrieve the rusty bait knife from the stern to cut the leader. That's when time stopped, the screamed bleat telegraphed to the fish, so it ran, and Stepwell fell down, so the thing dragged him clear to the water before he braced his good foot on the Man, hauled in enough slack to save his ass from the deep. That's when Jacky cut the leader, gave Stepwell the look and they both knew what it meant.

"No," he said, "Uh huh."

They could have cut it aloose.

Set her free.

But they didn't.

And once a man such as those from whence they'd come commits to the deed, no matter how drastically over the top, they would not turn loose. They wouldn't.

So it wasn't about the fish—anybody can tell you that. It never was, was it? But what's behind the fish, laying out there in the holes deep beyond time and space and what has been and will be. And in the forests of that night lives untamed all we ever feared or fought or desired and laid hands on together, so that tie would bind one man to the other for the rest of their lives on earth.

You can't just walk away from a fish like that, can you? But that's what they asked of him, Weldon Stepwell, goddamn insisted upon, as if the world would up and end if he didn't.

21.

From behind home plate, Perry Wiseman commanded a view of Little John Field such as he'd never imagined from left field. Coach had run the lime lines left and right with the wheeled liner, framed the batter's box pretty as you please. It had a bite to it, the lime, lay down the raw red dirt raked smooth and flat all around the infield where the bags shone in the afternoon sun, the smell of fried fish and hushpuppies, home style potatoes and all that iced tea sugary with lemon in paper cups. Jacky Thorpe holding down first, Hicks on second, with one-handed Lew Blanding in the deep gap at short. Bastard stood on the bag at third, Jimmy Patterson backing him up in case the throw out was wild in left. Mathis and George in center and right. Bill Lordes on the mound, smoking it. Fresh painted fence signs advertising the Bank & Trust, his own Hardware and Grocery, Arkansas Power and Light, Codger's. Four o'clock sun behind his back so he could see it in his pitcher's eyes, one for fast, two for curve, a full fist for throw out, which he'd just called, Stegall with a ridiculous lead off second—ten feet if an inch. Zero, Zero, the top of the sixth—he feels Stepwell back there still as stone, his vacuum of intergalactic space louder than the chatter that washed over the field of play. Clean up just stepped to the plate ready to swing, a righty, make him reach. Lordes about to pitch the throw out ball high and outside. Stegall juking it off second, about to throw Lordes into a conniption, gun it to Hicks for the rundown with Bastard, put old Speedy Gonzalez in a pickle.

Through the facemask bars, Wiseman sees all. How the field has greened since winter. The bright white lines. Bags secured on their hooks. How Lordes touches his thumb and forefinger of his throwing hand to his tongue. Takes the sign. Husky clean up practice swings so the bat's swish is clean and real. He felt Stepwell back there in the part of the bleachers they'd roped off for him and Floradee, the kids. Lordes, in the stretch, ready to fire. His own wife back there, Jeanine, little Perry. He'd only caught in three practices. Again, Coach made the sign for the throw out, two down, the stranding out at the plate. From ninety feet away, the quick release, red stitches spinning.

Stegall stole.

Running low, catlike.

God damn. He'd won the hundred at State—third fastest time in the world. Perry'd seen it, he had not forgotten. The way the world got quiet, something holy happening, had to be. How he'd walked back to the Arlington after and the woman drove up beside him in a T-Bird, asked if he wanted to have a drink with her at the hotel bar. Was he an athlete, did he have a room for the night. How she'd put him in mind of somebody.

High and outside, a heater. Batter couldn't touch it. No way. Perry stood to make the catch, both legs fully under him, ready to throw, rock and fire. Left hand full buried in Stepwell's mitt, Rawlings, made in St. Louis. He felt them back there, behind his back, collective breath held.

He caught the ball. Threw it. Hard.

Base coach at third made the sign for slide, get down. Stegall coming in hot, face first. Bastard blocking the bag, just like he was supposed to, glove open, then shut for the tag.

Got him first in the head coming in, then the shoulders.

Third base ump right there, squatting, a first cousin on his mother's side. Held his right fist up. Said, "Out."

The sound came all back on in a rush. Stegall leapt up

shaking his head. "Out," cousin said again. His right fist pumped in the air. On another day the dugouts might have cleared, punches thrown and landed. A big mess.

But not this time

Stegall smiled, looked at Perry and nodded. Guess you got me this time. Some throw. Where'd you get that from? Say.

He'd thrown out Gill Stegall. Stepwell'd never done that.

And when he turned to the home side of the bleachers, about to wave to Jeanine and little Perry, it was Floradee Stepwell he saw. It had been her that woman at the Arlington Hotel had put him in mind of, those green eyes, the lilt of voice from that day he'd clerked at the Bank & Trust, cashed her daddy's paycheck on the eve of the great tornado. Wiseman, overcome by the wall of sound, funny he'd never known.

He'd protested.

What on earth could be so important? This wasn't the time. What he needed was an early supper before dressing the fish, was there beer? He thought that the least he'd earned was cold beer. Early needed to watch this, Josie, how to nail the head to a tree with a sixteen-penny nail, make that a railroad spike for this hog, strip the skin off with needle nose pliers, head to tail. Cut the guts out, the gills. See what's been on big girl's menu, find the delicate egg sack, squeeze a little lemon and tabasco, go to town with crackers and cheese. Stretch a hose out back of the shed, lay her on the door propped up on sawhorses, you're going to need an ax for that backbone, broken every two inches for steaks, size of a dinner plate, the biggest. Mix egg, beer and stout mustard, whip it to a foam and get yourself three buckets of Crisco, melt it in the fryer, lay down a bucket full of Martha White's and cornmeal, fistful of red pepper. Sack of potatoes, bread and butter pickles, butter for the puppies, pickled jalapeños if they could find some.

So what's all this about him supposed to get dressed? Put on the blue shirt. Change his shoes? To get what they needed from the store—did they all need to go for that? Kids all dressed up. Josie with a ribbon in her hair. Earl wearing his Sunday coat. Just what was up, Dee? He wasn't changing shoes. You ever try getting a shoe onto that foot, stiff as a dead doe? They'd forgive him a little blood on his work shoes up to the IGA, wouldn't they—the Wiseman woman, Jeanine?

Why did she have to drive? What was wrong with everybody all of a sudden?

"Daddy?" Josephine said. "Daddy."

"What, hon."

She leaned up from the back seat, put a hand on each of his shoulders, coaxed him in. They drove then, past the stoplight Texaco—closed for the day. Codger's, empty. Eternally Yours, which they'd somehow managed to save, purple iris for the Hicks girl chilled in the cold room, baby's breath for the bridal bouquet, some extra for Daddy, when she could go.

"It's a surprise we're taking you to see."

Dee caught their eyes in the rearview, the same colors. Josie nodded. It was okay. It'd be okay.

"A surprise?"

And there it was, Little John Field, all those cars parked on the green grass next to the Highway, light poles stringered with stadium lights they'd paid for in full with gate receipts. A picnic going on out there, looked like. That hillbilly band from Booneville. Smelled like fried fish, potatoes, everything Weldon had just talked about. There was a sign with his name on it. The infield had been raked and lined, the outfield mowed. The base bags were bolted in. A bus said England Lions. Over there sat Gil Stegall smiling over a plate full of fried fish and the sides. There was coach. Bastard. Jacky and his wife. The hillbillies commenced to play "Ole Joe Clark." Umps had on their zebra suits. The wives were doing the serving. Fresh May Day. Everything right so far. Hadn't everything gone right? Since that far-off day when they'd all sat on blankets outside of St. Mary's waiting for him to live or die, and he'd hemorrhaged and slipped into the coma and lived and came out of it, and went to Boston to get fitted and was now returned, Weldon Stepwell, prodigal son, he'd come back to them, and everything was okay, wasn't it?

"What's this, Dee?"

"Your benefit," she said. "They've been planning it."

He stood out of the car, up on two feet, walked and did not limp. For the rest of his life, he'd be a man who refused to limp, just as Staggers had foreseen, along with the consequences.

"Why didn't you tell me?"

She should have had her hair done. They were all of them looking now. At her, the kids. The guest of honor.

Josie took her father's right hand with her left, walked over the green grass beside him. Floradee on the other, Earl trailing.

"It's a surprise, Daddy. Be happy."

And he did. He tried. What else?

Shook hands, chowed down, drank a ton of tea. Do you care for some more of those hushpuppies, Mr. Stepwell? Can I refill your tea? Of course, there's banana pudding for dessert. Floradee helped with the slaw—wasn't it good. That T-Bone Titsworth, he sure could flat-pick that gee-tar. Was it true Sheriff Kemp had got the jailbirds out to help get things ready? Bet they liked that, being out under the blue sky. Wasn't that Darla Diamond pretty in her Miss Dardanelle outfit, the scepter and crown, why she could sing the chrome off a trailer hitch, couldn't she? Would he throw in the game ball, just walk on in there, son, and give it your best. And that's what he did, Stepwell, walked out to the mound and took the brand-new baseball from Coach Stringham, hauled off and threw a dead-on bullet over home so you could hear it thwack, and that sound echoed off deep left, came back to them. He shook each of the player's hands, they'd all lined up, home and visiting.

Gil Stegall'd smiled, said, "Good throw."

"He's wearing my glove," he said in the bleachers, just as Billy Lordes threw the opening pitch high and tight.

"Why's Wiseman got on my glove?"

Jacky'd seen the look once before. Back in R'Ville after the double header, when the big redhead had joked about Lew Blanding, how it must be hard times, Danville having to field one armed boys. That look like he wanted to kill somebody when he'd beat up four men with his right arm tied behind his back, and they'd thrown him in the pokey and Dee refused to bail him out. A look that had brought on broken nose, teeth, that sound gets into your blood, your stomach. From the bleachers, Josephine on one side, Dee on the other. Perry'd just thrown a bullet to Bastard on third, cut down the base runner who just happened to be a Stegall, the fastest one of them, Gil, who'd danced and juked his way damn near into a rundown already while stealing second. Serve his ass right, get thrown down at third, zero-zero in the top of the sixth. But uh oh, what was he thinking up there, Stepwell? That browsy glower, his blood up.

From first, Jacky saw it clear as day, right when Perry spun to the applause, waved Stepwell's glove, that silly rich boy smile of his, daddy Codger lording it over everybody and their mother.

But it was a good throw, Butch, damn good. And they were teammates, cutting his leg off didn't change that. And Perry'd been out on that lawn with all the rest of them in front of St. Mary's. He'd give his life blood for Stepwell, too. And Horace Hicks had borrowed the mitt because the team didn't own one and truth was they needed it for a while. It was a good glove, a gamer, broke in already. Took half a season to break in a glove like that. More. None of them had wanted to catch. Coach had laid the job on Wiseman, given him the head nod that meant he'd been chosen. And he'd done his best. He wasn't no Stepwell, but he'd done his best. Hadn't he, so far? And now he'd just thrown out the fastest base runner in the whole Dixie League, maybe the whole goddamn world. Goddamnit, Butch. Don't give Perry that look.

It ain't right.

Stegall limped back to the Visitor's dug out, whamming red dirt off his chest with his throwing hand. Shaking his head. Where'd the boy get an arm like that? What had just happened?

Maybe Stepwell could have made that throw. Maybe not. But that skinny cracker boy behind the plate? Damnation.

Truth was, he was tired, Jacky. The fish had taken it out of him. He wanted the game to be over, drive on home, shower, slip between the cool sheets with Jane Ann. Let the moon come out, the stars. The food hadn't set right on his stomach, why on earth'd he eat like that before a game?

He'd almost got dragged down, Butch.

Catching one like that, you can't tell nobody about it, not in a million years. And they'd landed the white bellied son of a bitch, thrown it in the back of Jacky's pickup and trailered the boat. What was there to say? Guess we should weigh it.

Guess so.

Like they'd killed some brown river god.

On the day of the benefit, what had all been his idea—dreamed up in the reverie of White Horse catching the golden apple, the green field, shining barn, home. Buck fifty a pop, all the proceeds to pay off Stepwell's hospital bills. It was a good idea, maybe the best he'd ever had, Jacky Thorpe. It hurt his heart to see Stepwell up there feeling sorry for himself—he was better than that, he was. And for the first time what his mama'd always said to him made sense: *wish it was me instead of you.*

And maybe for just a second there on first, before the inning ended and the game wound into extra innings and ended in a tie because nobody won, maybe he did wish it was him instead of Stepwell. Because it wasn't any good blaming Perry Wiseman for anything at all that had happened to him. Truth was, everybody'd bent over backward for Weldon Stepwell, Perry included. And throwing Stegall's ass out on third, that was a good thing.

Holy, almost.

He needed to see that, Stepwell, and know that he was a part of it. They were here because of him, in his honor, out of love and friendship.

If not willing to trade places, they wished that Weldon had not fallen into the bucksaw up on Chickalah Mountain last August and were on his side to try and set things right.

All of them, to the man.

Three hundred some at the gate price of buck-fifty, bike, gun, vacation on beautiful Lake Ouachita at Shangri-La Resort, raffles, plus the matching funds ole Codger'd thrown in to cover costs, then some, looked like they'd clear five hundred—at least five hundred. Throw in the fish fry tips and donations, the gig fee the Yell County Yellers had graciously kicked back, and they were sitting on close to a thousand, and it's not just anybody walk up to you and put a grand in your front pocket, was it? Rumor was Perry Wiseman'd given or maybe let borrow a good deal more than that to Floradee, but that was a whole 'nother thing.

This was team money—Little John business.

What he needed was a talking to, Stepwell. And when the two teams shook hands in the infield, agreed to call it a tie because nobody'd won, when they'd agreed to sign and award the game ball to the guest of honor Weldon "Butch" Stepwell, and everyone agreed that it should be Perry who awarded, given he'd stepped into catch and had hot-flashed Stegall at third, that's exactly what Jacky boy Thorpe decided to do, tomorrow or next day, give Stepwell a talking to, but he of course hadn't counted on—though later he'd know that he should have—what happened next.

How Perry'd walk the game ball, wrapped in the leathery-sweat smelling catcher's mitt, up to the special roped off place for the Stepwell family, only they'd be gone already. Maybe he was tired, Butch, had been out late last night, hadn't he, something about a fish he'd weighed with Thorpe at the Texaco, over a hundred pounds somebody said. It'd been a hard way to go for the family, nine months into it now, and there'd been the whole Boston thing, and learning to walk again, and hey did everybody see how he didn't miss a lick, Stepwell, how if you didn't know you wouldn't know. They deserved to go home and have some rest, don't hold it again them. And there was the whole business of proceeds, maybe they should cut a check and deliver it all to them at once, the benefit money, game ball in the St. Louie mitt, and the announcement that thereafter, with his blessing, it was to be called Stepwell Field, where the Little Johns played.

That Perry Wiseman would let Sunday and church pass, make a call on the Stepwells at Eternally Yours Floral on Monday at 10:30, unannounced, accompanied by a photographer from the Yell County Record of Danville, Arkansas. On behalf of the team and the citizenry of Danville, he'd offer the gift package just outside the front door and the plate glass window wherein was written the name they'd taken from the silver service Weldon had bought for the wedding. Eternally Yours, what was painted in pink and green curlicues suggestive of flowers on the storefront they'd managed to save through the whole mess, no small part of which was due to Perry Wiseman, who met Stepwell on that very spot, offered the gift and his right hand to shake, just as the photographer readied his flash for the shot.

What he hadn't counted on, Jacky nor Perry nor any of the rest, was that instead of accepting the gift and shaking the proffered hand, Weldon Stepwell would throw a right cross that knocked Perry clean through the plate glass window, and that that moment would signal a whole new trajectory for everyone involved.

The event heralded all that would come.

In the team photo that has survived all of them, the players stare in two distinctly different directions: some face straight ahead, Lloyd George, Lew Blanding, Bastard, Stepwell, and the rest gaze straight into the eye of the camera, Coach, Patterson, Lordes, Wiseman. As if they see it coming, the whole sad story, that look on their faces, Perry at the far end, what did he have to fear? The ones who stare ahead seem alarmed, while the camera gazers appear serene. At far left, Wiseman looks into the camera, Stepwell straight ahead, a furrow darkening his brow where Dee'd folded a crease into his face that threatened, after some years, to tear. Of all them, only two smile, tall Jacky Thorpe, a big tooth grin aside Stepwell's glower. Through time and space, he grins. Straight into the camera, the only photograph ever taken of the 1949 Little Johns, the one that would get reprinted so often, whenever any one of them died or got elected to office or moved off to California to be a millionaire.

He hadn't counted on Weldon waylaying Perry through the plate glass window, nor the repercussions that would follow. But in that photo, the one that would pass down through the generations, you can see something's up, out there in the dark, some of them looking in its direction, some not.

And he didn't wish it was him instead of Stepwell. Finally, he couldn't. Best friend he'd ever had or no, but not that.

Not that.

PART 3

22.

24 April 2020
Friday

Joey Harvell
210 Humphrey Street
Salt Lake City, Utah 84102
801.843.6387

Mr. Jack Thorpe
6341 Highway 10
Danville, Arkansas 72833

Dear Mr. Thorpe:

I am honored to write to you today. My name is
Joey Harvell, and I believe that you played baseball
with my maternal grandfather, Weldon Stepwell, as
part of the Danville Little Johns Dixie League Semi-Pro
Team of 1949. Stephen Wiseman has suggested that
I call you to talk about the team and any memories
you have of Weldon, who you stand beside in the team
photograph passed to me by my mother, Josephine
Stepwell. I thought it would be better to write you
before I call, to let you know who I am, and that I'd
like to have a phone talk at a good time for you. Please

write back, if you can, and let me know a time and a day, and I'll be pleased to call you then.

I have a wife and a daughter here in Utah. My girl has the look of Weldon about her. She's a sophomore in college here, before all that shut down. She's an only child. Someday she'll be needing to know about her family.

I don't know why I'm telling you that. We've been on lock down for six weeks. Just like you, probably. How is it there, in Danville? We're well here. Mostly we are. I hope you're the same. And your children. I've got cancer. They caught it early.

Anyway, if you will, here goes:

What was it like, after the war, for the men to come home and play baseball?

Tell me about Danville then.

Did you know my family—Weldon, Floradee, Josie and Earl Stepwell? What do you remember about them? Do you remember the flower shop they ran?

Do you remember his accident, Grandpa's?

Do you recall any stories about Weldon Stepwell? Was he your friend?

My mama kept that team photo on her dresser for her whole life, and it's been up in my study for ten years. I've studied it. It's a professional shoot, lighted. You're beside Weldon, and your expressions couldn't be more different. He's brooding and intense. You're smiling. Half the men face the camera. The other half stare away.

What are they looking at, in the dark before you?

I am thankful, Mr. Thorpe, for your time and honored to correspond with a person who played ball with my grandfather. Growing up, I'd spend part of each summer near Mt. Ida on Lake Ouachita where he was

guide, hear his good stories and help him pick tomatoes and okra. I've missed him for a long time now and
working with material from Danville has brought him
and my memories into sharp focus.

Please write back, just a note will do. Let me know
when a good time to call might be. I'll look forward to
it. Thank you so much.

Yours,
Joey Harvell

ps., Weldon's great-granddaughter says hello. She's a
big fan. Will there ever be baseball again?

23.

The last torn in half, taped back together photograph she owned of Weldon Stepwell was of him in a Little John uniform, standing for the team photo with the rest of the backsliders and drunks. Two rows of them come back from the war, the Dixie League they called themselves. They ran Eternally Yours, Yell County's only florist. Name'd come off the plated silver set he'd bought for their wedding registry, Weldon, every last dented up run through the dishwasher spoon and salad fork advertising the lie across its backside. Eternally Yours, a downright hilarious promise from a man couldn't keep his pants on, even after the leg. Even Josie, who made her daddy into Jesus P. Christ after he hemorrhaged the second time and died, never argued that one. Sins of love misguided, Father Skully'd called it, well how about that? On the bottom row, there's Lew Blanding, hiding his blown up hand behind a jumbo fielder's glove. Coach squats over to the right, a husky sad-eyed man. He'd lost a son to one of those battles toward the end. "Dee," he used to say when she drove up for Weldon after practice, "I've been meaning to pick up petunias for Gladys. How long does it take to fall out of love?"

She'd laugh. Tell him they had a stash, fresh.

When what was left of his son came home draped in a flag, she did the arrangement herself, a purple spray interwove with scarlet gilia and lilac, a photo of big smiling Charley propped up beside the box.

In the back row, far away as he could get, there's Perry, scrawny next to Weldon, but smart as a whip, one day about to be rich as a Rockefeller. Wal-Mart money. Yell County truckers making runs from Bentonville, paid overtime runs in Daddy Sam's stock options which they did not hesitate to cash in at the grocery and hardware for slab bacon and a pound of sixteen-penny nails, who'd of guessed? Hadn't he been the sweet one, Perry? What on earth was wrong with the women of her people? Had they got you know what all twisted up in their DNA to make them such fools when it came to men? She'd married Weldon Stepwell for his letter jacket, and even more because ditsy Ruby Titsworth wanted him so bad, and she was from money back in Morrilton—bankers who'd steal you blind, steal your soul, even. And she had that long hair with the bounce to it, just like her daughter would later on, little floosy.

Perry Wiseman was not the sort to hit you in the head with a peanut butter jar, and she'd never even looked his way, well not much. A good man is hard to find, wasn't that what they said? Perry was one you could do with, sensible and kind and able to see what needed to be done and do it. Look how Perry's frozen there in 1949, neither worried nor happy, particularly, just gazing at the camera like he wanted it done. Jeanine, somewhere out there watching.

The tallest of the bunch wears that wild-happy smile— Jacky Thorpe. First baseman. The same girls wanted Weldon would've just as soon had Jack, though they were different as night from day. Kiddos can tell people, a gift we lose, some of us, as time goes by. Josie loved Jack Thorpe like she did her own Daddy, called him Uncle, him always underfoot, arm wrestling Weldon on the kitchen table, blowing duck callers, running trotlines out on Fourche LaFave. He'd been with Weldon after, on the day of the big Benefit the team threw, that hideous fish they wanted Dee to pose with.

He'd been the one to go back for it, the leg.

219

Just like it was happening that second, the ambulance sound, the one little window in the back door, all that green in full retreat, like flying in an airplane backwards.

The sound was the first thing she didn't want her daughter to hear, because no one who ever heard a man yell that way could forget. Not that. When the driver hit his brakes, they skidded sideways.

Into the sound.

Late summer, hot, the air still. No rain forever. The door opened. Doc Jenkins carried a hypodermic in each hand. They got him in. Left it lay out there. Fifty miles down Danville Mountain to St. Mary's. They did the tourniquet, tightened and loosened when Doc said. She asked him not to die, said I love you with all my heart, that she was his, for all time, that she was sorry, so so sorry. When he stopped breathing, Josie beat his chest, shouted NO, NO. NO.

She always heard her saying that. No.

Weldon's breath had caught. Like a tear in his throat.

Appeared the cupola atop ArkaTech, the big green lawn of St. Mary's where twenty-some, thirty, had gathered, on blankets, people she'd loved and hated. There was Coach. Lew letting people see the hand. Jack's wife, Jane Ann, running up beside the ambulance. Saying Deedee, what Weldon alone called her. What finally got her, broke the spell. As they wheeled him through the double door, she'd stripped off, Jane Ann, wrapped in a sheet for surgery.

Perry was there.

Here.

This photograph, souls under the lamp beside the telephone not so unlike the one through which her mother had said you're too late. He'd gone home. She'd never say goodbye, thank you, I love you, anything at all. Staring down dark-faced Danville men who'd made a minor-league baseball team named the Little

Johns—of all things. What she needed then was a Big John. The war was over. They'd survived. A whole season ahead of them, sweep the league, maybe, make it happen. Anything, anything at all.

Right?

Weldon would cut his leg off in the woods and bleed to death. Or not. They could forgive each other, renew vows, and put their whole hearts into it this time. Let sleeping dogs lay. The day she spun the butcher knife at him could unthrow itself and become something else. Make nice. Be sweet. Smile for the camera. Honey. She hadn't wished it on him, the bucksaw. She hadn't. Didn't have the outlaw in her like mama. Cruel blood. It was a long time ago. Things might have been different, and it wouldn't have to keep echoing through the walls of time. Over and over and over. That Stepwell tendency toward theatric catastrophe. Weldon with his leg, then the morphine. Perry Wiseman with his bagful of money, what came with it. Kept on coming, just kept on. The little slut and Boston and Weldon home clear as a bell, that pony tied to the shed, and the Hicks girl's wedding flowers, purple iris, Dad's favorite. Hadn't she ordered extra. To take him some. She was his favorite, his darling, the youngest girl, he'd sent her to school in Memphis with its Peabody Hotel and Lyle Lewis with his jewelry box full of it.

He'd had a spell, Mama said. He'd like to see her, if she had the time. It'd make him feel better, always did. Could she drive over? Just for a while?

And there was that window when she'd hesitated, but almost went, was in the car, driving toward Scranton and Subiaco and all those robed monks with their mouthfuls of dirt, an eagle living in the belfry tower, or was it a vulture—they were related, weren't they?

And there'd come Weldon, clear as a bell, changed, that whiskered head still breathing in the bed of Jacky's truck. Take your picture with it, dress it up in Sunday clothes for the

Stepwell Benefit, put a little hat on it, a bow, feed it all you can eat and a baseball game to boot. They'd rope off a special section for the family in the new-convict-built bleachers. Weldon'd throw in the game ball. Perry'd catch. Josephine and Early, little Catfish, they were family. About to stand and walk away from it all—*why's he wearing my glove?* Perry'd throw out a base runner. That fast one. They'd walked away from it.

Why they'd sent him the proceeds check that Monday morning, who knows. But there was Perry Wiseman with the County Record photographer, knocking on the glass. Smiling. Look at us, about to make your day. When Weldon hit him, he flew right through, and the glass stretched before it broke. Who knew that, that glass stretched? It made her sick all over again.

And that's when she *knew*.

He'd be sorry to beat the band. Sorry like no one's business. The sorriest man on a planet full to the sorry brim with sorry people. Sorry with a capital S. No one could touch him for being sorry, Weldon. Could they?

Daddy's heart attack was massive.

Here one minute, gone the next.

He hurt real bad there at the end. But it didn't last long, thank the Lord. God took him fast. Mama said it on the other end of the line, from a neighbor's house in Scranton straight into her ear. Through the Wiseman's borrowed phone. It was black. The receiver.

Had he heard about what happened. The storefront? Wiseman?

He had.

Had it upset him?

Had.

24.

Are you Joey?

Yeah.

This is Jack Thorpe.

Yessir.

Stepwell was as good a friend as I ever had. We all went and gave blood. They didn't expect him to make it through the night, but he did.

He liked to fight some. We all went over to this night spot. One of them said something and Stepwell was back there in the alley beating him up. We'd all scattered, and the police came. We all got away, he was the only one got caught.

I used to fish and hunt with him.

The bucksaw was like this giant tiller, push it right up to a tree and let it go. He cut one tree down and it fell into another and he must have tried to push it. Cut the one leg clean off and a good hunk out of the other. We all went and give blood. I was the one to go up and find that leg, a fellow who'd been up there told me exactly where it was, he wouldn't go back for nothing. I aint'a going back, he said. Went up and found it, the boot and pants and leg, put it in a mail sack. Had two choices, bury it in a cemetery or burn it. I took it to the incinerator and asked the fellow could I throw the leg in there.

He give me a funny look. Said, "Well I guess so."

Outside, motorcycles, Joey hears a whole tribe of them, how they roar toward the mountain. For the rest of his life, he'd be hearing those motorcycles, sirens, all across the flat Utah belly of ground where the lake once lay, shake like a bowlful of jelly when the four-mile fault line goes off. A morning when the intubated elderly lay dying up at ICU, freshly whisked there via ambulance from Friendship Manor Retirement Village across the street. The sign out front's shorted, so it flashes *Fried Man* in neon red.

A colleague once skated roller derby, her professional name was Donut Hurt. These quarantine days she skates the Jordan River, does trick jumps over trail roots so her wheels fly off when she lands two-footed, and astonished teens shake their heads, say *whoa*, that was some good stuff, and it surely must be the new world coming. Another reads Emerson: these, like any other, are good times to be alive if we but know how to live them. One's floated a desert river with her son who wrote a poem about how the ageless water flows from the old world to the new. He'd tracked down Jack Thorpe, last Little John. He wants to know what they're looking at, half the men in the photo. They've been encouraged to open up, Joey and his colleagues. Don't get all caught up in all of this.

You there?

Yessir.

So that's what I did, just threw it on in.

Wash your hands they keep telling them. Don't touch your face. Stay six feet away. Wear a mask. Social distance. Practice cough etiquette. Wipe off the commode when you're done. Wash your hands some more, sing the birthday song, sing it all the way through. You touched your face. Cheat, you cheat your whole family.

Eternally Yours.

Joey?

Yeah.

Jack Thorpe walks him through the photo, bottom left to

top right. Lewis Blanding could throw the ball and all he had was the thumb on his right hand; Baskin, Faye Mathison, a county clerk, Lloyd George, he was my cousin, Elmer Moore and Clyde Stringfield, our manager. Top left is Perry Wiseman, Joy Marcum, and Roy Shelton, he was the only one but me still alive in Memphis, but he passed; me and Stepwell, Jimmy Patterson, and Bill Lordes, he was an optometrist, framed this picture and give it to me.

What are they looking at?

I'd stripped to my undershirt. Those uniforms were hot and heavy.

After the accident, I tried to catch but got knocked all around. Was Perry ended up behind the plate. Wore Weldon's glove.

His wife, Mr. Thorpe's, had stripped off wrapped in a sheet and gone in for emergency surgery. She's gone these seven years. Little Jack lives a quarter mile down White Horse Lane. Can't believe he lived through that, they kept on giving him our blood.

I just now got this letter. Just opened it.

Can't get around like I'd like to. Fell down yesterday and fell down again today. I'll be announcing the games, though, if I can get up in that little thing.

Those light poles, ninety-footers, they're still there, they light up the football field. We borrowed four thousand and paid it back. In gate receipts. We paid it back.

He was handsome, Butch. Liked to fight a little. I went over to Ouachita to fish with him after, that little trailer with his garden. Shangri-La. He was big there.

Ever tell you about that fish? We oughtn't have kept her.

Dee, I knew her well. We'd come in from fishing. We made lots of parties then. It oughtn't to have happened.

What are we looking at?

25.

They'd all be nearly a hundred now, the Little Johns, men who'd fought the Germans and won, returned home to the states and Arkansas believing that the world was better for them and their people, about to sweep the Dixie League pennant, maybe, and so have true momentum to propel through whatever lay in ambush out there for the rest of their lives. Men like Jacky Thorpe and Coach Stringham, Bastard and Wiseman, Lew Blanding, with his blown off fingers. Gil Stegall, who one day'd drown in the Red River trying to save his boy. Men who loved their children, wanted to, who suffered mishap and sought recovery, who prayed and belly-laughed, whined miserably and farted. Hiroshima and Nagasaki behind them, Fat Boy and Big Mama and whatever other ridiculous names they'd come up with to incinerate all those blameless souls on the south China sea. But the plague had passed them over. Left their doors unopened. If you could just figure things out, it was a good time to be alive. 1950. The year Weldon came home clear as a bell. For a while, he was. Forgive and forget. Practice charity. Let the dead bury the dead. Live while you're alive.

Right?

What else?

They all work from home now—the three of them, Renee, Lara, Joey. School shut down the week of Spring Break. Renee's brother and family had flown out to ski, only they shut the resorts down, all of them, and instead they'd soaked in the hot tub at University Guest Plaza, and they shut that down too. It was give or take whether their plane would ever take off for Florida. They'd talked about having to steal the rental truck, a big-ass Mercedes SUV, driving the two thousand miles from Utah, the route they'd driven half a dozen times to spend a week with Poppy and Meemaw at Melbourne Beach, swelter in the ungodly heat, where he'd been when Mama drowned and they had to drive off to Arkansas for the funeral.

Eternally Yours, the name stuck.

Joey'd inherited the garbage disposal dented up silver, the phrase written in curlicue cursive on the backside, 1847, Roberts Bros. Heavy stuff, ornate with flowers. Like the Little John photo, a mystery to him. The heirloom he'd pass down through whatever generations to come.

Bad luck?

Albatross?

Things have gotten backwards since quarantine.

Shelter in place.

Time is squirrely.

What day of the week it was had sort of washed away. That's how it felt, like the colored chalk on the patio where he'd written I Love You after a snow. Truth be told, they were just words on a calendar, which in Joey's case, since he'd made his own since 1988 when he officially got his shit together after it had hit the fan again, reduced to S, M, T and so on. Or in some months like the one when he had the Guided MRI and he needed good mojo, Sun and Moon, Tew and Wind, Fry for Friday Night Fish Fish Fry, and Satyr. Renee's Sagittarius, and some dark mornings he imagined none of this had ever happened, that he was half man, half goat, buck snorting his way through the deer wood down at Fordyce, where his maternal grandfather once got the game warden so drunk he checked a spike buck whose nubbins had only just broke through, fried back strap in a cast iron with home potatoes and garden sass. In another world.

The Old World, Lara calls it.

When the days didn't seem made up. When things were real.

From whence arrived Jack Thorpe's voice. Mama, gone the ten years. Grandpa, thirty-two. So maybe none of this makes any difference to anyone but Joe now. Everyone who's ever told the story is dead but him, and maybe Jacky Thorpe. If he still lives. But if Mama was alive, she'd by god care. Kept the one photo on her dresser for her whole adult life, who'd turned me over to him at an early age, trusted him fully which maybe she shouldn't have come to think of it.

All that's beside the point.

This search for the last of the Little Johns, it's about ending this story for good and ever, about laying to rest the last tenuous cracked and splitting ligaments tying them to that perished time and place, and all the departed souls who shared it.

Here at the end of it all, maybe.

26.

No faded flower, Dee was southern auditor for the Arkansas Department of Education. She lived in a summit penthouse on the edge of Little Rock's Heights, with its thirty-mile vistas over the muddy river. Her photograph sometimes graced the Sunday Society Page. Dee Stepwell answered to no one, and this last thing was something for a divorced woman in 60s Little Rock. Faubus was Governor—best keep your head down. But at the end of the day, sunning poolside with the jazz blowing over from Park Plaza, after she'd had *just one* at the Summit House Bar and ordered up room service, when it got dark and the building swayed and she lay between clean sheets listening to the air click on and off, it was then she had started to pray, just for the talk of it at first, and then in earnest—*oh father God, let me love.*

But it was not to be.

Her divorce had been ugly, especially for Mama and Earl for whom the restraining order against their father had been viewed as base treachery. Uncle Earl had stood in cutoffs on top of the Dipsy Dumpster at the Summit House parking deck, like a cliff diver on *Wild World of Sports*, then, with a slew of shocked onlookers that included Joey and Dee, made both hands into fists and dove the three stories into the deep end of the Summit House pool, his way of saying hell no, Mama, you will not have your Memphis banker. Stepwells are like that, liable to lay hands on a butcher knife and throw it at your head to make a point.

After turning Lyle Lewis down, Dee's attention turned to me, and the view from the top of the Summit House is one I know by heart. At five, I walked naked into her shower, the steamy water jetting down her back, and she'd laughed and let me stay, though it became a joke between us, one she'd remind me of on those late nights watching the *Tonight Show* with Johnny Carson, who was from Nebraska, like her. Munching popcorn through hands of Canasta.

Grandmother's audits took her to places like Dumas and DeWitt, Paragould and Magnolia, rural towns where the sight of a well-dressed Little Rock woman with a briefcase, foreign car, and boy in tow caused double and triple takes. People stared at us outright. Add to this that Dee was a school auditor, which meant she was tasked with finding waste in budgets, ferreting out clerical errors and outright fraud. Her reports were delivered to state headquarters, and oftentimes school administrators were summoned to Little Rock afterward. A superintendent from DeWitt was sentenced to a year at Tucker. Townsfolk whispered to each other when we walked in the restaurant that inevitably occupied a part of town nearest First Methodist or Baptist where the bells would sometimes chime during our meal, and she'd say, "Darling? Won't you have a piece of pie?" and look at me through those guileless green eyes.

By the time I was in junior high, the whole family got Jesus. Weekends at the Summit House now included Sunday mornings at Faith Maranatha out on Kavanaugh, where well-heeled Little Rock folk spoke in tongues and prophesied, had demons cast out, and walked down the pitched aisles to receive healing and the laying on of hands, some of them stunned by the touch so they fell flat out on their backs and whacked heads on the floor, so they came too with Jesus P. Christ's own headache.

All this took place to the music of a six-piece band with this glorious red-haired woman playing a Flying V through a 100-watt Marshall amp. There was a Hammond 3-D organ, a sax and this soaring clarinet, even. They'd put the *Beatitudes* to music, *Psalms*. People would get up off the pews and dance the holy ghost dance, joy bubbling up from deep inside. I loved church on Sundays with Mom Dee, who'd taken to interpreting prophecy the year I turned thirteen. After somebody'd stood up, waved their arms and committed glossolalia, Dee'd decipher the nonsense. In a sweet, clear southern voice, she'd say how Magog had risen against Gog in the East, how the serpent was already afoot amongst us, sewing lies and deceit. God's children best keep their heads on straight—the day was at hand. Everybody'd say *Praise God* and *Hallelujah. Thine the glory* and *Jesus is Lord*. The band would fire up and this glorious raven-haired woman would belt out "I'm in the Glory Land Way," and I'd believe her with all my heart because if anybody'd ever been in the glory land way, it was her. *Praise Jesus*, Dee'd say. *Praise Jesus*, I'd say, and for my fourteenth birthday, she paid cash for a used Fender, a Pig Nose amp and six weeks of guitar lessons.

By the time I went to the University, Dee'd had the first of her heart attacks. It runs in the family—both her parents, eight brothers and sisters, her own children, me, probably, sometime down the road, everyone got a heart attack sooner or later. During one hallucinatory phone call, she claimed levitation, the four-poster bed floating to the ceiling, then falling only to rise again, a dark man up there trying to suck her breath. My girlfriend and I'd already gone through our first procedure at Planned Parenthood, and while it happened, I'd sat in my Cutlass Supreme under a leafy oak in the Summit House parking lot composing a letter from the blackness of my guilt. That very week, Doctor Drew Kumpure performed a triple bypass as we held prayer circle in the St. Vincent's waiting room—people gawking—my first experience with those bleak places, though I've had plenty since. Visiting her after surgery, I passed full out and whacked my head on the floor tile like the holy rollers from Faith Maranatha. Only when I woke up, I lay in a sweet-smelling nurse's arms. "Are you okay? Are you okay?" she kept asking.

I wasn't.

This evil spirit—really, really evil—scathed its way into my heart. The Stepwell business made itself known in me. It's an old story for my people, how the trickster revisits our generations. I drank Purple Jesus, swallowed Black Beauty, sipped psilocybin tea and woke up in Florida at a bus station saying "I'll pay you back, I promise" just like every other lost soul has ever said.

Dee wired the ticket. We prayed. She lay on hands. "*Get thee behind me Satan*," she spat. Real-deal energy passed from her hand into my head. "*Leave this boy's body*," she screamed. "*NOW*," and I could feel it go. Surely shocked neighbors heard it through the walls. And I believed. At twenty-five, I believed that my grandmother had cast demons from me, summoned down Holy Ghost who baptized with fire.

She hauled me back to Fayetteville where I got on with a professor who roofed summers, and saved enough for the house on Hill Street, re-enrolled at the University. A woman came to me from faraway, a sailor's daughter, she looked in my door one day. Pink moon at night, sailor's delight, she said, and love lifted me. My brother Jimmy died in a one-car crash. I graduated. Renee and I were married by a man named Lester at the Virginia Dare House in Greensboro, North Carolina. Our Lara was born, and life became something different than it had been—the great secret of the ages, what I'd missed all along. I found a calling, moved to Utah. I worked hard. I busted it. I had trouble with Mormons and then I didn't. My mother died under unusual circumstances. We buried Mama one June in a field of brown-eyed Susans, overlooking the Stepwell bottoms on the Trail of Tears. Dee pointed out the tree under which she'd married my grandfather. They'd held hands and leapt into Solgahatchia Creek. Her foot had touched an underwater tree root. *That's what love's like*, she said, *your foot on a tree root.*

There was a lost year. We got by. I quit weed. I gave up on Jesus as a person, but not as a principle. Spiritual guidance came. I practiced the Red Road Way. I went to Sun Dance— saw the piercings. I vision-quested, assisted *heyokas*, stepped in and poured the holy *inipi*. Time lay down. Grey came. I made peace and most times that peace was in me. My daughter turned twelve. She played piano. In the golden afternoons of my forties, I learned lamb curry and naan, the zing of fresh ground cumin and garam marsala listening to Lara play "Für Elise," or "Ode to a Wild Rose," and, finally, "For All We Know," the pink sunlight streaming in from the mountains that surrounded our valley.

The woman I loved went through her time. War came and there was rumor of war, and then war was everywhere. The State took up torture, and somebody published the pictures. Polar caps began to melt. The sea turned acidic. Great reefs began to die. There was drought and famine and some guy in the middle east lit himself afire, then a whole people caught fire. Australia flooded. A scientist said our species was driving like a bat out of hell at a brick wall, our collective ass was grass. Look at Venus, the famous physicist said, that's us in a thousand years.

Aliens visited.

The moon turned to blood.

A black Jesus held the spotlight—the *One*, they called him.

Katrina KO'd New Orleans. It rained 10,000 redwings one Christmastime in Beebe, Arkansas. A goose moved on top of the high rise across our street, stood up there honking like some frog-voiced prophet, and the guy they'd hired to kill it couldn't shoot to save his ass, so this goose stayed up there honk-honking nonstop, until its message was complete. In Japan, an earthquake shifted the earth's axis thirty feet. Five nuclear meltdowns happened all at once, and it rained uranium on Utah. After a routine colonoscopy, I hemorrhaged one-third of my total blood. The signs were all there. Surely the time was at hand. Surely the big shit was about to come down.

And then, on an afternoon in March when the pussy willow was blooming before a tail-end winter storm and I had not thought of Arkansas, nor my Mom Dee who lay dying in Lonoke Nursing Home, a package came UPS. It had a heft to it, and it was from home, ghost hands reaching to me. I put off opening it all afternoon, and then overnight, and then all the next day. Finally, when the box-slitter lay open the cardboard flap, the perfumed scent of Dee's skin. Inside was the old music box, the gift from the Memphis banker who would fill it with jewels—Dee's name carven on its face. Inside, many letters wrapped in red ribbons, some of these in my hand, my mother's and Earl's. The smell of them all was there before me. I cranked the handle three times and the melody tinkled out, just the way it had the last time, and I opened the note, written in her hand, weakly—

darling
we won't say goodbye
until the last minute
I'll hold out my hand
and my heart will be in it
for all we know
we may never meet again

The nursing home is on the old highway, just north of Lonoke Mortuary with the Church of Christ and a horse pasture in between. Renee, my wife, has a soft spot for Mom Dee. She spent her first night in the Natural State on Dee's couch in the Summit House, that wide swath of green Arkansas out the twelfth-floor window when we woke, the aroma of sausage and eggs and buttered toast greeting us from the kitchen. Lara, our nine year old, has brought a sketch in colored pencils of a dog named D.J. carrying a turtle in its mouth—her favorite from a weekend of storytelling with Dee. We park the rental under a big oak and the three of us, me, Renee, and Lara step out, press wrinkles from our clothes, and take our breaths.

Inside, a sort of lobby separates visitors from the home's inner-workings. *Sign in. DO NOT CROSS THIS LINE,* a hand writ sign says, only there's neither a line nor a sign-in book, nor anybody at all paying attention to comings or goings. The stench is intense.

"God, Joe." Renee says it and gags.

My stomach turns over—this stink's hard to believe, it has a real-deal personality, a mix of strong urine, feces, and the odor of popcorn from a lit-up machine in the hallway, cut with ammonia or Pine Sol or bleach maybe. An ancient woman in a wheelchair nods her head violently and sobs. She's run her chair into the wall. My first thought is to help her, and that's what I do, only she wails at me, spins the chair back into the wall, where she nods and sobs again. It's eleven a.m., we've been in Arkansas for two hours now, long enough to drive from Little Rock, take a room at the Day's Inn where we stayed after Mama died, still run by the Hari Krishna woman with luxurious curry leaking from the suite door behind check-in. Her children's sing-song voices are gone, they've moved off to college.

The main hallway runs past a fluorescent lit dining hall with an old stand-up piano at one end and a TV strung at the other. We find the main desk where a big whiteboard is scribbled with names of residents and their attendants, a few with red lines crossed through them, which I take as a bad sign.

There sits a woman I've seen before, I'm sure of it. Her crooked neck wedges a phone between her ear and shoulder. She looks me in the face.

"Hold on, Maurice," she says. "Hep you?"

"We're here to see Ms. Stepwell. Dee Stepwell."

She inspects the board, then thumbs a blue spiral notebook. "One sec," she says into the phone. "Ain't nobody here by at name."

A canvas laundry cart full of soiled sheets is parked in the wide hall. A whole troop, maybe a half dozen old folk wander by with this vacant look in their eyes—like a bad movie about a bad nursing home. They wear dirty pajamas and gowns that gape open at the chest and waist. Humpbacked, they're barefoot with gnarled toenails and shingles. They twitch and convulse.

"Dee Stepwell. We've corresponded," I lie.

"Stepwell?"

"Dee *goddamn* Stepwell," I say. "My grandmother".

The woman in the wheelchair stops running into the wall. She says *God. Damn. God. Damn.*

"Don't got no Stepwells. Is your name Joey?" Somebody's talking through the phone at her neck.

Lara walks off down the hall, at the end of which, I see now, is a glass door—a way out of here—with a cow chomping sweet grass in a field where daffodils bob on the spring breeze. Sun shines through that door.

"Daddy," she says, "Here Mom Dee is." Lara points at a piece of paper beside a door about halfway down the sunlit hall on the right. "She's *here*."

"Joey Harvell?"

"Yes."

"It's me. Tina."

Printed in blue ink, Floradee Stepwell. The room is poorly

lit, hot, and the smell has a bite to it. There's a bathroom, a vase of bristly roses on a TV, and a lavender gown hanging from a hook. One sheetless bed is empty. The other sits near a heavily blinded window. The heat's on full blast—the wall unit purrs. The gown rings a bell. A tiny body lay in the bed, a toothless skeleton of a body, a worn out done with body that is no way in this world Dee.

"It's not her," I say. And I'm right. It isn't. They've got the names mixed up.

In grade school I'd carried a photo of her in my first wallet. That's my grandmother, I'd say, and watch the school kids gawk. One of my best tricks, producing this smiling movie star of a woman from my wallet. Later, in my twenties, I'd walk her around the University, all these sidewalks imprinted with the names of graduates from across the ages. We'd walk year to year and she'd tell what had happened *in that* year *and that*, and I'd watch the scruff-bearded professors gaze at her sidelong through thick glasses when they passed. She was a beautiful, sure, but there was something else—a *thereness*. She was all there, even in her eighties, our last time home, when we made memory soup and cornbread, lit the bronze menorah and ate till we were silly.

"She's not here," I say. "They've got the wrong person."

Tina—I can't place her for the life of me—stands in the doorway, behind Renee and Lara, looks on their faces. "You don't reckernize me?" she says.

Then, as if from dream, the thin voice speaks.

"Darling?"

When I turn around, one lid opens and out shines an emerald green eye.

The *Revelation of St. John* was hell on wheels for a fourteen-year-old who'd learned the E-A-B7 progression on a dented-up Fender and met eyes with the raven-haired beauty as she finger-picked Beatitudes. *Blessed are they*, she sang, *which do hunger and thirst after righteousness: for they shall be filled.* She parted her lips and tilted her head just so. I mean, the two taken together, the woman and the word, made a dent in my adolescent soul such as I cannot say. I hungered and the word was my solace. *I am he that liveth and he who was dead. I own the keys of hell and of death*, the book said, and, *Woe, woe, woe, to the inhibitors of earth.* By the time I hit the part about the angels of God pouring out vials of destruction on the fearful and unbelieving and the abominable, I was cooked. Add to this that Mom Dee actually *believed* the whole nine yards. In fact, she was absolutely certain that it was all happening right in front of our faces, that the rapture was at hand and we were all about to be lifted up into the clouds with Christ Jesus, only many, many, many would be left behind to suffer unspeakable grief, it was possible for me to do things, think things, even, that could get me left behind. The God of the John's Revelations was pissed like you couldn't believe, and the whole earth would suffer his wrath. And even worse, the last thing Revelations says is that if anybody added to or took away anything from the book, God would visit upon them every plague he'd ever invented—boils and warts and worms and rivers of blood. This was serious mojo. Once, I tore a single page of Luke and lit it afire just to see. And my Bible was full of places where I'd added words, especially Song of Solomon, which was sort of X-rated, where I went the eve after the guitarist parted her legs and I caught the slightest flash of garment, and the raven-haired woman looked me in the eye and I knew she knew. I guess I had it coming. Sometime down the line, the deep shit would rain down on me.

Upon seeing the three of us, Dee's recovery is nothing short of miraculous. Before afternoon, she's managed to dress and I've hauled open the blinds so sunshine streams in through the big double windows, which I crack, so fresh air's pouring in to boot, and we can hear birdsong and the whistling dove make on the wing. Renee picked a bouquet of fence line daffodils, set them shining on the windowsill in a glass vase from under the bed. I've sprinkled sage and cedar in all four corners, while Renee and Lara hit the Tastee-Freeze downtown for a chocolate malt, which Dee sucked down straight away. Renee's brushed my grandmother's hair out, found a package of Nair and removed the hair that had sprouted on her chin. The lavender robe has been shaken out, and Dee's wearing it, as I go through a stack of unopened mail, I find on the broken television beside the dried-up vase of roses Earl sent down from Oklahoma. Lara's found a piano out in the main room dining hall, and I can hear the notes she plays faintly.

"I broke my tail bone, honey," Dee says. "Last week."

We've managed clean sheets, and the controls of the hospital bed so she's propped up at forty-five degrees in good light. Renee's dusting, humming under her breath. I've pulled a chair bedside and hold one withered hand.

Her broad smile is slow in coming, her eyes twinkling. "But you can't put your butt in a sling," she says, and laughs. "*Ha*. Does it hurt?"

"Like hell," she says.

"Lara brought this," I say, and unfold the piece of sketch paper where a sloppy brown dog carries a snapping turtle between its jaws.

"*D.J.*," she says, and the smile comes yet again. We'd once kept a mongrel dog that adopted a loggerhead snapper, and the joke was that neither would let go of the other until it thundered. "Where's my baby?"

Through the open door, faint melody. "She's found a piano. It needs tuning."

"Read to me from my book. Over there."

239

On the dresser, I find Faith Maranatha has put together a memory book for her, signed by about fifty people with funny stories about Dee, touching ones, bits of prayer and scripture, and even a semi-dirty joke about a donkey and three ducks. Renee joins us, looks me in the eye, so it hits me that this is a last moment, why we've come. And just as I read the first words of a seriously moving tribute signed by the preacher himself, this woman with a gout-purple foot wheels herself into the room.

"Got a question for Missus Stepwell," she says.

Renee bristles. "Excuse me?"

This woman with her cantaloupe-size foot wheels herself right up to where we sit, cranes her neck to see Dee. "How many hogs was it, Missus Stepwell, that Christ cast demons out of?" Her eyes smolder. She looks at me, then Renee, then back at Dee. "Afore they jumped off a clift and drowned."

Dee meets her gaze. "*What?*"

"It don't have to be zact." The swollen foot lay on a silver prop out in front of the wheelchair. "Just close. *Almost.*"

"Leave my room," Dee says. "*Get out.*" The words come out like dry husks.

The gout-footed lady snorts. "Don't seem like too much to ast. Not for somebody says she done read the good book through twenty-seven times."

Renee shakes her head.

Dee's eyes flash.

"Leave."

"They was *about* two-thousand. I'll ast you a new one tomorrow," the woman says.

It dawns on me, *dawns* is not the right word, more like claws its way into my chest like a cat on a screen door in August, that this woman has been here before, and will come again, that I have let my grandmother lay here going on four months now.

Renee shuts the door behind the wheelchair woman.

"Tomorrow's my appointment at the beauty shop. I missed last time," Dee says, and then she falls asleep.

That night I dream wildly. At Day's Inn, in the queen bed nearest the parking lot adjacent to a Burger King, where Lonoke County folk order Whoppers with everything at the drive-thru, I am visited. She comes to me, and it is as if I share her dying moment, very intimate, her voice is faint and I smell the lotion on her face. She says that she has loved much. Me and Renee and Lara, Mama gone these eight years, the host of her brothers and sisters, her mama and daddy, all these friends and lovers. *Weldon.* She looks forward to seeing us again—she *will* see us again. She turns her face so I see her eyes, and she holds me with them a last time. And then, in the dream, she quits breathing. I wake in a cold sweat, hear my wife and daughter breathing in bed across the dark room, a little red light blinking on the ceiling.

Out in the parking lot, I roll and smoke a cigarette. It's the eighth of March, a hint of flowers on the breeze. They'd run a flower shop together, Dee and my grandfather. Then he'd lost a leg in a woodcutting accident and got hooked on morphine. Story was, he turned mean. Dee'd thrown a butcher knife at his head one night after he'd passed out—I've touched the scar in the cherrywood headboard with my own hand.

The next morning dawns bright with sunshine. We dress in our good clothes and are at the nursing home by 10 a.m. I wrangle a plate of sausage and eggs from the kitchen, platefuls of wheat toast, oatmeal, OJ, and some sliced peaches, carry it all into Dee's room. She's awake and lucid, the bed cranked up so she's sitting up clear-eyed. Renee and Lara open the blinds and the good warm light shines through the vase of daffodils. The smell lay down some, or we're getting used to it. Lara's DJ is taped to a windowpane, the colorful snapper all lit up with a piece of the dog between its beak. There's no sign of the gout-foot lady, and the attending nurse today is this tiny Vietnamese woman who said for us to call her Sally, which comes out *Si-We*, and she smiles a big warm smile and I like her.

A tray holder swivels up from the bedside for Dee's tray. "Thank you, honey," she says. "Will you help me?"

One of her arms is broken, too frail to set. Her other has an IV run into it.

"While it's hot," I say, lift the cover off a plate.

We meet eyes.

"Thank you," she says.

I fork scrambled eggs and hold them into her opened mouth, hold the pint milk carton's straw for her, then the peaches and cream. Lara spoons strawberry jam on a wedge of toast, and Renee slices a sausage. We feed her that way, and she eats and eats. It's the first time in a while, Si-We says. "You good for Ms. Stepwell," she says. "Maybe she get out of bed later?"

"Maybe," Dee says. "What day is it?"

"Why today is Sunday, Ms. Stepwell." Si-We's smile radiates. "The Lord's day."

"We brought this," Lara says, and takes out a make-up kit, brush and comb. There's nail clippers and little scissors, another package of Nair.

"Beauty shop," Dee says.

From across the room, I watch my daughter brush my grandmother's hair while Renee works the hand of a broken arm. Though Dee falls asleep straightaway, they do her face, her lashes. Renee rips open the pack of Nair and each of them takes a leg, then wrap her in the lavender gown—the exact color of Arkansas redbud in springtime. Her favorite was the shimmering white dogwood at Easter, each petal nail-scarred the way Christ had been.

"There," my wife says, and the three of us stand around the beside where Dee sleeps.

"She's beautiful," Lara says.

That afternoon, our last, Si-We winks at Lara, then lifts Dee into a wheelchair. "For special treat," she says. We are led through the hallway into the main dining chamber where gather a multitude of the elderly and afflicted come for the early bird Sunday supper. Many wander behind walkers as if lost, and the sound of them taken all at once dizzies. Si-We pushes my grandmother up beside the piano at the head of the room, motions for Lara to sit down and play. Dee is bewildered—she looks at me as if I'm the moon. "All listen," Si-We says, loud. "Must be listening."

Grandmother reaches for my hand.

Si-We claps both hands together, yells, "*Be still.*" The overhead lights blink off for a moment. Someone screams. The light comes on, and it's all quiet.

"Should I play it now, Daddy?"

Before me, their faces. All of them. "Yea, sweetie. Play."

Only a little out of tune, my daughter sustains the first notes with one pedal. Dee's face brightens. "I knew you'd come," she says. "Will we dance?"

Mom Dee lifts one hand. We meet eyes. I feel her—all there.

The thoughts converge, and before I know it I've taken the hand and pushed her out in front of the rest, some of whom clap hands. She smiles, shuts her eyes, concentrates. I imagine her mind's hinges opening, light playing over what she's loved most in this world and lost. We dance that way, while my daughter plays the song she's learned from the old box with the name carved on its lid. We turn circles upon circles. Another couple joins. Voices rise to meet the notes, and it strikes me that this melody has words that I remember.

27.

Last week, or yesterday, who can tell anymore, we played some ball. Up on Stillwell Field in Fort Douglas, the army base set up to keep an eye on the Mormons after the Civil War, then turned into a prisoner of war camp during WWII. Where my office is. We drove up to the green grass, the three of us. A bevy of co-ed volleyballers had set up anew on one end of the field, dive-bombing spikes on each other's heads, and down on the other end a troop of graybeard professors, high by the look of them, playing Frisbee golf. All masked. We had the whole center of the field for a game of Indian Baseball, what Poppy'd taught Renee and her brother Rock when he was home from Viet Nam, before they put his name up for full Captain, which is a big deal in the Navy. I've seen men on base go into conniption fits when he drives us onto base, saluting up a storm like he's the president or something, which I guess makes no difference, now, given the current and maybe future.

Just across the street from my office, which was once the Commander's Quarters, a nice room with a backdoor and covered porch where I sometimes meet with students on wicker chairs, spring breeze in our faces the warmth of the sun of the Old World. A photo of Renee is framed on the wall, her brother's wedding, the blue pool and deep greens of Florida, violently blooming. The three of us outside Alf's up on Alta Mountain. Lara as a toddler. Our house in a snowstorm, glowing from the inside out.

I've read that UV light kills the virus, only we'd have to have enough poured over our heads to fry—how about that?

And sometimes I walk out the door, down the patio stairs and stand on the green lip of field, snow-covered Wasatch Mountains saw-toothing the very near distance, and think, goddamn, how lucky I am to be able to work here and do this, holy moly, what did I step in or some silly shit, and not see it coming, cancer or us on the field last week or yesterday, two months or another lifetime into global pandemic, playing Indian baseball on the shutdown campus of Spring 2020.

Turns out Lara can hit the ball.

She caught Renee's short popup and stood to the bat. Took a few swings, the aluminum bat swishing. Then *whammo*, she hit it just shy of the coed volleyballers. A pretty one in a red bikini underhanded it back to me.

"Sorry," I said.

And after about three rockets across the field, the girl said, "This is getting old. Can you please be careful, please?"

Cease and desist. From forty yards, I gave her the sign, caught it all in a glance. The flagpole across the street at the gazebo, foothills just starting to bloom, Renee at sixty, fit, there for me, she'd said. Snow gleams on the mountains. Backcountry, they're skiing the deep stuff, the rotten foundation won't be laid till next year when I'd be sixty and see my grandfather stare at me through my own eyes. A jolt. After the surgery and catheter and walking the road outside my house at 2 a.m., because you can forget sleep. Those men in the photo, they maybe see what I've missed, how those golden afternoons returning from Alta Mountain, when we'd skied our butts off, my and Lara at twelve, fifteen, eighteen, and she'd let the seat fall back far as it would go and fall asleep while I listened to Blue Grass Express and the great Salt Lake Valley opened beneath Little Cottonwood Canyon, it would never get any better than that, not ever. But I didn't know, couldn't see, our lives happening.

My daughter, bat in hand, the graybeard Frisbee throwers and the coeds, "all of us in this together," I kept hearing, on this green field of future, going back to the ones who'd looked off their patios and front porches and counted themselves lucky. A dog eats out of a pizza box behind the Officer's Quarters. We saw it walking back to the truck, still wearing our ball gloves, the sun on our faces. Past the office I haven't inhabited since before, ghostly and dark and empty now, bugs in the toilets, the plants all dead.

"That was fun," Renee said.

And we climbed into the nice, new truck. I'd averaged two-hundred miles a month before, I'm not sure after.

28.

From the study window, east facing, he had a full view of the football stadium, a big silver U on either tower. On game days, this close to ground zero, the place is a circus. Or used to be, back in the Old World. Which revisits them out of the blue today. Online finals are all done, and whatever students had made it back from Spring Break—not many, President Watts had put out the STAY HOME order, but some had come, only to get kicked out of the dorms to stay with friends, some of whom lived on University Street because it was party central, back in the day, and these students, they've been on lockdown, watching Netflix, eating who knows what, all those delivery pizzas with the drivers wearing shorts and whatever masks they could scrounge, rubbing hand sanitizer on blue-gloved hands, eyeing their paper money like it was evil, because maybe it was. They say the virus can live on cardboard for twenty days. Truth was, you can't trust anything anymore. The mail, the fence gate, the garbage bin, the soles of your shoes—it was all fair game for Covid, the word which puts him in the mind of covert and livid, sort of spliced together, add the 19 and voilà, just what the doctor ordered.

Only not quite, because there's this new thing called quarantine fatigue. Which is sort of like, lock people down, we're talking young people in their prime with spring in their blood, say, for six weeks or so, feed them delivery pizza and jellybeans leftover from Easter, and the liquor stores are starting to be shut down, in Moab, Murray, St. George, just a few, sure, but there's that new layer of anxiety—he's not immune from it. So lock everybody up with shitty food, then threaten to shut down all the liquor stores in the state, add to this the whole mess about the ten thousand ceiling fans and refrigerated trucks idling outside hospitals from here to Timbuktu, and everybody and their mother having this weird-ass dream where you're being stalked by camo-wearing peckerheads with guns, and you get what happens next, last Wednesday of April, on their street with its full view of the U. of U. Stadium on one side and Mt. Olivet Cemetery on the other, ground zero, the circus.

The street erupts.

Close enough to campus to hit with a rock, housefuls of what will become known as the Covid Generation pour onto the street, renters and evacuees and kids recently fired from the ski resorts with nowhere to go. Folks who'd lived a month and a half in dark rent houses with clogged up toilets because the sewer system was maxed out, who'd smoked through their household stash and then ground the seeds and stems and smoked them too, vacuumed up what they could from sour carpets, and understood that they themselves were living in a vacuum, so that the world outside had ceased to mean what it had meant in January and February and the front end of March, even, when the plague was just the punch line of a party joke.

And then the earthquakes started.

As if God and Jesus and the Holy Ghost just had to be sure they all got the goddamn point, earthquakes came, the first one at sunrise on March 18, apparently having the decency to hold off on the 19th, it being Vernal Equinox and all. 5.7, the first one, a thousand some aftershocks so the ground between Great Salt Lake and University Street school looked like Jell-O, which was the official State Food, what kind of people on this earth would choose Jell-O as their state food? So they were a people who'd lived with earthquakes felt in seven western states, who would not have lifted a brow should a plague of frogs descend upon them, followed by the Pale Rider, a great bugling summoning the dead from their graves for the Apocalypse everyone had waited for. The shit had hit the fan. Out of dope, liquor stores closing, school all but disappeared, the ground perpetually unsteady beneath their feet, and in a 4.6 aftershock, Angel Moroni, atop the Holy Temple, had the trumpet ripped from his lips, hurled to the ground so the golden idol stood up there bewildered, for once in a hundred years not blowing.

They poured from doorways off front porches in bikinis and American flag swimming trunks, bare white skin to the sun, set up beer pong tables and blared bad music from Joey's college days. Boston, ELO, Journey. Bad even then. They don't social distance nor wear masks. The beer bongs come out and a bevy of blondes from next door dump a bottle of champagne over each other's heads and dance the hootchekoo. Forget the cops, the landlords who've been forced by the governor to let this month's rent slide, the utility people and the dog catcher. Fuck it all—the limbo since spring break, the shutdown parks, the can't drive to the next county, and the summer ahead of them they'd no doubt be spending with parents who would not countenance such a display as was going down on Wednesday or Thursday, but pretty sure not a Friday, right at the end of March, no it was April, last day of the month. He sees the party catch its breath, Joey Harvell, the coeds dumping a second bottle of champagne, the pong game firing up, a loud afternoon and night ahead. Renee'd call the cops. They wouldn't come. They'd wake the next morning to vomit on sidewalks, the streets glistening with broken beer bottles for a solid block, cups from grain alcohol punch glowing Easter egg red all the way to the law building. And Renee'd say she hated living there, it was the central disappointment of her life.

He saw it coming.

He thought he did.

And then the next thing happened.

"I want you to see this," Renee said. She led him through the house, said, "Look."

Across Fifth South, Friendship Manor, a retirement home for the elderly and disabled, stood fourteen floors facing south. In wintertime its shadow covered their house entirely for half the day. Three or four times a week, firetrucks slammed right up to the glass doors in front, followed by an ambulance out of which crawled EMTs in full protective gear pushing a silver gurney inside, and after it was all done it'd take the firemen an hour to disinfect everything, even their shoes. They'd drive away with a skin-and-bone body covered with a sheet and leave the rest to the fire boys who'd laugh, joke with each other, who'd cook the *chile verde* that night, spraying the soles of each other's shoes—it was something to see.

Only not today.

They walked outside and saw.

Across the street, under the good sun, stood a man with a stand-up bass that was hooked to what sounded like a good amplifier and P.A. Beside him was who turned out to be his brother, strumming what looked to be a Martin guitar and just then singing, "don't think twice, it's alright" into a silver mike on a stand. A heavy-set woman with ribbons in her hair played a tambourine that resonated off the tall building and across the street.

"Open up your windows," the woman's amplified voice, and sure enough they did, the old folk, open up their windows.

The trio moved from Dylan to Johnny Cash and the Dirt Band, "Will the Circle Be Unbroken" and "This Little Light of Mine."

Lara clapped along with them.

People stopped and got out of their cars.

The post lady sat the mail down on the neighbor's front step. It was last day of April, six weeks into quarantine, when the double doors of Friendship Manor opened and out they came. He'd taught there once, had taken students with him sometimes, workshops, they auditioned, scored and costumed a musical comedy once on Valentine's, and one of the numbers was how Don and Marian Shelby had gone on a dinner date to a steak house in Michigan sixty years earlier and fallen in love. The couple'd wept to see the students perform their meeting, how happy they were on their night. Genevieve and Maxine and Lydia, who he'd set up on a pen pal project when Lara was in third grade. Harriet Bean had been a telephone operator in Kanab on the day the USS Utah was sunk at Pearl Harbor, and all the young people had gathered that night on the outskirts of town and fired pistols and shotguns and rifles into the dark, they just did, shooting at that unseen thing that had taken their namesake down that very day.

From the old world.

Out they came.

Wearing masks and rubber gloves and pajamas, some of them, onto the parking lot there the trio had turned it up and launched into a version of "I'll Fly Away," the gospel tune he'd had played at Mama's funeral, because she loved it, and it seemed to connect him to his roots back in Danville, where his people were from. They were singing along, the elderly and infirm, some of them dancing right over the parking lot where not two days ago the fire truck and ambulance had sat waiting and they'd seen it through their blinds and knew it was coming for them. It was. It surely was.

For one and all.

In the shadow of a coliseum and cemetery, they poured out of their quarantine houses and made song for the first time in many a dark day. The old folk saw his tiny family and the goings on all down the street, waved for them to join, big holy smiles on their faces. Lara crossed over first, Renee followed. Some of the people who'd pulled over left their cars right on the street, and the post lady carried over her bag of undelivered mail. They were playing "The Old Country Waltz," and the kids on the street had got wind of it, the old folk shaking their asses. With him came a host, the beer ponged and champagne-drenched, singing voices of young and old intermingling, and time came back to them again for a while there on the parking lot, buoyed by each other—*ain't got no excuses, we just want to play, that good old country waltz, today.*

"What do you call an earthquake during a pandemic," a man Joey'd seen walking in the cemetery with a crooked snake stick asked through his mask.

He shook his head, Joey. Bright sunshine in his face.

Behind him stood a woman who looked for the world like Mom Floradee, the last time he saw her at the nursing home in Lonoke.

This was like that.

His bright eyes twinkled.

"A panquake," he said, laughed through the mask.

That second he imagined Friendship's east wing residents rising up before light, the Oquirrhs going red across the valley, letting eyes fall on Mt. Olivet Cemetery where the forty acres of tall trees made a good shade on the hillside from Foothill to the freeway that rolled on out to sunny California.

Open up your windows! Open!

Had Floradee been like that in the end, the season of flowers for which she was named, had someone called out for her to open up her window, sing, "I'll fly away. Sweet Jesus. I'll fly away."

Grandmother, his refuge, his protector.

All of them thrown together in a parking lot with little yellow lines marking places numbered surely as the cemetery plots beyond.

"That's funny," he said. "Panquake."

Lara danced, waving both arms, beside her mother. Over there the girls whose hair is champagne-matted. Mayday just around the bend. There's talk of opening things back up, the parks, drive-in movies, maybe. Summer was coming on, maybe the virus doesn't like the heat. It was possible, wasn't it? Somebody said the ultraviolet rays killed it. Flowers were blooming, iris bedded in front of their house, just now catching the sun so yellow stamen gashed the flouncy petals. Purple, it had been one of Dee's favorites. He knew because she cried one time when he brought them in a glass vase for Mother's Day. He'd said, "Don't be sad Mom Dee," and she'd hugged him and cried into his shoulder. "I'm not, honey," she said, placed them so the sun shone on them through her sliding glass.

It took his breath. He'd never seen it from across the street. His house, where they'd lived and walked and breathed and birthed a child. Where they'd locked down together for fifty days in ten-by-fourteen rooms that would surely reek of them forever.

This is what they look like from across the street—purple iris. What they'd planted that first fall against winter.

29.

The morning birdsong takes him to the dirt road and mailbox close enough to smell the lake, strawberries on the air and birds going off before light, the one-legged man in the trailer kitchen making oatmeal, the aroma of coffee and tobacco, radio tuned to the morning weather forecast, high pressure for the Ohio Valley, the threat of thunderstorms for the Deep South. Hot and humid conditions in the Heartland to the upper Midwest, continued storminess in the Appalachians moving into the Atlantic Corridor. Wind with occasional showers for the Northeast. Heat and continued drought for the Southeast, from Raleigh down to Savannah. The High Plains were chilly through the week with late snowfalls for the Intermountain Region and high heat in the Desert Southwest. Texas and Oklahoma were still for the next few days, calm and still and average through the weekend. A low moved into the Pacific Northwest by Friday, would affect the regional weather all next week, and Santa Anna winds would bring the threat of fire to the Pacific Southwest with the foothills especially vulnerable through week's end. 5 a.m. Tuesday, May 24 forecast from the National Weather Service in Oklahoma City. Again. High Pressure for the Ohio Valley, the threat of thunderstorms for the Deep South with hot and humid conditions in the Heartland to Upper-Midwest.

In the trailer with its Scotch-taped picture window, under

covers on the pull-out couch, with the maternal grandfather most like a father to him in this world, his face clean shaven, making oatmeal in the kitchen before light, the hiss of butane with birdsong and the smell of ripe berries through the open windows.

A duck call blown forcefully in a small room is loud.

"Wake up and pee, Joey," the world's on fire.

How he woke that morning in the long-gone world, before all who'd ever heard this story save him had disappeared.

30.

Top L-R: Perry Wiseman, Joy Marcum, Roy Shelton, Jack Thorpe, Weldon Stepwell, Jimmy Patterson, Bill Lordes

Bottom L-R: Lew Blanding, W. D. Baskin, Faye Mathison, Lloyd George, Elmer Moore, Coach Clyde Stringfield

31.

Our iris—this is what it looks like to the resident elderly from their side of the street, pretty, really, a thing to admire. The house seen from across the street, stadium on one side, cemetery on the other, a state highway in between. How it was when the virus made the leap from whatever intermediary host had carried it to the brink of that first human in Wuhan, a spark before the fire. Mother's Day this weekend, falling on Renee's mother's birthday, Meg, all our mothers gone now, who to mourn the children?

Renee was to retire in two weeks.

Thirty-seven years of special education, the last half-dozen in a lockdown facility for kids banned from regular school, anger or drugs or general fucked-upedness, but who could cast the first stone into that lake water?

Staying home had hit her hard. Cleaning one room a day. Not flushing their toilet paper because the city sewer lines were maxed out. The little silver can with its flip up lid smelled like exactly what it contained morning, noon and night.

Two-thousand-six-hundred and something died yesterday, and as many the day before. They were moving from red to orange. He felt for Lara, she needed somebody to love. She needed her life. She needed to get up from that bed and run like hell, up into the foothills where arrow root sunflowers were mock-glorious under May sunshine, and the snowmelt glacier lilies blooming wildly. Two months into lockdown today.

He fried fish for last night's dinner. Lara made coleslaw, Renee oven fries. This morning he hit 190, the first time he'd weighed himself since.

Renee needed foot surgery.

The Hall's cough drops she'd bought for him at Smith's had little motivational snippets written on each wrapper. Tonight was Full Flower Moon. Venus had reached a brightness that cast shadows.

Keep your chin up, today's wrapper said.

32.

What they're looking at, in the photo, had Mama wondered, did Dee know? Better than half of them staring straight ahead, the ballpark at night, I'm guessing, and the rest into the camera eye, the ones in front squatting, Coach in a catcher's stance. Some holding their gloves. One with a B on his shirt. Jack Thorpe in an undershirt—"those jerseys were hot and sweaty."

They're not dirty yet, so before a game, the lights on, the ones they'd paid for with half the gate receipts and a promise. Men who'd kicked Hitler's ass and were home to play ball. Their wives out there, sons and daughters. The other team warming up maybe. Scoreboard with zero-zero in the top of the first, shiny plates on hooks with black numbers. It was a summer night, the stars streaming down overhead. Standing and squatting in green grass, their spikes sinking into the soft ground. Someone spoke a prayer through a loud speaker, then a tape recording of the Star Spangled Banner. It meant something being there, this moment in time.

Every one of them dead now.

History colleagues are posting up snippets of their daily lives since the Virus and Quarantine, the earthquakes and all. One who'd had breast cancer all last year floated a desert river with her son who'd turned twenty-one at the put in. They'd never really talked before that day, not through the divorce nor college applications, they just hadn't. He'd been in New Zealand, the boy, when the shit hit the fan, had to fly home and lock into a bedroom for fourteen days, have his food shoved under the door like a dog. And they'd talked for the first time down on the river where there was this energy, the colleague said, it had been there all along. They'd celebrated his twenty-first birthday under the blue sky in the house of the falling rain—that's what she called it, house of the falling rain. Another had hiked with his wife on the deserted campus, a strange bereft energy there too, and they'd walked up on this sign in the dirt advertising TRUTH. It was the week virus deniers had marched on the Capitol, President Yammer-Hammer'd encouraged them to drink Clorox to ward off the virus. It was all a hoax, fake news, the mass grave, the refrigerated trucks idling outside hospitals, bullshit perpetrated by socialist liberal Satan-worshipping cannibals. One woman had bought a pet rabbit, named it Black Rabbi, another'd spotted a bobcat and wild turkeys. Rumors were that wild hogs had burst into a Spanish town and eaten a baby. A stampede of elephants had drunk all the rice whiskey somewhere in India.

Drunken elephants, hilarious.

Air pollution had plummeted. People were exercising in their basements. Renee and Lara were, down there doing jumping jacks and knee-lifts, buoyed up by livestreamed faces who cheered them on. His peas were up, blooming, garlic and turnip greens, mesclun mix lettuce. They'd gone in for chicks, thirteen of them in the coop, now, imprinted on the one survivor of the October raccoon attack, the one-eyed black sexlink Lara'd named Cyclops.

Summer classes had started.

There was talk of de-escalating the threat from orange to yellow. They could do a river trip, the three of them, up to the Green where there was good trout water. Primitive camps on the east slope of the Uintas, lots of distance, coyotes yip-yapping under the moon and stars. Italy had got its shit together, Spain, a little. Utah still had a slew of hospital beds, ventilators, had got their hands on two-million Chinese masks or something.

Good days to be alive if we but knew how to live them.

Sure.

They'd hiked the foothills yesterday, Butter and Eggs blooming, bluebell, balsam root and death camas. Up to the creek, hear it running, a sound that made Joey have to pee somewhere deep inside.

He'd decided to have the surgery, the prostatectomy. He'd arrange it today with Amanda, his cancer doctor's secretary. For mid-September, that would be a good time. Just before the autumnal equinox, enough time to heal for the holidays. Halloween with everyone dressed in a coronavirus spiked head, the grim reapers and refrigerator truck drivers, people wearing ventilators, walking Clorox bottles, some dressed as big needles full of vaccine—wouldn't that be nice, a vaccine? If they still weren't face-to-face, he could teach from bed, couldn't he? no problem. Newly retired Renee, she could make coffee, unload the dishwasher. The elections were just around the corner. A miracle could happen.

They hadn't started coughing, not yet.

What would they do if they got it? they asked each other. Well, what would they? Self-quarantine in the basement? Set up the groover down there and push plates through the cracked door? What if it's Renee? Lara? There's a photo he'd framed for their thirtieth wedding anniversary. Of him and Renee on a bridge in Paris with the Seine flowing behind their backs, a cathedral, the Champs-Élysées, a piece of Notre Dame back there. A glass-floored wedding boat had sailed below, the bride and groom on a platform where music played, jazz, floating to them over the water. Just as it approached the bridge, the couple leapt hand in hand, and then the boat went under, so they never saw them land, the bride and groom. "That's what it's like," Renee said, "Isn't it?"

261

"What what's like?"

"Everything."

She was right.

It was.

Hand in hand in the falling jazz. Broken ankle or sweet baby's arms. Who cared? They'd made it. Thirty years. The first of his people maybe ever in history to make it that long. She took her phone out, Renee, held it at arm's length and snapped a picture of the two of them, wind in their hair, him graybeard grizzled and her with that surprise look she got sometimes. Later, it would make him happy and sad at the same time, the photo, through knee-deep shit and joy to the world, they'd hung tight. They'd had their moments though, hadn't they? That mess in D.C. Lara's birth had made them better people. It had. Everything got right when mine became thine. Love had saved their lives. The photo was proof. And it could happen again, couldn't it? They were happy in that picture, not the namby-pamby kind of happy, but deep down inside joyful happy that afternoon in Paris, when the glass-bottomed boat passed under them, even though they never knew what happened when the bride and groom landed. And it made him sad because the shadow of cancer wasn't on his face yet, they were unclouded by that at least. And for a long time he thought that was why the photo worked a sadness in him, because of the Big C to come, but that didn't seem right because his heart hurt worst when somebody he loved was hurting. So there was something else behind the photo, and now he knows, they'd never seen it coming, not in a million years. No one had. The genie that jumped their bones from the Old World to the New.

He didn't know what they were seeing, those men in the Little John photo that's worn and creased and nearly torn half-in-two down his grandfather's face, but it was something real, out there before them. Maybe that's the point. Why it's come to him. The thing to meditate on, but maybe not understand.

He'd called Joey to him, before he died. Grandpa did. He'd checked into the Vet's Hospital in Little Rock for the back surgery he'd needed the last time down in the silver Airstream on Lake Ouachita. He hurt. And though he didn't show it, he must have been scared. There was a window, looking out on a grimy highway that ran over the Arkansas River past the airport toward Memphis. He wore a gown, the little white bracelet with his full name on it, date of birth, social. Fasting for tomorrow morning's surgery, when the doc would nick an artery and he'd damn near bleed out for a second time, only now he wasn't a thirty-year-old athlete, was he? The coma lasted a week. A sister thought he might wake up if he heard Joey's voice.

He didn't.

When he visited before surgery, they were alone in the room. Jewell was off somewhere, no one else was around. "Joker," he said. "You remember that bridge?"

"Yeah. I do."

Late of the afternoon, on some days, they'd drive Old Lake Road right down to the water where a sunken bridge lay, remnant of travel from before the Ouachita river's damming. The white lines ran straight into the clear lake so you could see them down there, two stripes for no passing, one for the fast lane. He'd stripped naked, Grandpa, hopped the pilings on the one foot and swum out into the sun-shafted water. The Ouachitas were deep green around them, ancient mountains where the continent's lone diamonds were forged in the fossil throats of extinct volcanos. Quartz crystal shone on the banks.

"Hey piss ant," he said this one time. An afternoon when Mama'd called long distance, said she was coming to get him, that they were leaving Arkansas forever.

The old man swam a circle, he was looking for something. Joey was twelve, about to be thirteen. Life was catching fire.

"Looky here," he said. Then the old man stood on top of the water, held both hands out and caught his balance, then just levitated there for a moment, the sun in his eyes. *Ha!* he yelled, dove off and swam.

He'd since seen the bridge at low water. They'd camped there once, Joey and Renee, drinking beer by a wood fire, leaves turning all up the mountainside. He'd told her the old story. On her dare, he swam out into the icy water, climbed up on the now-exposed beam, held hands out in a hollow imitation of the old man's miracle.

She clapped. And her approval echoed off the blazing hickories.

Later, they confessed love by the wood fire, and slept under a sky that offered frost before morning. What he didn't tell her was how his body'd turned on him, that happens to all of us, right? How it had been that summer before the divorce when life'd caught fire and grandfather had leapt atop the blue water and stood there for a shining moment. Wild August smoldering in his eye, he touched foot to the phantom bridge, then swam to Joey a moving maze.

What if they got it?

So what if they did?

It was out there in lurk, just out of the corner of their eyes, braced for the ambush. So were the silver clouds sailing down over the stadium and cemetery this morning, a chill come on in May, a good time for the river. Maybe break quarantine, head north and west into Wyoming, a wild country in the dark of night, not unlike Chickalah Mountain must have been for Jack Thorpe driving up to get the leg, that catwalk overlooking Boston Harbor where the wind slapped Grandpa down. For Mama in her eternal fleeings from Arkansas and everything it had come to stand for. For Joey and Renee when they first drove Highway 80 west, limped into Rawlins, Wyoming after a hard road day, and it was Rodeo Weekend, fringed riders galloping horseback down Main Street firing off six-shooters just like it was the Wild flipping West, the snow-clad Medicine Bow behind them as backdrop.

For his green-eyed grandmother and mama who'd twisted the tourniquet while flying down Chickalah Mountain, the white lines shining toward the hospital and all the water that would come under that bridge.

For them, this moment, plague at their doorstep.

The stairs where iris blooms and the post lady sometimes rests her load on a hot day, takes off her mask and breathes. In Utah, home beneath the stadium and adjoining cemetery. Where headstones shine so fiercely that they are sometimes mistaken for swimming pools by those who pass overhead, flashes of light where might lay the young and in love and not entirely afraid.

ACKNOWLEDGMENTS

I'd like to thank writers from Novel Writing Workshop 2020-2021, whose commitment and hard work buoyed my own efforts, and whose novels were created in concert with this book. I'm grateful to Kim Davis and the folks at Madville Publishing for seeing this through in a good way, as well as for their encouragement and support. For the gift of this story, I'd like to thank my mother, Jackie Gills, and grandmother, Edith Treadwell, from whose lips I learned the family history upon which this fiction is loosely based. Finally, I give heartfelt thanks to my wife and daughter for reading and offering valuable suggestions to this work in manuscript form.

Many thanks to the editors of *New Madrid*, *The Oxford American*, and *Mayday* where portions of this manuscript appeared in different forms.

ABOUT THE AUTHOR

Arkansas native Michael Gills is the author of eleven books of fiction and nonfiction, including the novel *New Harmony* (Raw Dog Screaming Press) Book 4 of the *Go Love Quartet*. A fourth collection of short fiction, *Burning Down My Father's House* will be published by Texas Review Press in 2023. Other work has been nominated for the PEN/Faulkner Award for Fiction, and won the *Southern Humanities Review*'s Theodore Hoefner Prize for Fiction, *Southern Review*'s Best Debut of the Year, recognition in the *Best American Short Stories* and *Pushcart Prize Anthology*, and inclusion in *New Stories from The South: The Year's Best*. His undergraduate novel writing workshop has been featured in *USA Today*, and several of his students have gone on to publish books of their own. Gills is a Distinguished Honors Professor at the University of Utah, where he lives in the hills with his wife of thirty-five years, Jill.